Advance Praise for
Under All the Lights

"A triumphant and tender story filled with thoughtful characters whom you'll be rooting for throughout."
—ROD PULIDO, author of *Chasing Pacquiao*

"A compassionate and heartfelt story of survival. Ameyaw tackles difficult topics like sexual assault, homophobia, and the price of fame with nuance and a necessary tenderness. Readers will love returning to these characters, and will find healing in the pages."
—JEN ST. JUDE, author of *If Tomorrow Doesn't Come*

"*Under All the Lights* explores themes of identity, acceptance, and using art to find your way through trauma with empathy, compassion, and nuance. A heartfelt, tender story about letting yourself be seen."
—MARIKO TURK, author of *The Other Side of Perfect*

"*Under All the Lights* brings Ollie's journey to the sweetest conclusion. A great story to share with teens looking for strength and an ending that fills them with hope."
—K. ANCRUM, author of *The Wicker King*, *The Weight of the Stars*, *Darling*, and *Icarus*

"[A]n intensely beautiful exploration of the self and how the mind navigates the complexities of love, identity, trauma, and familial expectations."
—ALEEMA OMOTONI, award-winning author of *Everyone's Thinking It*

"Bold and gentle, *Under All the Lights* is the best kind of encore. Ameyaw is finely attuned to her characters as Ollie is thrust out of his comfort zone into the spotlight."
—TRYNNE DELANEY, author of *A House Unsettled*

"Ameyaw imbues what sounds like every teenager's dream—touring with your musical idol—with the kind of grounded, realistic emotion needed to make the story truly sing. In *Under All the Lights*, we stress, sweat, and crush right alongside Ollie."
—ALEXANDRA MAE JONES, author of *The Queen of Junk Island*

"Told with deft tenderness and clarity, Ameyaw's story features characters brimming with so much empathy and passion that readers will count them as friends by the final encore."
—DERRICK CHOW, author of *Ravenous Things*

"A poignant page-turner with a compelling cast that will tug at your heartstrings. I adored this book."
—RISS M. NEILSON, author of *Deep in Providence*

"A timely and heartfelt story of self-discovery, resilience, and healing. Ollie's journey is one that deserves the spotlight!"
—ELIZA MARTIN, author of *Harvey and the Extraordinary*

UNDER
ALL
THE
lights

MAYA AMEYAW

annick
press
toronto • berkeley

We acknowledge the support of the Canada Council for the Arts and the Ontario Arts Council, and the participation of the Government of Canada/la participation du gouvernement du Canada for our publishing activities.

Library and Archives Canada Cataloguing in Publication

Title: Under all the lights / written by Maya Ameyaw.
Names: Ameyaw, Maya, author.
Identifiers: Canadiana (print) 20240310950 | Canadiana (ebook)
20240310969 | ISBN 9781773218632 (hardcover) | ISBN
9781773218649 (softcover) | ISBN 9781773218656 (EPUB) | ISBN
9781773218663 (PDF)
Subjects: LCGFT: Novels.
Classification: LCC PS8601.M49 U53 2024 | DDC jC813/.6—dc23

Published in the U.S.A. by Annick Press (U.S.) Ltd.
Distributed in Canada by University of Toronto Press.
Distributed in the U.S.A. by Publishers Group West.

Printed in Canada

annickpress.com
mayaameyaw.com

Also available as an e-book. Please visit annickpress.com/ebooks for more details.

Author's Note

Under All the Lights was written with the intention of depicting healthy examples of cultivating queer community while dealing with challenges related to external and internal queerphobia. While themes of finding healing and support are woven throughout, please be aware that there are many heavy subjects discussed that may be difficult for some readers. These subjects include depictions of biphobia, anxiety disorders, eating disorders, substance abuse, racial discrimination, sexism, and mentions of physical assault and sexual assault. Several detailed experiences of panic attacks are portrayed on the page. If you are sensitive to any of these subjects, please proceed at your own pace and comfort.

There's courage involved if you want to become Truth.

—Rumi

1

My heart sledgehammers against my rib cage as soon as I spot my dad at the kitchen table. It's ten on a Saturday morning—I expected him to be over at my uncle's house watching their weekly soccer game.

He raises an eyebrow suspiciously when I don't say good morning. I walk quickly past him and drop my duffle bags by the back patio door.

"You're leaving soon?" I hear him ask over the soaring vocals of the post-punk ballad blasting through my headphones.

"Yeah," I mutter, keeping my head down as I pull my headphones off. I turn fully away from him and crouch down to try and locate the travel mug I thought I packed last night. If I keep some distance between us, maybe I can get to the car without him getting a good look at me. I just have to get some coffee in me, grab a couple of snacks for the road, and then Soph and I can take off for the festival.

Caffeine is my first priority because I stayed up way too late working on a new song last night. I'm exhausted, but I'm glad I got it all down instead of falling asleep and forgetting the chorus that popped into my head while I was listening to one of my favorite indie folk playlists.

"Olia, wait!" my mom says, bounding into the kitchen. "You're not leaving without having some breakfast. There's fresh kahwa, did you have some?"

I nod and straighten when I finally locate my travel mug. "Thanks. Just about to grab a cup."

"But don't just drink that—you have to eat something! I made baghrir," she says, handing me a plate piled high with spongy hot cakes.

I put the plate down and bite at the inside of my cheek, containing a sigh. "Mom, it's fine. I already had some cereal earli—"

"And I have some pastries for Aisha, make sure you give them to her," she says, stuffing containers into my hands.

"Mom."

She grimaces at my annoyed expression. "It's just a treat for later. A little baqlawa. I didn't mean—"

"Don't worry." I take a deep breath and smooth out my expression. After Aisha's accident at her dance recital last year, I made my mom promise to stop pressuring Aisha to eat more whenever she's over here. And to stop commenting about her weight since it's triggering for her eating issues. "It's okay, I'll give them to her."

She smiles at that but frowns when I hand back a bigger container loaded with couscous.

"We can't bring a ton of food, though. We're only gonna be in the car for a few hours and then we won't be able to take any outside food into the festival grounds."

"What will you eat then?"

"We'll just buy food there," I say, brushing past her to finally fill my mug.

She sighs loudly as she carries the containers back to the fridge. "They'll only have expensive junk."

I shrug as I take a sip from my steaming mug. She's right. And I'm not exactly thrilled to spend the little money I make at The Vinyl Underground on ten-dollar hot dogs. The festival tickets on their own took me ages to save up for. Working at a record shop/concert venue does have some cool perks, but a big paycheck isn't exactly one of them.

"Do you have enough money?" I hear my dad ask.

I'm still turned away from him, looking out the kitchen window at Sophie's old, beat-up station wagon. She's standing by the open trunk, struggling with a folded-up tent.

"Yeah," I say to my dad even though I'm not totally sure. I'm surprised he asked at all—I can't remember the last time he offered me spending money.

"Here," Dad grumbles.

I have to face him now. Turning around, I see he's holding out a twenty-dollar bill.

"Oh." A fifty would have helped more, to be honest, but it's better than nothing. I manage a smile as I take it from him. "Thanks, Dad."

When I meet his eyes for a second, I see his gaze go to my right ear. His face sours. *Shit.*

"Earrings again? I thought you stopped that girly nonsense."

I stare at the floor unable to move, my mouth going dry and bitter.

"Isaac, enough," Mom scolds him before Sophie comes bursting in the back door.

I finally unfreeze, glancing over at her. "Ollie, can I take your stuff out to the car?"

In two long strides I'm right next to her, picking up my backpack and guitar. "I've got them. Okay, bye—"

"Just a minute," Mom calls out, and I resist the urge to roll my eyes. "Sophie, be careful on the highway, all right? And Ollie . . . you be careful too."

I cringe. "Yep, okay, see you—"

"I mean with Aisha," she continues. "You two be safe."

Sophie stifles a snicker.

"Yeah, I got it," I grind out, my face flaming. I love my mom, but she's so goddamn annoying sometimes. I resist the urge to pull my headphones back over my ears to drown out my embarrassment.

Aisha and I have been dating for almost a year, but this is the first time we'll be alone overnight together. We decided when we first started dating to take our time with stuff, but things have been getting more intense lately. A couple of nights ago she asked me to sneak into her house to sleep over. I didn't because honestly, I'm a bit terrified of her dad and what he'd do to me if he caught me in her room. Besides that, I'm worried about freaking out while we're together. I haven't had a panic attack in a while, but every time it happens, it's beyond mortifying. I know I shouldn't feel that way, but it's impossible not to.

I'm probably being way too presumptuous anyway. Just because Aisha invited me over doesn't mean she wants to have sex. And just because we'll be alone this weekend doesn't mean we have to.

I mean, obviously I want to. A lot. Enough to bury a pack of condoms at the bottom of my bag. But the real point of this weekend is to relax and be in the moment for once instead of overthinking everything. All I have to do is chill out and enjoy some good music with my friends—it's that simple. And maybe vlog a few of the performances for my YouTube channel. I mostly post original songs and a few covers on there, but some of my viewers have been asking for vlogs. There's no pressure on that, though. No one I'm going to the festival with even knows about my channel except Aisha.

"Listen to your mother," Dad says, and I risk another quick glance at him. "You don't want to ruin your life having a baby at seventeen. And we can't afford to take care—"

"Dad, stop!" I can't help glaring at him.

He shakes his head and sighs. "I'm not saying that just because Aisha is . . ." he trails off, looking away.

Fucking asshole. I know exactly what disgusting, stereotypical bullshit he was about to say.

"Oh good. It's not *just* because of that. Great."

"I mean, she's a very smart girl," my dad says, shrugging. "She has her whole life ahead of her. And if you get your grades up when school starts next week, maybe you will too." He laughs, but it's clearly not a joke. "Your college applications are coming up soon, aren't they?"

"Right," I mutter. So much for chilling out and not worrying about the future. My grades have never been good enough for me to go into engineering like him, but that doesn't seem to stop him from hoping. I have no idea how to break it to him that I don't plan on applying to any of the fancy colleges he wants me to.

If I told him I wanted to be a musician, he would laugh in my face. Even though I'm in the music program at my school, I'm painfully aware that being a singer/songwriter isn't something I could make a living from. Producing other artists' music is a way more practical career—if I can even get into a production program. My grades last year weren't stellar. Between working and not being great at school in the first place, my B- average has turned into a C. Not exactly what college administrators are looking for.

My mom and Sophie stare between us in horrified silence for a moment, then my mom jumps into action again.

"Just take this one container of dolma dalya. You can eat it in the car." Mom puts it in my hand after I've hoisted my bags onto my shoulders. "And come here."

She manages to trap both Sophie and me in a bear hug and kisses our cheeks.

"Ugh, stop," I complain, but I don't pull away until she lets go. This is the last weekend before school starts and Sophie moves out. She's going to an art college downtown, so it'll just be me with my parents until I graduate in the spring.

After Soph and I say goodbye to Mom, I glance back at the kitchen table. Dad's already disappeared without a word.

"Are you okay?" Sophie asks as we get to her car. She bought it last week with the babysitting money she's been saving up for years. And now here she is, back on babysitting duty.

I shake the thought away. She's not babysitting me. Soph wanted to come this weekend. Feist is headlining and I can't even count the number of times we listened to our worn vinyl copy of *Let It Die* together. I'm really glad she's coming with us, and not just because she offered to drive me, Aisha, and my best friend, Neil.

Sophie and I used to hang out a lot more when we were kids. Not that I'd ever admit it out loud, but growing up she was basically my best friend. To be real, she was my only friend for a while there.

Ever since I can remember, talking to people has just been . . . hard. Sophie, on the other hand, has always been the life of every party. And, lucky for me, she always had my back when kids got on my case. But when she went to high school I was on my own. That also happened to be the year I suddenly wasn't just the weird, quiet kid with the stutter anymore. That was the year I had my first ever crush on a guy—and he happened to be a bully who definitely noticed. Let's just say he and his friends got *way* more inventive with their insults.

"I'm fine," I say finally as I fight to get my bags into the overflowing trunk. "Jesus, we're only going for two nights. Do we really need all this stuff?"

"The tents and sleeping bags took up more space than I thought," Sophie says as we manage to shut the tailgate. "*There* we go. Time to hit the road!"

*
*

A few hours later, I glance at my phone and groan. "And . . . we've officially missed the first set."

Sophie turns around in line to roll her eyes at me. "Can you relax? We're almost inside."

I peer over her shoulder toward the festival gates, tapping out a rapid-fire rhythm against my leg. "We would already be inside if you didn't drive so slow."

"I was driving the speed limit. It's not my fault everyone else was speeding," she mutters.

Aisha lets out a sigh beside me and I bite my tongue, cutting off my retort. I guess it's not the end of the world, but I can't help being annoyed that we're already off schedule. A lot of the bands playing in this festival have never played at The Vinyl Underground—and I've been wanting to see them for a while. Especially Jesse Jacobs, a new Indigenous indie pop rock artist whose debut I've been listening to constantly for the last few months. His sound has been super inspiring for me—I even covered his latest single on my channel. At least we won't miss his set since it's not till tomorrow.

Neil pats me on the back and smiles. "Don't worry, we'll still catch most of the acts tonight." He glances toward the parking lot, his grin growing wider. "And look who finally showed!"

I follow his gaze and see Ebi and Khadija, two of our theater kid friends, bounding up to us.

Ebi and Khadija both seem thrilled to see Neil. It can be a little infuriating hanging out with someone who is so universally liked, but I've mostly gotten over it. I met Neil in ninth grade when he randomly came over to me in the caf one day. I was sitting alone, and he started talking to me like we'd been friends forever. Before long, we were hanging out pretty much every day. He always stuck up for me when assholes would make fun of me.

"Aisha, you look fabulous!" Khadija says, taking her by the hand and twirling her around. "Loving this outfit! A bit of an upgrade from your neutral hoodie collection."

"Gee, thanks," Aisha says, crossing her arms over her cropped floral tank.

She does look extra great today, but I haven't said anything because I was afraid it might make her uncomfortable. It's been a struggle for her to feel okay with looking a little different now that she's been eating enough.

Khadija winces. "Sorry, that wasn't—"

"How was your drive?" I cut in as I slip my fingers through Aisha's again.

"Awful," Ebi answers, setting his bag down. "Especially right by the Falls. We didn't move for like an hour. Thanks for saving us a spot."

"We're moving!" Sophie calls from ahead of us, and we all rush to catch up to her.

I tune out everyone around me as I try to calculate how many more minutes I'm going to miss of the second set.

Aisha curses under her breath and I zone back in, glancing at her. "What's up?"

She's squinting toward the gates with her brow furrowed. "I don't think they're letting people bring in snacks."

"They usually don't at these things. We'll grab food inside—" I clamp my mouth shut. I could kick myself for not remembering to offer Aisha any of the food my mom gave me. On the drive over, Aisha shared a new single from a band she wants to check out this weekend and I got entirely distracted jotting down some new lyrics that came to me while we were listening.

"Do you think they'll let me bring in a few protein bars?" Aisha asks.

I look to the front of the line again as we move forward. They're doing full bag checks. Judging by the pile of bottles by the gates, they're not even allowing outside water.

She follows my gaze and swears again. When I shoot her a concerned look, she squeezes my hand and manages a smile. "It's fine. They'll probably have a few food trucks that aren't, like, deep-fried everything."

"Yeah, they should have some healthy stuff."

Nodding, she reaches into her bag and pulls out a handful of protein bars, chucking them into the closest garbage can.

"Don't look so worried," she says, kissing me on the cheek. "It'll be fine. Let's just focus on having an awesome weekend, okay? We're gonna see so many amazing bands!"

I slowly break into a smile, her excitement trickling into me. If she says she'll be okay, I should trust her. And she's right, I need to chill out. Even though we missed a couple sets, there are still a ton of acts I can't wait to see. With senior year starting next week, this is my last chance to not have a zillion things to worry about, including the huge question mark of my future.

"Wait." Aisha gives me a funny look and then touches my earlobe. "When did you get your ears pierced?"

My face grows hot as I remember my dad sneering at me this morning. "I've had them pierced since ninth grade," I say.

"You have? I've never seen you wear earrings before."

"Yeah . . ." Honestly, when I talked myself into putting them on this morning, I was a little surprised the piercings hadn't completely closed up.

Pretty soon after Neil and I started hanging out and he introduced me to his super open theater friends, I started feeling comfortable wearing earrings and even nail polish sometimes. My dad made lots of snide remarks about it then, too. But at the time, I was slowly starting to stop caring so much about what people thought of me.

All of that changed after what happened with Thomas. He was a guy Sophie dated a few years ago for reasons beyond my comprehension. After they broke up, he started talking shit about her in front of me at school. When that didn't get him the reaction he wanted, he started picking fights with me. Sophie didn't know how much it had escalated until I ended up in the hospital. And she still doesn't know about—

Not now. I squeeze my eyes shut as my throat starts to tighten.

"Hey." Aisha squeezes my hand again. "What's wrong?"

I shake my head, opening my eyes. "Nothing. I'm good."

"Okay . . ." She can clearly tell something's up, but she lets it go. "Well, I like them. They look really good on you. Where'd you get them?"

"Just found them at a thrift store," I say as she leans in for a closer look.

Her fingers trace the tiny, gold, spiral-shaped emblem hanging from my ear. "Do you know what this symbol means?"

"Unalome. It means, uh, the journey to enlightenment. The spirals at the bottom are supposed to be all the chaos at the beginning of the journey, and then the path starts to straighten out the more lessons that you learn. Or something like that."

I cringe. It sounds so corny when I explain it—nothing like how it feels when I'm meditating or translating my thoughts about spirituality into my music. After what happened with Thomas, I started seeing a therapist who suggested meditation. Developing a practice has helped with some of my anxiety, but it's still a daily struggle.

When I focus on Aisha, I can tell she doesn't find it stupid, thankfully.

Her eyes soften. "I love that," she breathes and then kisses me right where my neck meets my ear.

I love you. The words are right on the tip of my tongue, but I bite down, containing a groan as she pulls away.

We still haven't technically said "I love you." I've almost said it so many times . . . but she always looks so terrified when she can tell I'm about to.

I've been working on a song as a way of finally saying it out loud, but I've been stuck on how to not freak her out or make her feel like she has to say it back if she's not ready.

Neil clears his throat loudly, and Aisha and I finally break away from each other. "Sorry to interrupt, but the line's moving. Let's go."

As we inch toward the gates, I close my eyes for a moment. Focusing on the distant sound of drums, I inhale the smoky musk of newly lit campfires, letting go of the tension in my shoulders. I give Aisha's hand a gentle squeeze and when she squeezes back and grins at me, I can't help thinking that I'd be totally okay waiting in line the rest of my life as long as she's next to me.

2

"You good, dude?" Ebi asks. I snap my head up from my phone.

"Uh . . . uh, yeah." That's all I'm able to stammer out. I used to get teased about my stutter when I was younger. It was never so bad that I was diagnosed with a speech disorder, but I've always tripped over my words when I'm nervous.

He gives me a sideways look then wraps his hands around the barrier in front of us and glances up at the vacant stage.

Could you please *just act normal for once?*

Once we got inside, it took us a while to hike over to the camping area and set up our tents. When we were done, everyone else decided they wanted to go to the beach and take a dip to combat the oppressive heat, and I wanted to catch an act happening at a stage halfway across the grounds. Ebi is the only one who opted to come along with me. Which is a nice break from socializing as a bigger group. But somehow, I'm still managing to be weird and awkward.

Ebi started at Huntley in tenth grade and almost immediately became one of the most popular kids in our grade. He starred in our school's musical two years in a row and probably will again this year. Considering I've had lunch with him and Neil basically every day since we met, it's truly pathetic how inept I still am at talking to him.

Ebi and Neil are both ultra extroverted, but Neil never seems to care if I don't talk that much. I think maybe long silences make Ebi uncomfortable, though. The entire walk over to the stage he tried to keep the conversation going, but I didn't manage to get out more than a few coherent sentences. I figure not saying too much is better than stuttering and babbling on like an idiot. Ebi probably doesn't even care—he's used to me being quiet. That doesn't stop my brain from worrying about it though.

Finally, the band we're waiting for takes the stage, the lights brightening. The crowd roars with excitement and it's too loud to worry about being social for a while. I haven't seen this act before and I'm completely entranced by how good they are live—all my buzzing thoughts still as the hypnotic baseline booms through my chest. I nod along to the beat, letting the music take me over for a few songs before I suddenly remember I wanted to vlog a bit this weekend. I take my phone out of my pocket and start recording the set. The sun's lazily descending in the humid evening air. The view is picturesque, shades of magenta, violet, and lavender blazing across the horizon behind the stage.

My mind starts up again, but instead of worrying, I feel myself moving into a state of flow, some lyrics I've been stuck on for my latest song finally falling into place. I switch from my camera to my notes app and jot them down before they float away.

When the set ends, I turn to Ebi and smile, feeling much more relaxed. "I'm gonna stick around—Midnight Cavalcade is coming on in a few minutes. Do you wanna check them out too or are you heading back to camp?"

"I'm sticking around," Ebi says, shooting me an easy smile. "My friend Dev is gonna meet us for the next set."

"Okay, cool. Aisha said she's heading over here. Is Dev from school? I don't think I know—"

"One sec," Ebi cuts in as his phone starts ringing. He picks up and starts speaking quietly in Igbo.

I focus on my own phone again, reading through my song notes. Hopefully I'll have some time this weekend to try and nail down the melody on my guitar.

Ebi starts yelling and I look up, blinking at him. I don't think I've ever heard him sound even remotely annoyed at anyone.

He hangs up after a moment and I raise my eyebrows. "Everything good?"

"All good," he says quickly. "Anyway, yeah, Dev's not from school. We started talking on a music forum a while back. When they told me they'd be coming to the festival this weekend, we decided to link up in person."

I nod. "That's cool."

"I have a feeling the two of you will get along. Dev's a musician too—they're a drummer."

I nod again, biting down the urge to say I'm not a musician. I do kind of like the way it sounds, but I have a feeling Dev's an *actual* musician. Like someone who's played real gigs, not just an art school kid with a tiny YouTube channel.

Ebi continues when I stay quiet. "So . . . you excited for senior year?"

I shrug. "Not particularly."

He laughs. "I'm not looking forward to summer being officially over either. Do you know where you're going to apply to college yet?"

My stomach begins to turn. "Probably some music production programs."

"So you can produce your own music?" Ebi asks. "You were great at back-to-school auditions last week."

I snort, shaking my head. I was so checked out I can hardly even remember how I did . . . but at least it was better than last year's auditions, when some jerks laughed at me and I froze in front of everyone.

"Thanks, but I'm probably gonna stick to producing for other people."

"Gotcha. You *do* have a great voice though. Like I could definitely see you up here performing one day!"

I don't think he's bullshitting me or just trying to be nice. He means it.

My face warms and I stare at my feet. "I don't know about all that."

I started my channel to get some objective feedback, and I can't deny it's been overwhelmingly positive. But being a good singer is only half the battle. The thought of being up on a stage like this is downright terrifying. I almost throw up every single time I have to perform for a grade.

But if I'm being perfectly honest, sometimes I *can* picture it. Like when I catch myself imagining what it would be like if my anxiety didn't exist and I could get up onstage without a second thought. How it would be to feel totally uninhibited, to feel the same high I can sense my favorite musicians get when they're in their element.

"Maybe you'd consider trying out for the musical this year?" Ebi asks, pulling me from the daydream. "I know show tunes aren't your thing, but I'm gonna try and convince the theater director to let us do a *Rocky Horror* adaptation this year."

"Cool!" I'm a rock opera fan, so that does sound intriguing. But even the thought of auditioning—let alone actually performing in a show like that—makes me feel a little nauseous and lightheaded. "I'm not sure about trying out, but I'll definitely be there opening night with Aisha."

"If you're not up for performing, we could use some help with stage production . . ." Ebi raises his eyebrows hopefully.

Since I do sound and lighting for shows at work all the time, that sounds like something I could handle. And I probably need at least one extracurricular to put on my college apps.

"I'll think about it," I say after a minute.

"Think about what?"

I turn and find Aisha beside us. She wraps an arm around me as Ebi fills her in.

"We could really use Ollie on the crew for the musical this year."

Her eyes light up. "Ooh, that sounds fun!"

"Aisha, you should join too," Ebi says. "We could use some more dancers."

"Sure you don't need me to sing?" Ebi scrunches up his nose and she laughs. "Just kidding. Fully aware that my voice sucks. But yeah, I'm not sure I'll have time to help out. I'll uh, be starting ballet again this year and between that and Modern . . . I'll have to get back to you."

I squeeze her hand. After her accident last year, she took a break from ballet to focus on her health, and I know she's been nervous about returning to it.

"Dev!" Ebi says, dragging me from my thoughts.

I look over as he embraces someone with short black hair.

"So great to finally meet you!" Dev says.

"You too!" Ebi turns to the rest of us. "Dev, these are my friends Ollie and Aisha . . ." His phone starts ringing again and he frowns. "Sorry guys, just give me a sec." He answers it, stepping away.

There's a beat of awkward silence before Aisha speaks up. "How do you know Ebi?"

Dev scratches their head and laughs. "Uh, from online actually. We met on a forum and then we started our own music blog—" They stop short when Ebi shouts into his phone again.

We all exchange surprised looks.

"Whoa," Aisha says when Ebi ends the call. "What's up?"

"Just African parent things. You know how it is." He tries to smile, but he still looks upset.

"What's going on?" Dev asks carefully.

"My mom's pissed about my hair." Ebi's hi-top fade is currently bleached blond. A look I could never imagine pulling off, but it suits him so well it barely even registered when he and Khadija met up with us earlier. "She keeps spewing random Bible verses at me to try and make me feel guilty or something. Woman's completely off her rocker."

"That sucks," Aisha says. "What's the big deal though? Your hair looks great."

"No idea." Ebi shrugs. "Well . . . maybe she's getting closer to clueing in that I'm into guys, I guess? Because only *the gays* bleach their hair, obviously." He snorts and rolls his eyes.

"I feel you on that," Dev says. "My parents were pretty awful when I told them I was nonbinary and stopped dressing femme."

"My dad's sort of the same way. This morning he freaked when he saw my earrings." The words tumble out of my mouth before I can stop them.

Dev nods sympathetically, but Aisha's eyes widen at my admission. When I peek at Ebi, I catch him giving me an all-too-knowing look.

Shit. I frantically try to think of something to say to backtrack. Something about my dad's reaction being about his outdated perceptions and nothing to do with my identity. I come up blank, staring down at my sneakers.

The thing is, Ebi already knows that I'm bi. I mean, I haven't come out to anyone besides my therapist and Aisha, but I know he can just tell. Part of why it's so difficult for me to act normal around Ebi is because I'm a little envious of how confident he is with his sexuality. He's still in the closet with his family, but him and his ex were really open at school. No one ever gets on his case about it, unlike how I used to get teased. I got an inkling of what that kind of fearlessness could feel like back in ninth grade. Then Thomas came along and snuffed it out. When Ebi started at Huntley the next year, he saw right through me even though I was doing my best not to even think about that part of myself. To be real, it's not much easier to think about it now.

The frantic thudding of my heart reverbs in my ears, muting the din of the crowd. What if Ebi mentions it to Neil or Sophie? I don't think he would out me on purpose, but what if he assumes I've already told them? It's not that I think Neil or Sophie would react badly. I'm just not ready to talk about it with more people in my life.

"Your parents are from Turkey, right?" Ebi asks. "Are they religious?"

"Uh, well . . ." I'm not sure how to respond without rambling on about my family history. "My parents were both born in Algeria, but my dad is part French and Libyan. My mom grew up Muslim and stopped practicing, and my dad's family is agnostic. Anyway, sorry about your mom."

"Thanks. And yeah, sorry to hear that about your dad," Ebi says, and Dev nods understandingly.

"Me too," Aisha says quietly, and I finally look up again. She leans in and kisses me before pulling back, breaking into a sad smile. I'm utterly unable to look away from her.

"Okay, that's enough. I'm too single to deal with this right now." Ebi rolls his eyes at Dev and they laugh as Midnight Cavalcade starts playing.

Forcing my racing thoughts aside, I focus on the warmth of Aisha's fingers wrapped firmly around mine. This is the same band we saw on our first date, and I'm suddenly transported right back to that night at The Vinyl Underground with her in my arms just like this. Everything stopped mattering except for us. The sun's fully set now, the warm lights of the stage illuminating the night. My mind shuts off as the music envelops us completely.

3

I'm buzzing in the best way by the time Midnight Cavalcade finishes. Their set was really inspiring, and best of all, there was a surprise appearance from Serafina, the band's breakout ex-lead singer. The crowd went wild when she came on and they played a few of their old classics together. Now I'm antsy to get back to camp so I can grab my guitar and start on the melody I made notes on earlier.

Dev walks with us back to our camp and Aisha gives me an opening to explain the full lore of the band's split—something I'm intimately familiar with through fan forums.

"My band actually opened for Midnight Cavalcade once," Dev says when I'm finished. "They did a surprise show at this tiny local venue in Regina. We were the hometown act."

I try to keep my jaw from hitting the ground. "That's amazing! How long have you been with your band?"

"A couple years. We've been touring off and on since we graduated high school last year, playing whatever small gigs we can book.

We're on a break right now, so I've been traveling and doing odd jobs whenever I can find them."

"That's cool," I say. Dev sounds pretty happy, but it must get hard sometimes, living on the road and trying to find work in new places. But it seems like they really love it.

"We're actually going to be looking for a new bassist soon. Ebi said you're a singer, but do you happen to play bass too?"

"Um . . . yeah."

"That's awesome. I could let you know when we're auditioning?" Something about their hopeful expression makes me hesitate. I'm imagining myself up onstage again, but this time not having to deal with the stress of being in the spotlight. Excitement sparks inside me, but I quickly come back to reality.

I shake my head. "I'd love to try out, but I'm starting my senior year next week. Let me know when you guys are looking for gigs again, though—I might be able to get you in at the small venue I work at in Toronto."

"I hear you," Dev says as we arrive back at camp. "And that would be great!"

Aisha squeezes my hand, studying me curiously. I'm pretty sure she noticed I sounded a bit bummed. I squeeze her hand back and give her a genuine smile, and her face relaxes. It was fun to imagine what traveling as a musician would be like for a second, but it would be super difficult to be away from each other.

"Hey everyone," Ebi says as we approach. Neil, Sophie, and Khadija are gathered around a small firepit set up in the middle of our tents. I tuck away the urge to go work on my song since I don't want to be antisocial. "This is my friend Dev."

Dev gives a hesitant smile. "Hope you guys don't mind me crashing your camp for a bit."

I wonder if Dev came to the festival alone or if they have some other friends at their own camp. I know lots of people go to overnight festivals by themselves, but that's yet another thing I don't think I'd be brave enough to try.

"The more the merrier," Khadija says. "We got deep-fried s'mores!" She holds up a bunch of them attached to long wooden sticks. "Honestly the best thing I've *ever* eaten. Consider yourselves blessed that we saved these for you."

Ebi and Dev go over to grab a few.

I glance at Aisha. "Do you want to find some actual food?" Ebi and I grabbed burritos on the way to watch the set, but I don't know if Aisha has eaten since we got here.

She shakes her head. "I had some roasted corn on the cob after our swim."

I frown. "That's all? We can get something else . . ."

"I think all the food trucks are closed now," she says.

Neil glances at us. "Aisha put me to shame and downed *three* entire cobs."

A wave of relief passes through me.

Aisha laughs as she grabs a couple of the deep-fried s'mores sticks Neil's holding out. "I guess you were saving room for these atrocities? They look kinda disgusting."

"Don't knock it till you try it," Neil says, passing a few to me as well.

"Thanks." I sit on a log next to Aisha.

"These are surprisingly good," Ebi says as he chows down across the circle. "Definitely verging on deep-fried Mars Bar territory."

Dev nods and lets out a sound of agreement with their mouth full.

"I know right?" Sophie chimes in.

Khadija holds her s'mores stick above the fire. "Cheers!"

After we finish eating, Ebi and Khadija predictably break into show tunes, singing at the top of their lungs. We all join in, and after a while Soph manages to convince me to grab my guitar for some instrumental accompaniment.

"Ollie, why don't you sing that song you wrote for Aisha?" Neil asks suddenly, and my blood slushes to a cold stop.

She told him about that? The song I wrote about Aisha was the first one I ever posted online. It was a spur-of-the-moment thing after I recorded the video for an assignment. My music composition teacher said all these nice things about it and gave me an A+ even though I hadn't been brave enough to perform it in front of my class. Not just because it's embarrassingly sappy . . . but because the lyrics allude to what happened with Thomas.

Writing about that was extremely difficult, but it did help me sort out some stuff. And when I first sang it for Aisha, she was more understanding and supportive than I could have hoped.

I never asked her not to tell Neil about the song, but I assumed she wouldn't because she promised to keep my channel a secret.

Aisha shoots Neil an annoyed look then leans toward me. "Sorry. I didn't tell him about your channel or anything," she whispers.

"Ollie, you wrote a song for Aisha?" Sophie asks. "Aww, *that's so cute!* Can we hear it?"

Ebi, Dev, and Khadija chime in, urging me on.

Aisha shakes her head. "How about we sing something else?"

"I can play it," I say quietly, and she gives me a disbelieving look.

I make myself smile and keep my breath steady. Within the warm circle of the fire, surrounded by friendly faces, performing doesn't feel quite so scary. Maybe it's the support I've been getting online combined with how encouraging everyone's being right now, but I'm pretty sure I can handle this. I can just sing the first half of the song that's about Aisha and avoid any mention of Thomas. I can do this.

Everyone cheers while Aisha keeps staring at me. "You sure?"

I nod then focus on my guitar again and start.

When you danced
I tripped and fell
Fell into a waking dream
You're inked inside my memory
It never stops
You're on repeat
At night I can't
I never sleep . . .

I keep my gaze on Aisha and everything else melts away. It's hard to believe the way she's looking at me. I know exactly how much she's feeling right now because I'm feeling all of it, too.

I stop after the bridge like I planned. Aisha smiles sadly when she realizes I'm not going to sing the part about Thomas. She wipes her eyes then kisses me while everyone whoops and claps around us.

"That was so good!" Ebi says. "See, Dev? I told you he's a great performer!"

"Totally!" Dev smiles at me. "It's too bad you're not free to gig with my band. We could use some backup vocals, too."

"Look at you, getting offers to join a band," Khadija says, shaking her head. "Soon you'll be leaving us little people behind."

"Ollie, that was beautiful," Sophie says. She looks a little teary as she smiles at me across the fire.

I try to shrug off my discomfort at the excessive praise, staring down at my guitar. "Thanks, everyone."

Neil pats me on the back. "Got anymore for us?"

"Uh . . . Anyway, here's 'Wonderwall.'" I loudly strum the opening chords and everyone cracks up and then starts booing.

"Come on," Dev urges. "I'd really love to hear more of your stuff."

I bite my lip. Since they were all so nice about my first song, I don't think it would hurt to play one more. I choose another one of my originals that's gotten some good feedback on my channel. This time, I start to actually have fun with it. Surprisingly, it doesn't feel that different from playing in my room at home. Aisha's grinning at me and I'm grinning right back, my entire body warm and light. I'm thinking about watching my favorite musicians onstage earlier, wondering if this is how they feel when they're in the zone, everything flowing perfectly. After I finish, I get way too many compliments again, and then we sing a few more show tunes.

A little while later, Ebi goes to walk Dev back to their camp. After they say their goodbyes, I glance at my phone and realize just how late it is.

"I'm going to bed too," I tell Aisha. "I wanna get an early start."

She nods as she gets up and takes my hand. We say good night to everyone and head over to our tent.

"Jeez, it's so dark in here," Aisha says, unzipping the tent.

I turn on my phone flashlight as I step in after her. When I glance over, she's in the middle of taking off her shorts.

She laughs when she catches me frozen by the entrance. "Are you just gonna stare, perv?"

"Sorry." I clear my throat, trying to swallow down my pounding pulse. *Stop acting like a freak.* I force myself to turn away from her as I unroll my sleeping bag.

"Oll, I'm only kidding." Her voice is right next to my ear now and then she's wrapping her arms around my shoulders. "You can stare."

She kisses the back of my neck and I turn toward her, meeting her lips with mine.

After a few airless minutes, Aisha pulls back to look at me, her face serious. "Hey . . . I'm glad you felt okay playing tonight," she murmurs. "It was really sweet of you."

I nod wordlessly then press my forehead to hers.

She takes a deep breath. "And I'm glad—I'm glad you were comfortable saying what you said about your dad in front of Ebi and Dev."

I lean back and sigh. "Yeah, I'm pretty sure Ebi kinda knew about me anyway."

She takes my face in her hands. "I'm still proud of you. And . . . Ollie, I love you."

I'm speechless. I get how scary this is for her. From the beginning, it's been incredibly difficult to get her to open up to me about anything she's feeling. Never mind something as inescapably vulnerable as this.

I blink hard as my own eyes start to sting. "I love you, too. N'habek hataa i t'harkou lil njoum."

I lean into her, but she pulls back again.

"Wait, what does that mean? It sounded so pretty."

My pulse drums up to a lightning tempo as I try to come up with something that makes sense. The literal English translation from

Arabic is something along the lines of *I'll love you until the stars burn.* Which would sound slightly unhinged to repeat in English.

"Just that I'm in love with you," I finally get out, pulling her to me again.

All my fears about what she might be expecting from me tonight gradually begin to unravel. No matter what happens, I know she won't think any less of me. I know I can totally trust her.

*
*

The muted turquoise haze of dawn is filtering into the tent by the time I pull away from Aisha again. I sit up in the sleeping bag we're cocooned inside of.

"You okay?" she asks.

"I'm okay." I take a steadying breath. "I was just wondering if you wanted to . . ."

She looks at me sideways when I don't continue. "What?"

My face heats up as I scrub a hand through my hair. "You know. Have sex."

Her eyes widen as she sits up next to me. "You wanna have sex?"

"I mean, if you want to, yeah. I, um, have condoms."

Her mouth opens, but no sound escapes her. She seems way more surprised than I expected.

I shake my head, glancing away. "Forget I asked."

"No, it's okay," she says as she takes hold of my hand. "I just . . . I thought you didn't want to?"

My brow furrows. "What do you mean? Why would you think that?"

"When we first got together, you asked me if it was okay if we never had sex. Remember?"

I blink at her for a second until it comes back to me. She means the first time we hooked up, the week after her accident. The same night that I came out to her.

"I didn't say I never wanted to. Just that I wasn't sure if I uh, could," I mutter, wincing. "I've been doing okay for a while though, so . . ."

She squeezes my hand a little. "So you wanna try?"

I nod. "If you feel ready."

She's quiet again for a long moment.

I lie back down and rub my eyes. "I didn't mean to spring this on you."

She settles back next to me, resting her head on my shoulder. "It's okay. But . . . I don't want to this weekend. Like, I'd wanna get on the pill, even with condoms."

I turn toward her and kiss her temple. "Okay. That sounds good."

She runs a hand through my hair and considers me closely. "Are you really sure you're ready?"

"I haven't had a panic attack for a few months," I murmur.

"I know, but you still never talk about what happened with your assault. I mean, you never talk about it with me. I know you do with your therapist."

I pull away from her, sitting up again. She means the thing that happened with Thomas that was so much worse than getting beat up. The reason why I can't just be excited when we're alone together— why I'm constantly worried I'll freak out.

"Ollie . . . Sorry for mentioning it," she says, gently taking my arm and pulling me back to her. "I didn't mean to upset you."

"You didn't," I say, though it's an obvious lie. "I just don't know what you want me to say about it."

"I don't mean you have to tell me details. I just wish you felt comfortable talking about it with me at all. We've been together for almost a year, and you've never said a single thing other than telling me it happened."

"What does it matter?" I sigh out. "Look, whatever I tell you, I know it's just going to make you sad."

"You had to go through it. I can handle just hearing about it, I promise."

I force myself to relax my bunched-up shoulders. I hate even thinking about it, much less talking about it. Doing it in therapy is hard enough.

I open my eyes again after a while. "Okay, thanks. I don't want to talk about it right now, though."

I glance away from her pitying gaze. Why do I feel like I'm disappointing her? I get that she just wants me to be okay and to stop feeling so guilty. I hate that after all this time it still feels like I'm partly to blame. But I don't see how talking would help with that.

"That's all right." She puts her head back on my shoulder. "Love you," she whispers.

I whisper it back and watch her eyes fall closed, her breath slowing. Instead of drifting off too, my mind whirs with the events of the evening, turning them into new lyrics. I think about the song I'd been planning to use to tell Aisha that I love her. Since we've already said it, I guess it's not as big of a deal, but it'll still be nice to surprise her with it soon. Maybe whenever we figure out when we're actually going to sleep together. I jot some lyrics on my phone until my eyes are too heavy to keep open, then finally close them against the early morning light.

4

I wake up drenched in sweat, the sleeping bag plastered to my skin. I peel it off with a disgusted groan and see that Aisha's up and gone already. When I glance at my phone, I jump up. It's close to noon. Just great. I missed two more bands I wanted to see this morning. Why didn't Aisha wake me up when she was leaving?

I'd only brought two pairs of jeans this weekend, and it's way too hot to wear them. I throw on some swim trunks and my lightest undershirt before I stumble out of the tent, squinting against the glaring midday sun.

"Look who's finally up," Sophie says from a picnic table where she, Ebi, and Khadija are chowing down on what looks like either gigantic waffles or oversized funnel cake.

"Aisha didn't wake me." I sit down next to Sophie. "Do you guys know where she went?"

Khadija shakes her head as she pushes a whipped cream-topped funnel cake/waffle monstrosity my way. "Neil went off to find her a little while ago."

When I tense up, Ebi gives me a reassuring smile. "Don't worry. Neil said she was going to find some breakfast and didn't think to bring her phone."

I nod slowly and grab a fork, doing my best to quell my nerves. Everything's probably fine. They'll be back soon.

Sophie grins at me. "If you hurry, we can still catch Feist in a few minutes."

I shoot her a smile in return. "Okay, cool. Just give me a sec," I say as I start stuffing food into my face. "Ebi, Khadija, you guys down?"

"For sure," Ebi says. "I'll check and see if Dev can meet us there too."

Khadija grins. "Let's do it!"

*

I check my phone a couple of times on the way to the stage, but there's nothing from Neil.

"Hey." Sophie loops her arm through mine. "Relax, everything's fine."

I let out a breath and nod, trying to bring myself back to the present. We have a pretty great view of the stage, and the set is just starting. Dev arrives and squeezes between Ebi and Khadija. Everyone screams as Feist floats onstage in a long, flowy dress. Instead of starting with one of her massive hits, the opening notes of "L'amour ne dure pas toujours" filter through the speakers.

Sophie squeals and shoots me an excited look. This has always been one of her favorites. Personally, I find it a bit too sad.

She starts singing along and turns to me expectantly. Rolling my eyes, I join in as Ebi, Khadija, and Dev look on and laugh. Not in a mean way, though. This is actually pretty nice. The worry nagging at the back of my mind fades as the set continues. The slightest breeze starts up, providing some relief from the humidity.

While everyone is busy jumping and dancing along to a more upbeat number, Ebi turns to me. "I forgot to ask you something yesterday."

His expression is more serious than usual, and my heart starts to pound. God, I hope he doesn't bring up what I said about my dad. "What's up?"

"I hope I'm not being too pushy, asking you to join the musical and now this, but I was wondering if you might be interested in writing for our music blog?"

Dev turns to smile at us. "Yeah, we'd love to have you contribute."

I let out a breath. "Oh yeah, you were saying you guys started a blog, right? What kind of stuff do you cover?"

"Don't worry, it's not just musicals," Ebi says wryly. "We cover all kinds of genres. It's an online journal, but we're planning to launch a print issue soon, too."

"Yeah, I'll be renting a tiny studio space when I'm back in Regina. The logistics have been kinda difficult, but we've been making it work so far."

"That's super cool! You guys really want *me* to write for you?"

"Yeah, of course!" Ebi says. "Your music knowledge is off the charts. Like all that Midnight Cavalcade tea you spilled last night. And you always clean up at our trivia nights . . . when you actually show up," Ebi teases.

"Thanks." I can't help but smile. I glance over at Sophie and Khadija, who are still dancing their hearts out beside us. "So is there a theme for the upcoming issue?"

He gives me a careful look. "The theme is queer identity in music." I look toward the stage as he rushes on. "But contributors don't have to identify as queer. Allies are welcome too."

Dev clocks my hesitation and chimes in. "Right, everyone is completely welcome."

I hate that my discomfort is obvious and that Ebi, and most likely Dev, know exactly where it's coming from. That I'm not just an "ally."

Despite my significant social shortcomings, I get that Ebi is trying to connect with me and get me out of my shell. Which is honestly really cool of him. I need to get over myself.

I glance at them again and give a genuine smile. "Okay. I'll get back to you with some pitches."

"Bet. No pressure or anything," Ebi adds, clapping me on the shoulder.

"We can add you to our contributor Discord group too, just so you can get a sense of what everyone else is working on," Dev says. "You can introduce yourself in the intros channel whenever you want. And just a heads-up, a lot of contributors go by nicknames and don't use photos of themselves since some of the stuff we publish is anonymous."

"Okay, that sounds cool. That would be great if you could add me," I say as my phone starts to ring. When I see that it's Neil, I pick up immediately. "Hey man, what's up? You seen Aisha?" I plug my free ear to try and hear him better.

"Yeah. I found her."

My stomach plummets at his tone. "What's wrong?"

"I spotted her pretty far from our campsite, at the other end of the grounds. When I asked her where she'd been she said she got breakfast and checked out some bands, but I think she was lying."

I frown. "Lying about having breakfast?"

If she was lying, Neil would know. He's known her since they were just kids, when she first developed her eating disorder. She told me after her accident that her mom and her old ballet teacher put her on some messed-up diet when she was only twelve.

"Yeah. And I don't think she saw any bands either. I think she went for a super long run. She used to do that in the morning a lot."

"Are you sure?" I shake my head. I can't imagine running for even five minutes in this heat, but since Aisha's used to ridiculously intense dance training, I know it's possible Neil's right.

"Pretty sure. I told her I think she's been restricting and punishing herself because she thinks she ate too much yesterday. She got pissed at me and stormed off a second ago. She didn't look too great. I think she was dissociating."

Aisha was diagnosed with a dissociative disorder last year. "Shit. Did you see where she was headed?"

"The main entrance area. I'm going after her."

"Okay, I'll meet you there."

Ebi and Khadija exchange concerned looks as I hang up.

"What happened?" Sophie asks.

"Neil said Aisha's not feeling well. I'm gonna go meet up with them."

"Do you want us to come too?" Khadija asks.

"No, I don't want to overwhelm her. I'll check in when I find them." I take off before they have a chance to respond, pushing my way through the crowd.

*

I find Aisha and Neil on a bench near the front gates. Aisha's holding a water bottle, sitting back with her eyes closed.

Neil jumps up to meet me when I'm a few feet away, and my stomach turns at his expression.

"Is she still not doing okay?" I ask.

He shakes his head. "She's been completely spaced out. She hasn't said more than three words in, like, twenty minutes. I think we should probably take her home."

I nod. "Okay, just let me talk to her first."

I'm bummed about having to leave early, but making sure she's okay matters more to me than seeing a few more bands.

I slide onto the bench next to her. She's opened her eyes, but she's looking at the ground now.

I wrap an arm around her shoulders. "Hey."

She finally looks up, her eyes widening when she registers my presence. "Sorry. Was I zoned out for a while?"

"It's okay," I say quietly. "Do you wanna go home?"

Aisha pulls away from me, her brow furrowing. "No, we're supposed to stay another night."

"We don't have to if you're not feeling well."

She lets out a shaky breath. "I'm sorry. I . . . I thought I would be okay without my protein bars, but . . ." she trails off for a long moment. "You guys should stay. I'll call my dad. He can pick me up."

"But you'd have to wait hours for him to drive up here when we could just leave now."

Aisha shakes her head. "There's no reentry. You won't be able to come back in for the rest of the weekend."

"It's fine. We can just grab all our stuff at camp and head out."

Obviously it's not the ideal situation, but all that matters is getting Aisha out of here. I push away my disappointment about the weekend being cut short.

"But you wanted to see Jesse Jacobs perform tonight," Aisha says. "Let me just call my dad."

"Okay, but tell him we're driving back because it'll be faster." In the back of my mind, I'm aware that her dad, who's not exactly fond of me, might find a way to blame me for this. Maybe he should. I can't believe I didn't make sure she'd be okay with the food here.

She leans forward and covers her face with her hands. "I'm sorry I ruined this weekend."

I kiss the top of her head. "Don't say that. You didn't ruin anything."

Neil clears his throat and I look up to find him standing in front of us. "We should head back to camp to pack up. I just texted Sophie— she'll let Ebi and Khadija know."

I nod as Aisha pulls away from me again, wiping her eyes. She stands, crossing her arms. "All right, I'm ready."

*
*

The ride home is awful. Traffic is better, but we're completely silent the entire way, which makes it feel twice as long.

When we pull up to Aisha's house, she glances at me for the first time since we got in the car.

"Call me later?" I ask.

She nods before grabbing her bag and taking off. I know she's upset at herself and not me, but I have no clue how to fix that.

We drop Neil off next and then a few minutes later Sophie and I are back at our place. Mom's waiting for us in the living room when we get inside.

"Poor girl," Mom says, shaking her head once I explain what happened.

I look at her sideways. I know she's worried about Aisha, but from how worn her face looks I know something else must be up.

"Mom? What's wrong?"

She's quiet for a long minute, the record player's soft murmur the only sound in the room. I shoot Sophie a worried look.

"There's something I've been meaning to tell the both of you," Mom finally says with a sigh.

My stomach starts to coil in on itself. I don't think I've ever seen her look this serious. I already feel awful, but I have a feeling that things are about to get a lot worse.

"What's going on?" I ask.

"Isaac?" she calls for my dad, and I glance over at Sophie, frowning. He's usually in my parents' room watching the news right around now and my mom rarely disturbs him. "Isaac, come down here!"

I hear his footsteps headed down the stairs and he walks into the living room looking bleary-eyed. "I thought you were coming back tomorrow?"

"Ollie's girlfriend wasn't feeling well so they came back early," Mom explains. "Come sit down. Let's tell them now."

"Tell us what?" Sophie asks as Dad sits across from us in his worn recliner.

"Your father was laid off from his job last week."

"I wasn't laid off," my dad grumbles, shifting in his seat. "The entire company is shutting down. After twenty years you'd think they'd have some loyalty to their employees, but they're leaving us with nothing."

Mom sighs. "The point is, money's going to be a lot tighter with only my paycheck until your father finds another job. That might take some time and . . ." She looks to Dad. He stays quiet, his mouth set in a firm line.

"And what?" Soph asks.

Mom keeps her eyes on Dad, but when he says nothing, she finally continues. "Our emergency savings have run out. We can't afford the mortgage here anymore."

"We're losing the house?" I blurt out. Money's never been great, but we've always had enough to get by.

"We'll find a more affordable place," Mom says.

I nod, but this doesn't feel real. We've lived in this house my entire life. My parents moved here when they got married, a few years before Sophie and I were born. Sophie's moving out next week, and I'll be leaving next year, but that doesn't change the fact that I thought this would always be home. The place that I could always come back to.

"So, you guys aren't gonna be able to help me out with tuition?" Sophie asks. Her voice is quiet.

Mom shakes her head. "I'm sorry, honey. And Ollie . . . I don't think we'll be able to help out with your school fees either."

Dad gets up, heaving out a sigh. "Good night."

Mom gives him an irritated look, but she doesn't protest as he leaves the room.

After he's gone, we all just sit for a moment.

"It's okay, Mom," I say. I'm entirely numb, but I force a small smile. "I can pick up some hours at my job and save up. And I can sell some records."

But I know none of that will make a real dent. I thought my parents would at least be able to help me out a little. I guess I'll just have to take out a ton of student loans and be saddled with debt that I'll probably never be able to pay off. The small fantasy I had about being a traveling musician and surviving on odd jobs like Dev seems even sillier now. Not only do I have to worry about supporting myself, but now my whole family's future hangs in the balance. My gut pinches harder, and I swallow down my nausea.

Mom reaches over and gathers me in a hug, kissing my cheek. "Everything's going to be all right. Things will be different, but we'll still have each other."

Sophie leans in, hugging us both, and I close my eyes. I clench my hands to stop myself from shaking.

Mom's right—even if things are changing, we'll find a way to get through it. But as much as I want to believe that, the unsteady, sinking feeling inside me refuses to go away.

5

"Not your best work, Mr. Cheriet." Ms. Lin smacks my History quiz down an inch from my face.

My head shoots up from my desk as I blink into full consciousness again.

I press my hand against my right ear as casually as possible, hoping she doesn't spot my earbud. Slowly reaching into my pocket, I turn the volume down on the hyperpop playlist I put together to get me through classes without choking on the oppressive boredom. But apparently even that couldn't keep me awake this morning. History almost always makes me sleepy, but aside from that, I've been working pretty much constantly since school started a week ago, picking up as many shifts as I can.

Ms. Lin's already moved on to Aisha, handing back yesterday's pop quiz in a much gentler fashion.

Aisha glances at me once Ms. Lin's moved on from our row.

"*How bad is it?*" she mouths.

I grimace and put my head back down, closing my itchy eyes

against the searing burn of the fluorescent lights. I'm too chickenshit to look. The dates of senseless wars always blend into mush in my mind. Never mind that they're wars we originally studied before the summer break.

Aisha snatches my paper off my desk. Her eyes widen. "Jesus, Oll."

"Miss Bimi." Ms. Lin's back at the front again, her eyes sharp with a final warning.

"Sorry." Aisha lowers her face toward her notebook, and Ms. Lin turns to the blackboard.

I reach for my quiz, but Aisha doesn't hand it over. Instead, she wraps her fingers around mine and squeezes tight for half a second. Thankfully, she's been feeling better since we got back from the festival last week. She said being away from her usual food routine was a big part of her getting triggered.

I watch her lips silently mouth something, but my half-awake brain scrambles any possible meaning.

Pulling my gaze away from her mouth, I focus on her eyes again to find her squinting at me. "*What's wrong?*" she whispers.

I haven't been able to check in as much as I'd like, and I'm somehow even more exhausted this morning than I was yesterday. I probably look like shit. I shake my head and rub my eyes, wondering just how red they are.

"Just tired," I sigh out.

Her eyes soften and then cloud with concern before she surrenders my paper.

I want to tell her that I'm fine, but my head is a jumbled mess of half-formed thoughts. I haven't told her about my parents losing the house yet. I haven't even wanted to think about it. At least work has been a consuming distraction.

Sitting up, I brave a glance at my grade and wince. Fifty-one percent. Great way to start the year. I shut my eyes tight again.

"What time did you get home last night?" Aisha asks when the lunch bell finally rings.

I sling an arm over her shoulders as we head toward the caf. "Like two in the morning. The lead singer of the last set went MIA right before they were supposed to go on. I had to stay to deal with the refunds—it was a nightmare."

Aisha grimaces. "Shit, that sounds awful. Did you find out where the singer went?"

"Brad said the other band members found him passed out in a bathroom after I left, wasted out of his mind. I don't know why they keep booking them to play our venue. It's like the third time this has happened."

"Third time what's happened?" Neil suddenly appears next to Aisha as we walk into the lunchroom.

"Hey. Nothing, just work stuff." I don't want to get into it in front of him since he's in recovery. He's said he doesn't care, but it's still weird talking about drinking in front of him considering how bad things got last year.

"Okay . . ." he says slowly.

Aisha tightens her grip on my hand and quickly changes the subject.

After we grab food, we head upstairs to eat with Ebi, Khadija, and the other drama kids.

"Hey, guys! Ollie, you coming out to musical auditions tomorrow?" Ebi asks when we sit down.

I shake my head as I pull out my math textbook for a last-minute cram session. I have a test right after lunch that, thankfully, I got some warning about yesterday. There's no way I can bomb it, not after this morning. "Won't be able to make it."

There's no point in worrying about extracurriculars for my college apps until I can figure out if I'll even be able to afford college.

"No worries." Ebi moves on to try to recruit Neil. I let out a breath, relieved he didn't ask about the blog, too. Even though I promised myself to give it a try, I'm not sure if I'll have time for it anymore. I did accept Dev's invite to their contributor group on the way home from the festival, giving myself the username Cavalcader24. Everyone was really welcoming. I said hey to a few people who seemed cool, including a guy going by KamranTheSufi who listed an eerie amount of my favorite bands in his intro post. But I haven't looked at the group again since then.

"That sucks you have to miss auditions," Aisha says. "I wish I could try out, too, but I know ballet is going to be a lot this year."

I look up from my textbook. "Have things been going okay in ballet?"

Last year, her classmates were complete assholes, spreading rumors and making gross comments about her eating disorder, which made her issues with food worse. I feel bad I didn't remember to ask her about it when classes started last week.

She shrugs, focused on her spinach salad, and I give her a long look.

"What happened?"

"Not much. The other girls have been ignoring me like usual, no big deal. But yesterday, after class, my teacher asked me if I wanted to do a one-on-one contemporary study with her instead of continuing with classical."

"That sounds great," I say gently, squeezing her shoulder. "I'm glad you don't have to deal with them anymore if you don't want to."

"Yeah. I think she gets how hard last year was for me. I'm just not sure how I feel about switching from classical to contemporary. I told her I'd think about it."

"I'm glad your teacher's trying to help out," I tell her then turn back to my math textbook. I have to make sense of this before lunch ends.

"Do you want my math notes?" Neil asks me a few minutes later. "I have this weird feeling this is the first time you're looking at the chapter."

"That would be great. Thanks, man."

Neil shrugs as he hands his notebook over. "My notes aren't that great or anything, just to warn you. But we don't want you failing out the second week back, do we?"

When I don't even crack a smile, Neil snorts and claps my shoulder. "Hey, relax. You good?"

I lean away from him. The symbols and formulas on the page jump around and multiply. "Yeah. I'm just exhausted."

"You need to stop working so much," Aisha says.

I say nothing, not looking up at her. I know I should tell her about my family's money situation, but it's such a weird thing to bring up since her family never has to think about stuff like that. I don't want her to feel sorry for me. Well, any sorrier for me than she already does.

She doesn't feel sorry for you, I remind myself as I finally look up. I find Aisha and Neil communicating in their secret best friend code with their eyes. A common occurrence that I should be used to, but it sparks something in me closer to anger than annoyance.

She realizes I've caught them and puts on a big smile. "Neil and I have to stay after school for our Modern rehearsals. But I can stop by your place after to study for our next History—"

"I have work." The words come out harsher than I intended, and her eyes flash with hurt. "I picked up an earlier shift right after school."

She raises an eyebrow. "Got it."

I contain a groan as I try to focus on Neil's notes. I hate that I snapped at her and that we haven't been able to talk as much recently. There just aren't enough hours in the day. When I do get home from work, I barely sleep between trying to catch up on schoolwork and incessantly worrying about the future.

What if my mom and dad can't find a place by the time we have to move out? Would my uncle let us move in with him and his family? It's not like they have a ton of extra room. What if we're just out on the street?

I blink hard. Now's not the time. Not here. I try and make sense of the numbers in front of me again, swallowing down the sour taste of dread.

✳

At lunch the next day, I madly scribble down the last half of my English essay with my earphones turned up high, blocking out the theater kids singing beside me.

When I look up from my notebook to chug some coffee, I spot Aisha down the hallway, grinning at me. I smile dopily back, surprised she looks so happy to see me. She usually calls me after I get off work, but she didn't last night.

She starts squealing as she jumps into my arms, almost knocking me over.

"Whoa." I laugh as I take my earbuds out. "What's up?"

Aisha searches my face. "You didn't see yet?"

I tilt my head. "See what?"

"Okay." She squeezes my hand like she's trying to break it. "Don't freak out."

"About what?"

She holds up her phone. The YouTube app is open to my channel. My first video is playing; it's the song I sang at our campfire at the festival, "On Repeat."

"Look at the view count."

Squinting, I lean in. My eyes are too blurry with exhaustion to focus on the tiny numbers, but I think it says ten thousand views.

"Oh, cool," I say, smiling a little.

Last time I looked, it had a couple thousand. It's still weird to think anyone listens to my songs, never mind thousands of strangers. But since it's people I don't know, it's easier to compartmentalize putting all my personal shit out there like that.

"*Oh, cool?* Ollie, what the fuck? You have a *million* views!"

Grabbing her phone, I take a closer look. I blink a few times, expecting the zeros to decrease, but all of them are still there. My brain starts to shut down.

"I was looking at the comments and apparently Jesse Jacobs shared your video."

"*What?*" I finally croak out as she takes her phone back. How could he possibly know who I am?

I check my feed and see that my mentions have exploded. Scrolling back, I finally find the original post he tagged me in.

obsessed with this ♥

That's all he wrote besides linking my video. I scroll through the comments. They're all wildly complimentary, but I can't take in a full breath, like I've been kicked in the throat.

"Hey." Aisha rubs my shoulder. "This is a good thing. Everything's okay."

Jumping up, I jam my English notes back into my bag.

"Are you having an attack?" she murmurs. "Where're you going? Want me to come with—"

"No." It comes out too sharp.

I know I've hurt her feelings again, but I can't deal with this right now. I throw my bag over my shoulder and take off toward the closest exit.

Outside, I slide down the dusty red brick wall, my face in my hands.

A million people. A million people know what happened to me.

It's just a song. People won't know it's true. I take a deep breath, trying to rationalize, but I can't stop thinking about everyone at school who must have seen this by now. What if my sister sees it? Or our parents . . .

I whip my phone out of my pocket and log in to my channel. I'm a second away from deleting the video, until I remember that reuploads are a thing. The internet is forever. There's no way to erase this. My throat seizes and then squeezes completely shut, dread seeping into my bones.

6

It takes me a couple minutes, but I finally calm down enough to get to my feet. When I get to the doors, I can't muster the strength to go back inside. I head over to the bus stop instead.

On the bus, I text Aisha to apologize for being so short with her. She doesn't respond, but I don't really expect her to since she's in class.

I check my feed again. I can't believe how many notifications I have. Thousands of strangers are commenting about "On Repeat." It was weird enough that a small group of people were into my stuff. But seeing this much positive feedback . . . it's somehow exciting and terrifying all at once.

Thankfully, no one's around when I get home. Mom must be at work and I'm not sure where Dad is. I kick off my shoes and bound up the stairs.

Sophie's door opens and I flinch violently. She winces at my wide-eyed expression. She hasn't been home since she moved into her new place on campus a few days ago.

"What are you doing here?" I get out after a second. I brush past her and continue down the hallway to my room. "Don't you have class?"

"I mean, I could ask you the same thing." Her voice gets closer as she follows me. I have the strong urge to close my bedroom door behind me, shutting it in her face, but it's not like she would leave me alone if I did. I collapse onto my couch and rub hard at my forehead.

Sophie stares at me, but I don't say anything else, keeping my eyes trained on the rug. Sitting beside me, she pulls me into a firm hug. I want to push her away so badly, but I stop myself, keeping my arms limp at my sides.

"Ollie, are you okay?"

"I'm fine," I grumble.

Finally, she pulls back, her eyes teary. I only glance at her for a second then stare at the floor again. "I heard your song. You know, the last half that you didn't sing that night at the festival."

"I figured," I say shortly and then wince when I hear her sniffle. "Soph, it's just a stupid song, okay? It doesn't mean anything."

"Ollie, I know you didn't want to report Thomas for beating you up because you were worried he'd keep bothering us. But . . . why didn't you tell me?" she chokes out.

I scrub at my eyes. God, I don't want to do this with her. She already blames herself for bringing Thomas into our lives.

"Tell you what?"

When I glance at her again, it's obvious I'm not fooling her. She knows.

I spring up from the couch and head over to my records, flipping through them to distract myself from the unbearable humiliation of this moment. The knowledge that I'm weak and pathetic is an invisible stain on my entire person.

You're not weak and pathetic. My therapist's voice echoes in my head for the millionth time. *You didn't do anything wrong.* I pick out an ultraloud grunge album and stick it on the record player then head over to my desk without looking at Sophie.

"I gotta get some homework done before work, " I yell over the booming drums and guitars.

Sophie doesn't leave like I hoped. She comes over and perches on the edge of my bed. "We have to talk about this."

"No, we don't." I open my laptop. Even more notifications are waiting for me.

She reaches out and slaps my laptop closed again. "I'm so sorry. I was such an idiot back then. I should never have dated him."

I resist the urge to roll my eyes. It's not like he was ever *not* an asshole. It got to the point that I couldn't help snapping at him, telling him not to talk about her like that. And that's when he got obsessed with making my life a fucking nightmare.

I finally meet her eyes. "It's not your fault. Look, it was a long time ago. I'm good now. You know I've been going to therapy for a while."

"Well, yeah—I knew you were dealing with anxiety and stuff. I still wish you'd told me." She stands and tries to hug me again, but I swivel away from her and open my laptop back up.

"I'm good now," I repeat, doing my best to keep my voice steady.

Sophie sighs. "Just let me know if you do ever want to talk about anything."

I nod.

She peers over my shoulder at my feed. "Ollie, holy shit. Look how many followers you have."

I can only nod again. It's way more than when I checked on the bus.

"This is so crazy." She squeezes my shoulder. "My brother's famous."

I snort. "Uh, no."

"Uh, yeah. You should post something."

I never post, not even about my videos. My small following grew organically on YouTube. "Like what?"

"Like, thanking people for supporting your music."

"But then more people will start commenting."

She blinks at me. "You say that like it's a bad thing. Everyone loves your song. Everyone loves *you*."

I frown, shaking my head. "You're being ridiculous."

Sophie reaches over me and clicks my messages open. She scrunches up her nose. "Wow. These girls are really trying it. They must know you have a girlfriend since you talk about Aisha in your song."

"Jesus. Stop." I try to swat her away, but she dodges me.

"Oh my God, Ollie, look!"

She's scrolled down to reveal a DM from Jesse Jacobs. My heart starts to thud as I hurriedly scan the message preview.

Hey Ollie! I hope you don't mind that I shared your video.
I saw your cover of my song, then I found your original
music . . .

Sophie clicks it open before I can stop her. I elbow her away from my side.

"What did he say?" She peers over my shoulder again. I ignore her as I read the rest of his message.

> . . . and I thought it was brilliant. Your production is so polished and your lyrics really moved me. I'd love to set up a meeting with you and my label.

I stop reading, distracted by Sophie shrieking in my ear. "He wants you to meet with his record label?! They probably want to sign you!"

"It's just a meeting," I say, even as excitement pumps through me.

This is absolutely unreal. What if they *do* want to sign me? I've done my best to be realistic, to think of singing as just a hobby, just for fun. I produce all my songs on software I bought online. I'm not an expert or anything, but the end product usually sounds decent— it's why music production seems like a safe bet for college. The fact that Jesse Jacobs agrees is too mind-blowing for me to grasp.

"Have you heard of his label before?" Sophie asks as I open my email. Jesse asked me to send him my availability.

"I know they signed Jesse after his indie EP came out," I say as I type. "And they just signed Serafina, who used to be the lead singer of Midnight Cavalcade."

Sophie plops back down on my bed as she starts scrolling through her phone. "What's the label called? Middle Path?"

"Yeah."

"They're a new division of RMA Records."

I turn to her. "They are?"

RMA is one of the biggest record companies in the world. Their Canadian office is based here—I pass it all the time on my way to work. I thought Middle Path was a small new label.

Sophie grins. "Ollie, what if you end up signing a huge deal with them? That would be amazing!"

I can't even let myself wish for that. I guess they could offer me something, but big deals are super rare, especially for debut artists. It would still be incredible to be recognized that way. But I could never take it now that I have to spend so much time working to afford college and help out at home.

"This is wild," Sophie continues. "Mom and Dad are gonna freak!"

I bite down on a sigh. When they get home they'll start questioning me about the song, like Sophie just did.

"I have to get some homework done," I say, looking pointedly toward my door.

"But—"

"Can you give me some space?"

Her eyes dim and I grimace. "Okay, fine. I'm staying for dinner so I'll see you then." She heads for the door, shutting it behind her.

I lean forward, putting my face in my hands. *What is even happening right now?*

After focusing on my breath for a few minutes, I straighten again and manage to compose a normal-sounding response. I read it over way too many times then finally hit send, my heart going into overdrive.

I look through some of my other messages and see a lot from people sharing how much my song meant to them because of their own assault experiences. Sending a rote thank you doesn't feel right, but I'm completely unprepared to send anything more genuine. My windpipe starts to close at the thought.

I shut my laptop and reach for my phone to call my therapist's office. Nadine's not in today, but I set up an appointment with the receptionist for right after school tomorrow. God knows I need it.

I check to see if Aisha's responded even though school isn't out yet.

Aisha: *It's okay, Oll. I get that this must be overwhelming, but I'm really proud of you. Everything's gonna work out. Call me after you finish at the store tonight, okay? <3 <3 <3*

I send her some hearts back as my throat finally relaxes. Thank God she's not pissed at me. I'm lucky she gets how bizarre this all is.

I open my backpack, thinking I'll try to get some homework done for once to distract myself from everything else.

Forty-five minutes later, the front door opens and my stomach twists into an impossible knot as I hear my mom talking to Sophie.

"Olia, come down here!" Mom calls out.

I get slowly to my feet and head downstairs, my insides still writhing.

Mom throws her arms around me. "My girlfriends have been messaging me all day! Why didn't you tell us you had been posting your music?"

I shrug as I step out of her grasp. She takes my arm and leads the way to the kitchen. "You can pick what you want to have for dinner tonight."

"Can we get pizza?" She hardly ever lets us order takeout.

"I second that," Sophie chimes in.

Mom sighs but doesn't protest even though I know she meant she wanted to make me something.

"Olia . . ." I avoid her gaze. I know she wants to ask about the lyrics, but she contains herself when she sees my expression. She just hugs me again, way tighter this time. "I love you so much, honey. You're such a brave boy."

"Thanks. Love you too." I resign myself to being trapped in her arms for the next few minutes, grateful she can't see me blinking my eyes dry.

Sophie wipes at her own eyes then picks up her phone. "Where do you want to order from?"

*
*

Dad's over at our uncle's house, so when the pizza comes, the three of us eat in the living room while we listen to Mom's old album. She recorded it before Soph and I were born. Mom always says it's no big deal since there were only a few copies ever made. It's unbelievable to think I could have the chance to record my own album soon . . . but the thought is bittersweet. Even if I could somehow find the time, I wouldn't be able to give up school or work and make music a full-time thing. And that's if I could even afford to accept an offer in the first place. Mom said that when she recorded her album, she ended up having to pay out of pocket for some production costs.

When Dad gets home, he looks at us sideways. Mom usually makes us eat at the kitchen table.

"Isaac, did you hear?" Mom asks.

I stop chewing and hold my breath, unable to look at him. I don't know exactly what his reaction will be, but I know it won't be good.

Dad hadn't said much when he saw the shape Thomas left me in, but I could just feel that he'd lost respect for me. He must have thought I was useless for not defending myself better. And now he knows what really happened. What I let Thomas do to me.

You didn't let him. My therapist's voice again.

"Did I hear what?" Dad asks lightly.

I hold in a sigh of relief.

Sophie grins. "Ollie wrote a song that got a ton of views online and now he has a meeting with a record label!"

Dad blinks. "A record label?"

"It's RMA," Sophie continues as I give her a sharp look.

His eyes light up in recognition. "That's a big company. That's great news, Olia. Congratulations."

I shrug, hoping he doesn't ask to hear the song. "Thanks."

He smiles at me briefly, continuing into the kitchen.

Mom reaches over and puts an arm around me. "Don't mind your father. He's just stressed."

I nod, not sure what she means—that went about a million times better than I expected. Dad's not a big music guy, so maybe he won't be that interested in hearing the whole song? I cling to the thought tightly.

"I gotta get to work now," I say, dragging myself off the couch.

"But we're celebrating tonight," Mom says. "You should call in."

I shake my head. "I have to cover for my coworker." I really can't afford to miss any shifts right now.

Mom's face falls a little. "Okay. We'll do something on the weekend."

"Sounds good." I peck her on the forehead. "I'll be back late."

I hug Sophie then head out the front door, avoiding Dad in the kitchen on my way out.

I put my earbuds in, turning on Jesse's album as I walk to the bus stop.

It's still not sinking in that he likes my music. And that he wants to set up a meeting with RMA. A nauseating mix of giddiness and nerves bubbles in my stomach. I breathe deeply again, channeling all of my energy into clearing my mind. Finally, Jesse's warm and completely effortless voice floods my senses, shutting down all of my thoughts.

7

The next morning, I get up and take off for school, but a few minutes after I leave, air stops entering my lungs. I can't stop thinking about how everyone was staring at me when I left yesterday, morbid curiosity written across their faces. Facing a whole day of that . . . I just can't do it.

I stop at the edge of my neighborhood, where my quiet residential street meets a major intersection. The booming engines of passing semis make me want to plug my ears, but I can't move a muscle.

There's the sound of a throat clearing, and I look up to find an older guy in an orange vest standing at the crosswalk, looking at me expectantly. I realize the light is green and I'm supposed to be crossing the street right now.

Ducking away from his gaze, I spin around and walk back the way I came. I grip my backpack straps as hard as I can to keep from shaking, concentrating on getting one foot in front of the other until I reach my backyard. I scale the tree outside my bedroom window to avoid my dad and quietly cross my room when I get inside. I climb straight into bed, not moving for the next three hours.

Both Aisha and Neil call around noon, but I can't make myself pick up. Neil texted me a couple of times last night, too. I know he wants to talk about the song, but I can't handle that conversation right now.

I text them and say I have a migraine, doubting they'll buy it. A second later, a notification pops up and I groan—I thought I'd turned them all off. It's from the contributor Discord group. I'm about to clear the notification, but then I notice that someone's written out my full name.

My breath catches. I open the chat to see Dev and KamranTheSufi excitedly talking about how much they love my song.

Dev doesn't say anything about it being me. I wasn't too worried that they would since they emphasized anonymity within the group, though their username is just Dev and I told them mine. I lurk for a while as other contributors join the conversation. They're talking about how much they like my music—not just the song that's going viral but the less popular ones on my channel too. It's kind of sweet how supportive they're being despite not knowing it's me. Still, I don't feel up to adding anything to the conversation. I like some of their comments then finally toss my phone aside.

Thankfully, Aisha and Neil don't call me out for lying and I'm left in peace for a few hours until I have to head to therapy. I definitely won't be short on material for the session.

While I'm walking to the office, I get a text from Ebi.

Ebi: *Hey, congrats on your song blowing up! I can imagine it's probably a lot, though. Let me know if you ever want to talk. Also, Dev wanted me to tell you they're sending good energy your way.*

Ollie: *Thanks, man! I appreciate that.*

Ebi: *I'm around whenever you're up for talking. Anyway, I know you have a lot on your plate so I understand if you don't have time to contribute to the blog right now.*

I worry my lip between my teeth as I try to work out a response. It was really nice seeing all the positivity in the contributor group. Honestly, it would be cool to be able to connect with them more, especially in a way that feels anonymous and safe. Now that basically everyone everywhere knows who I am, I could use a space where no one knows my real name.

Ollie: *I'll try to still put something together. Probably under a pen name.*

Ebi: *Sweet! Reach out anytime if you want to talk through ideas with the group.* ☺

Maybe I could review some albums by some queer artists? I think that might be doable, but I'll have to psych myself up for it. I let out a sigh as I put my phone away and step into my therapist's office.

"Hey!" Nadine grins, as usual, as I collapse into the seat in front of her desk, which is cluttered with arts-and-crafts knickknacks. "Haven't seen you in a bit. How were your first couple weeks back at school?"

"Uh, not great," I sigh out, trying to arrange my thoughts in some semblance of a coherent order. "Actually, pretty horrible."

"What happened?" From her genuine surprise, I don't think she's seen the video.

I stare down at my hands and take a deep breath before telling her about my song going viral.

"Ollie, that's unbelievable!" I look up to find her eyes wide and her mouth ajar. "Congratulations!"

"Thanks," I mutter. "The thing is, the song mentions . . ." I trail off and shut my eyes for a second. "It mentions what happened in ninth grade. So now everyone I know knows."

"You wrote a song about your sexual assault?" she asks quietly.

I only nod, opening my eyes but still not looking at her. "It's really about Aisha, but it was kind of the way that I told her about it. And like, worked through some of my feelings."

"I see," Nadine says, and I finally manage to meet her gaze. She smiles gently. "That was a really courageous thing to do."

I shrug, knowing what's coming next.

"And it must have taken a lot of courage to post it online," she continues predictably. "What made you decide you were ready to do that?"

"Posting didn't feel as scary as, like, performing at school. It was just a low-pressure way to get feedback from people who don't know me."

Nadine nods. "Got it. And I guess you never thought that this many people would see it. How have you been dealing with more people in your life knowing about it?"

There's a strong part of me that just wants to lie and say I'm handling it okay. I'm embarrassed about the way I reacted to Sophie yesterday. But I have to face this and be honest if I'm going to actually work through it.

Taking a steadying breath, I tell her about how I completely shut Soph down when she asked me what happened with Thomas. Nadine has tried to convince me to tell my family about it a lot over the last few years, so she knows this is pretty much the worst-case scenario for me.

She's silent for a long moment. "I know you've felt like you'd only be hurting the people in your life by telling them. But now that this has happened, maybe you could consider that opening up might help resolve some things for you. It sounds like your sister just wants to be there for you. And I think that everyone else in your life wants to support you too. If you're ready to let them."

I think about Aisha asking me about it that night at the festival and how I just . . . couldn't.

I know Nadine's right in theory. Basically everyone I know has been trying to be there for me. But it's so much harder to translate that knowledge into opening up outside of this office.

*
*

On Monday morning, I'm able to get myself all the way to school. From the moment I walk in the front doors, even more people stare at me than on Thursday. I ignore everyone's gazes as I head straight for my locker.

"Hey, Ollie." I stop dead in my tracks—Neil's suddenly standing right in front of me. "Are you good? I didn't hear back from you all weekend."

I move around him, and he falls in step with me. I feel bad for not returning his calls, but I just haven't been looking forward to this.

"Sorry, I've been busy."

"No worries," he says easily. "I just wanted to say congrats on your song and everything."

"Thanks," I say as I reach my locker and struggle to get my lock open. I can feel Neil watching me, and my face starts to burn.

"Look," he says quietly after I finally get it open and start unloading my textbooks. "I really appreciate you being there when things weren't going so great for me last year."

I meet his gaze again, unable to keep the surprise off my face. I don't think Neil's ever willingly mentioned how much he struggled with his drinking last year.

I nod. "Of course, man."

Neil scratches the back of his neck. "And if you ever want to talk about anything . . . I got your back."

I resist the urge to look at my feet and nod again. "Got it. I appreciate that."

"Is it okay if I hug you?" he asks, and my stomach squirms.

This is part of the reason I didn't want people to know. It's nice that he asked; I just wish he didn't feel like he had to. Like I need to be treated with kid gloves. It's especially annoying because he's right.

I dap him up before leaning in for a side hug.

He pats me firmly on the back. "Love you, dude."

"You too, man," I mutter, grabbing the last of my things from my locker. I'm doing my best to take in what Nadine said about accepting support, but it still feels so awkward.

Neil nudges my shoulder. "Looks like you have a fan club already."

I follow his gaze down the hall and see a small group of freshman girls whispering with their phones pointed my way. When they see I've caught them, they scuttle away.

Neil laughs. "So what's it feel like to be famous?"

I roll my eyes as we head toward first period. "It's seriously not that big a deal. Random people end up with a million views on videos all the time. It'll probably blow over soon enough."

"Hate to break it to you, but your video has like ten million views now. I guess you haven't checked recently?"

"That's funny," I snort as I glance at my phone. My breath catches when I see that Jesse finally responded to my email. "Oh shit."

"Did you just check? I told you."

"No, I heard back from Jesse Jacobs. He told me last week that he wanted to meet with me and his record label. They just got back to me—they want me to come to the RMA offices after school."

"That's sick! Sophie mentioned you'd be meeting with them."

I turn to squint at him. "When did she tell you about that?" I ask slowly. As far as I knew they hadn't been in contact since we got back from the festival.

He reddens. "Uh, she texted me. She's, um, she's just been worried about you."

I contain a sigh. I still haven't spoken much with Sophie since she asked me about what happened.

The bell rings and Neil claps me on the shoulder. "Good luck with your meeting! You're gonna kill it!"

8

I take the subway down to the RMA offices right after school. I've passed the sleek, forty-story building on my way to work a million times. I sometimes imagined it might be a cool place to work someday, but I'd never dreamed of being here under these circumstances.

What circumstances? This could be nothing.

At the main desk, I check which floor the RMA offices are on then make my way over to the elevators.

I groan internally as I catch my ratty old band tee and jeans in the elevator mirrors. I wish I'd had time to go home and change into something less casual, but I didn't want to risk being late.

"Can you hold the door?" someone calls out behind me. I quickly turn and press the open button as a guy around my age steps in. "Thanks."

I nod as I stare up at the floor numbers rapidly increasing. My pulse pounds in a concerning staccato rhythm as I surreptitiously wipe my hands on my jeans. What if this goes horribly? What if I stutter in front of a bunch of execs and humiliate myself?

"Ollie?"

I stare at the guy beside me blankly until it clicks. It's Jesse Jacobs. He's replaced his signature shoulder-length black hair with a low buzz cut, but I recognize his sharp cheekbones and beautiful dark brown eyes.

Beautiful? I cringe at myself, but that doesn't stop me from taking in just how stunning he is in person. He stares right back at me for a long moment, then breaks into an incapacitating smile.

"Hi, Jesse." I stop short of saying his last name out loud. I don't want to sound like an overexcited fanboy. "Sorry, I didn't recognize you with—" I gesture to his head as the bell dings for our floor. *What the hell is wrong with you? Get it together.* "Good to meet you."

"Likewise!" He's still smiling at me so brightly I have to look away as we step out of the elevator.

The receptionist looks up as we approach her desk. "Pierre and the team will be with you two in a few minutes."

We head over to a waiting area, its walls adorned with platinum records of some of my favorite bands. I take a closer look and see that a lot of them are signed.

"This is cool," Jesse says and I look over at him again. He's examining the records on the opposite wall.

"Haven't you been here before?" I ask and he turns toward me. I immediately turn my gaze back to the records, not wanting to stare at him too long again.

Jesus Christ, why am I acting like this? I talk to talent all the time at work, and I've never felt this nervous. None of the talent I've ever worked with looked like Jesse, though.

I can't believe I even just *thought* that. It's one thing to occasionally notice people are hot, but this feels different.

I try and focus on Jesse's response. "No, I got into town earlier today. I'm from Vancouver—I've met Pierre before, but I've only spoken to the rest of the team online."

I nod as he comes to stand right beside me, hoping he can't sense how my heart has picked up speed again. "So how do you like working with them?"

"It's great," he says, but I catch something flash behind his eyes that worries me. "I mean, this is all recent for me. I never thought my album would get this much attention. It's kind of wild."

That's an understatement. When I first heard his music a few months back, he had only a few thousand listens on Spotify. Now his album's topped all the North American charts. "I can't imagine. Well, I mean I guess I sort of can now . . ."

He laughs. "Yeah, I hope you don't mind that I shared your song. I just think you're—"

"They're ready for you!" the receptionist calls out.

I shut my eyes tight for a moment, trying to breathe normally.

"You ready?" Jesse asks.

I nod, but otherwise I don't move a muscle. I feel his hand on my shoulder and my eyes snap open. Miraculously, my pulse slows down, and my thoughts stop racing.

"Hey, it's gonna be fine," he says as we move toward the exec offices. "Everyone's excited to meet you."

Jesse knocks on the first closed door, and it swings open, revealing a man in his forties in jeans and a T-shirt. Thankfully it doesn't seem

I'm underdressed in current company.

"Hey, Jesse! Good to finally see you again," the man says, looking him up and down. "Wow! You didn't mention you were going to cut your hair!"

Jesse keeps his face neutral. "Should I have?"

The guy laughs, but it sounds a little awkward and forced. He turns his attention to me. "And you must be Ollie! I'm Pierre, head of the Middle Path division here."

I nod and try to smile in a way that doesn't look panicked. "Thanks for inviting me today." *Inviting me for what, I still don't know.*

"Of course. Come in, come in." Pierre gestures us inside where two other people are seated around a table. "Grab something to eat if you like."

There's coffee and snacks on a side table. I'm too wired to eat or drink anything, so I just take a seat. Jesse sits next to me.

"I'm Helen," a blonde woman in her late twenties says. "I'm head of marketing. And this is Jonah." She nods at the guy on her other side. "He'll be helping me out with notes and our presentation today."

Jonah picks up a remote and switches on a large monitor.

"So, let's just get into it, shall we?" Pierre says with a grin. "We absolutely love 'On Repeat' and your overall sound on all your songs. It's a great mix of accessible indie pop with some really unique contemporary folk and art rock. We think you'd be a great fit with us here at Middle Path."

I blink at him. He can't mean what I think he means. "How so?"

"We normally wouldn't be making an offer so quickly, but since your song has been getting so much attention, we want to move fast in case you have other interest."

"Interest from who?" I blurt out. Then my brain catches up and I realize he means other labels. "I mean, I don't have any other interest."

Shit, maybe I shouldn't have told him that? I don't know if this is going to be something I'll be in a position to negotiate. He said they're making an offer, didn't he? Or am I losing it?

A slide titled "Contract Proposal" pops up on the screen, which confirms that this is happening.

"All right, let's just give you a rundown of our pitch," Helen says. I do my best to stop from checking out. "We want to capitalize on this moment that you're having. Jesse is starting a cross-country tour in October and we'd love for you to open for him."

Jesse's beaming at me. I can't make my face move.

"If you could vlog the tour on your channel, we think that would be a great way to get you even more exposure. Along with documenting your process while writing your album," Pierre says.

"Album?" I know I must sound like an idiot, but I'm still not wrapping my brain around this.

"Sorry, I'm getting ahead of myself." Pierre laughs and turns to Jonah. "Next slide please?"

The slide that pops up is labeled "Tour Budget and Album Advance Breakdown." All the numbers have way too many zeros behind them. I squeeze the arms of the chair to keep myself still.

Jesse bumps my knee with his and I zone back in. "You okay?"

"Uh . . . yeah, sorry," I choke out. "This is just a lot of information at once."

"Totally understandable," Helen says in a gentler tone. "I know it sounds like a lot, but we promise, we try to keep things low-key here."

"That's right," Pierre chimes in. "We're very flexible. For instance,

Jesse wasn't interested in getting a tour bus—he'd prefer to travel in his van. Which is totally fine with us!"

Jesse shrugs. "Yeah, I don't know what I'd need a whole bus for. Ollie, you'd be welcome to travel with me. I do cross-country trips a lot."

"It could be like a fun road trip!" Helen says before I can respond. "And van life is very in right now, so it'll be great for Ollie's vlogs—"

"Hold up a sec," Jesse says to Helen. He studies me. "How does this sound to you? Would you want to open for me on tour?"

"Sure," I find myself saying. Even though performing night after night sounds beyond terrifying . . . it also sounds thrilling. I can't stop staring at the advance numbers and thinking of how many problems money like that could solve. There's no way in hell I can turn down an opportunity like this. "I mean, yes. That sounds incredible. But, uh, how long is the tour? I'd have to miss school."

"Three months—until the end of the year," Pierre says.

I wince. "It's my senior year and I have college applications coming up . . ."

"What are you applying for?" Pierre asks.

"Music production."

He laughs. "Well, I think you've got that covered already. Once the tour is over you can record and master everything here."

Helen jumps in. "Or, since we love the DIY vibe your music already has, you're welcome to do it on the road with your own software."

I nod and try and get my thoughts together. "This all sounds like a dream come true, but I have to talk to my parents."

Pierre nods. "For sure. We'll let you go over the whole contract proposal with them on your own." He hands me a thick stack of papers. "Thanks for coming in today. We can touch base next week."

Jesse and I head out of the office and back toward the elevators. I grip the contract as hard as I can to keep my hands from shaking.

"Sorry, again," Jesse says as we step into the elevator. "They're just really hyped about all this. I mean, I am too, but I know they can be intense."

"No. I mean, yeah, that was great, I'm just . . ." I trail off, not able to think of a word to describe how I'm feeling. I should be more excited, but part of me still can't accept what just happened. Also, performing in front of thousands of people isn't something I can conceptualize.

"I get it. When Pierre first told me Middle Path wanted to sign me and sent over the contract . . . Honestly, I'd never seen that much money in my life. Took me some time to wrap my head around it," Jesse says as we reach the ground floor. "I'm headed over to my hotel, but do you need a ride home or anything?"

"That's okay, I work a few minutes away," I tell him. "But thank you so much. Seriously—you have no idea how much it means to me that you want to work with me."

We're standing just outside the front doors, and I find myself utterly unable to look away from his smile.

"No problem. I'm psyched about this! I hope everything goes well with your parents."

"Thanks. Okay, guess I'll see you—"

"Wait, can I get your number?" he asks.

"What?" I squeak out, my heart starting to race again.

"Can I have your number?" he repeats slower, breaking into another distracting smile. "So I can check in with you about everything later?"

"Right. Yeah, for sure."

After I recite my number, he grins at me again. "Bye, Ollie."

He takes off toward the parking lot and I find myself staring after him for a moment before I snap out of it and head toward work.

Holy shit. I take off my backpack and shove the contract inside. This is completely unbelievable. How did all of that happen in less than an hour? I want to call Aisha to tell her everything, but she's still at dance rehearsal.

Well, not exactly everything. I obviously already knew what Jesse looked like, but the moment his eyes met mine in the elevator it was like . . .

I shake my head, making myself focus on what's important right now. The tour. And the freaking huge record deal. Excitement finally starts to pump through me as I remember all those dizzying numbers. I'm praying my parents are going to let me take time off school. I mean, they'll have to, right? If I take this deal, I'll be able to help with money while my dad's looking for work. But I know he won't be thrilled about me putting off school. I'll have to figure out a way to show them what this opportunity would mean for our whole family. And not just for them but for me. Even daydreaming about this kind of thing has always felt so stupid. Now that it's happening, there's no way I can let it slip through my fingers.

9

Later that evening, I sit in the living room with my parents while they pore over every page of the contract.

"Hmm." My dad sits in his recliner, squinting at the small print, even with his reading glasses on. "Are you sure this isn't some type of scam?"

"Yes. I talked to Brad at work earlier," I say. The store was dead and there weren't any shows to set up for, so I had lots of time to run the contract by my boss. "He's been working in the music industry for, like, thirty years and he's talked to tons of different artists about their contracts—a lot of them have worked with RMA. He said none of the language is predatory."

Dad frowns. "Predatory language?"

"Basically, asking me to pay for anything out of pocket or trap me into doing things I wouldn't feel comfortable with—"

"But are you comfortable with *any* of this?" Mom cuts in, looking up from the other half of the contract. "They want you to sing in front of big crowds, Olia. But you've always been so shy. You don't even like singing for us at home."

I cringe internally. I hate being called shy. I know she tries, but she doesn't fully get that my anxiety is more than that. But obviously mentioning that now wouldn't be a good idea.

"It's time for him to grow out of that anyway," Dad says.

Yep, I'll just grow out of a medical condition. That's a totally reasonable request. I swallow down my annoyance. I do want him to say yes, after all. "I'll figure it out."

I've had to help out with equipment in front of a packed house at work for years now, with no issues at all. I just have to figure out how to not be terrified when all the attention is on me.

I push the thought away. "So, you'll let me take off school to go on the tour?"

"I didn't say that," Dad mutters. "What about your college applications? You can't afford to miss school right now."

I've prepared for this question. "College admissions will use my grades from last year to decide if I get in or not."

"Your grades this year are still important," Dad says. "Colleges can rescind offers if you do badly."

"Yeah, but I could make up the time I miss in summer school," I say quickly. That would suck, but it'd be worth it.

"Hmm." Dad focuses on the contract again. "There has to be a catch, though. These numbers are ridiculous."

"It's a bigger deal than normal because my song has so many views online. They already know I have an audience." I thought Neil was kidding at school, but the last time I checked, the video had over twelve million views. "I guess the catch is that they want me to make videos and do social media stuff more often. Which I can handle." At least I hope I can.

"And this contract is only for one album?" Mom asks. "You don't want to be stuck working with them forever if new opportunities come up."

I know she's speaking from experience. She worked with a tiny label when she made her album. "Yeah, it's just a one-tour, one-album deal. One year. That's it."

Mom nods. "Your father and I will have to look this over a little more, but if you're sure you feel ready to do all this, then I think you should go."

I break into a grin. "Wait, really?"

"Anissa." Dad shoots her a sharp look. "I don't think we should rush into a decision."

Mom meets his gaze unblinkingly. "He's going to be eighteen next month. It's his choice what he—"

"But he's still living in *our* house."

"We're not going to have this house for much longer if you keep being so stubborn," Mom snaps. "First you won't accept your brother's help. Now you won't let Ollie do this?"

My uncle's help? I catch Dad giving Mom a scathing glare. He tosses the contract on the coffee table then storms out of the room.

Mom puts her face in her hands.

"Hey." I slide closer to her on the couch, slinging an arm around her shoulder. "What did you mean about Uncle?"

She gives an exhausted sigh as she lifts her head again. "Your uncle told your father on the weekend that he wanted to give us a loan to help us out with the mortgage. Your father refused. He said he doesn't want any handouts."

I shake my head. My dad's always seen everything in black-and-white, but turning down my uncle's help when we desperately need it seems extreme, even for him. "A loan isn't a handout though. Why wouldn't Dad just take it?"

"There's no explaining your father's pride," Mom mutters. "He wants to do everything himself. I wish he could understand that being part of a family is about helping each other when we can."

"Mom, I get that. And I . . . I really want to help." I can't just let her deal with this all on her own. I still have my own future to worry about, but I don't want to leave her hanging out to dry. "If you let me go on the tour, I'd be happy to give you my advance money for the mortgage."

"Olia . . ." Tears form in her eyes. "That's so sweet of you. If I can get your father to accept your uncle's loan and then with your help too, we would have more than enough to tide us over until he finds work again."

Relief washes over me. I wasn't sure how deep in the hole my parents are—or exactly how much the deal would help.

I hug her tight for a long moment before I find my voice again. "Okay, that's great. I can try and help Soph out with her school fees too."

I don't mention my own college fees. The truth is, if this works out, I'm not totally sure I'll still want to go to college. I mean, this is basically the dream. I think about Dev and their band again, how tempted I'd been to join them. But this would be on a completely different scale. I'd be front-and-center in front of thousands of people.

As much as I've daydreamed about something like this, now that it's within reach, anxiety and dread threaten to overwhelm the relief I felt a minute ago.

"Thank you, wlidi. My sweet boy." My mom wipes her eyes then takes my face in her hands. "And don't worry, I'll handle your father. Olia, I'm so, so proud of you. This is what was meant to happen. This is what you're meant to do."

She gathers me in her arms again, and I squeeze my watery eyes shut.

I don't know if I believe in fate, exactly. But it seems so beyond the realm of simple luck that this happened right when my family needed it the most.

But it's not like I'm going to get a giant check in the mail all at once. The advance money comes in installments. I'll get a bit when I sign the contract, a bit when I post all the videos I'll have to film, a bit when I finish writing the album, and the rest when I finish the tour. And like Mom said, none of that is stuff I'm comfortable with. If I'm being real, I'm not sure if I'll be able to do any of those things at all.

You have to. There's no way in hell I can chicken out on this. At least Jesse will be on tour with me. Having him at the meeting earlier was the only thing that helped me to not completely panic.

My chest starts to rise and fall more slowly as I calm the rhythm of my breath. All I have to do is take things one step at a time. After Mom talks to Dad again, I can sign the contract, get it back to the team, and go from there.

*

"So what was Jesse Jacobs like?" Aisha asks me as soon as the bell rings at the end of History. She's looked like she's practically bursting to talk to me since I got to class.

"Oh. Uh . . ." Jesse's smile pops into my head and I shove it away. "He was cool. I was super freaked out, but he helped me keep it together. And he texted me last night to ask how I was feeling about the contract."

"That was nice of him," Aisha says as she loops her arm through mine. "Oh my God, I still can't believe this is happening! Well, actually I can believe it. Remember I told you last year that you'd probably be off on a big tour soon?"

"Yeah, I remember." I never in a million years thought she'd be right. I kiss her cheek. "I'll miss you, though."

Her smile is wistful. "Me too, but it'll only be three months."

I wish Aisha could come on tour with me. It's always so much easier for me to sing in front of other people when she's there, cheering me on.

"Still not sure how I'm even gonna do this," I mutter.

"Hey." Aisha stops walking and turns to me. "You've got this, Ollie. Trust me, everything will work out."

"I don't know. The label wants me to start posting vlogs over the next few weeks. I'm a little nervous about it." Talking in front of a camera isn't exactly my forte. What if I don't get as many views as when Jesse shared my video and the execs start to question why they asked me to join the tour?

"You've made a Q&A video before and that wasn't a problem, was it?"

"Uh, it kinda was." I stuttered so much in that video. I could barely deal with knowing Aisha had seen it when she told me she found my channel. The thought of being so awkward and unsure of myself way more publicly is kind of horrifying. "What if I just screw everything up? The tour and the videos . . ."

Aisha looks at me carefully. "You know that you don't have to go through with this if you don't want to, right?"

"But I do," I say, my voice a little more forceful than I meant it to be.

I wince, but she doesn't look upset, just confused. "What do you mean?"

I remind myself about my conversation with Nadine. I know Aisha only wants to help and that she'll get it, even if she can't exactly relate. And I don't want to keep snapping at her. "My dad lost his job recently. Going through with the tour and everything will help keep my family afloat for the next little while."

Her eyes widen. "Ollie, I'm really sorry to hear that. Why didn't you say anything?"

I glance away from her hurt expression. I hate that she might feel like I didn't trust her. "I don't know . . . money is just hard to talk about. But we should be okay if I somehow get it together."

The bell rings and Aisha gives me a sad smile and a quick peck. "I get it. That sounds like a ton of pressure. We can talk more later and I can help you film if you want. I'm sure Neil would be totally happy to help you with filming too."

"Thanks, that would be great." I find myself smiling. The dread that's been growing inside me might be starting to wane, tentative excitement finally creeping in.

10

My fingers shake as they hover over my keyboard on Monday morning. I take a long moment to calm my runaway pulse, then finally press "send."

I did it. I'm doing this.

Over the weekend my mom convinced my dad to let me go on the tour and drop my classes for the rest of the semester. Signing a digital version of the contract and emailing it back to Pierre just now made it official. It still isn't sinking in.

My boss told me he was okay with me taking a leave of absence on the condition that our venue would be a tour stop. Pierre agreed, adding it as a final show at the end of December. I wish it could have been the first show of the tour instead—I could have used the home-court advantage. But The Vinyl Underground is booked solid all fall.

We'll start in Montreal and work our way to the West Coast before swinging back east. We'll mostly play smaller clubs and theaters—

with the exception of a stadium show in Vancouver that I'm trying not to think about. I'm psyched I'll be able to see the historic venues some of my favorite indie bands have frequented for years. Not exactly psyched about the fact that I'll be the one onstage—at least not yet. Jesse's coming back to town for rehearsals a week before we leave, so I'm hoping I'll feel more confident after that.

For now, I have to focus on filming my first video. Pierre suggested something short, just announcing that I'll be opening for Jesse. Sounds simple enough, but the thought of posting on my channel now that it has so much attention still makes me want to curl up and die.

Oh, boohoo. People want you to know they like your music, how awful. I need to suck it up and get to work . . . but I stay in bed for most of the day. I spend a bit of time lurking in the contributor group, and I see that KamranTheSufi posted about the article he's been working on for the upcoming print issue. It's about how queer Islamic poetry has influenced some of the music he's been writing. I reply to his post and say that I'm looking forward to reading it. He responds right away, telling me to just call him Kamran, and we end up chatting about some of our favorite bands. He even introduces me to some queer Iranian underground artists that I haven't heard of.

After we finish chatting, I finally get up and put on one of the artists Kamran said I should check out. The driving beat is super catchy and energizing and I find myself tapping my fingers against my closed notebook. The lyrics touch on the idea of widening narrow religious ideals into more fluid spiritual beliefs that don't constrain people's identities. Something I've wanted to write about myself, but haven't been able to find the words for. I eventually flip my notebook open, but each time I try to form a lyric it feels forced. Letting out a groan, I lie back and continue to lounge around instead of getting any work done on the video. Maybe once I listen to a few more of the albums Kamran suggested I'll get into a more creative mood.

I'm sitting on the floor, needlessly sorting my mountain of records, when Neil and Aisha burst into my room.

"We're here to save the day," Neil says. "Aisha said you need help filming a video for your adoring fans."

"Our showcase rehearsals let out early," Aisha adds as she sits down next to me. "How're you feeling? Is it weird to be off school?"

I shrug, opening my laptop on the carpet beside me. "I know I should just get the video over with, but I've been scared to even look at my channel since everything happened. Not mad about missing school, though."

Neil swivels my laptop toward him. "I'm guessing you don't want to hear your view count now."

"I'm good," I say as Aisha leans over to take a look.

"There's literally thousands of comments." Aisha falls quiet. "Looks like a lot of people are *very* interested in more than just your singing."

Neil snorts. "That's a tame way of putting it. Some of these comments are . . . let's just say *creative*."

"Okay." Cringing, I grab the laptop, shutting it again. "Let's just do the video now."

"I've been getting some weird comments about you on my socials, too," Neil says.

I shoot him a sideways look. "You have?"

"People figured out I know you because you've posted pics with me," he says before turning to Aisha. "I'm sure you've been getting way more out-there comments than me, though."

Aisha fiddles with one of the records scattered on the carpet around us. "I guess."

"Have people been saying rude shit to you?" I ask carefully, my stomach knotting up.

"Uh, it's mostly nice stuff, like people saying we're a cute couple. But yeah, it's whatever. Don't worry about it. Didn't you say you wanted to film now?"

I shake my head. "But some people have been saying messed-up stuff, too?"

She nods, still not looking up at me.

Neil and I exchange a worried look.

"Aisha . . ." I take her hand, threading my fingers through hers. "I'm so sorry that's been happening. Why didn't you say anything?"

"Because it's no big deal. It's just random people on the internet, who cares? I privated my account so it's fine now." She pulls her hand from my grasp and gets up. "Don't worry about it."

"But—"

"Really, it's okay. I promise." She grabs my camera from my desk and shoots me a small smile. "Come on, let's do this."

I sigh but drop it. It makes me sick to think that she's been dealing with this and didn't feel comfortable telling me. Why do people have to be so goddamn horrible? Aisha's already had enough shit to deal with from the awful girls in ballet.

When I glance at Neil, he's frowning at Aisha. He flashes me a hesitant smile. "Okay, you ready, man? Do you usually write a script for your videos or just go off-the-cuff?"

"Usually just wing it."

Aisha sits in front of me and turns on the camera. She holds up three fingers, counting me down. "And . . . go," she says.

She raises an eyebrow when I remain silent.

Filming videos alone is hard enough—it's somehow embarrassing even when there aren't any witnesses.

"I'll count you down again," Aisha says after a second.

Neil gives me a pat on the shoulder before sliding out of frame and moving next to Aisha.

Christ, this is a nightmare. I already know I'm about to stutter up a storm.

I make myself start. "Uh . . . Hey. I'm Ollie. Welcome to my channel."

"*Louder*," Aisha mouths.

I clear my throat and start again. "Hi. I'm—I'm—I'm Ollie. *Shit*." My face flames and I rub my eyes. Why do I *constantly* have to be such an incompetent loser?

"It's cool," Neil says calmly. "Forget about the camera. Just talk to us like you were a minute ago."

Right. Like it's that easy. I shake away my irritation. I know he's just trying to help.

"Look at me, okay?" Aisha says and I focus on her reassuring gaze.

Sucking in a long breath, I start again. I get through welcoming new viewers and announce that I'm going on tour with Jesse.

"And . . . cut!" Aisha shuts the camera off then leans in and kisses me on the cheek. "Great job!"

"That was less than a minute," I mutter, rubbing my forehead. "The label said my videos have to be at least ten minutes long."

"Maybe you could add some other clips? Do you have any footage you haven't posted yet?" Neil asks.

"I recorded a couple of sets at the festival," I say.

Aisha's eyes cloud, and I think she's feeling guilty about us leaving early that weekend.

"On second thought, maybe I should save that footage for a separate video," I say quickly.

Aisha focuses on me again and nods. "How about a Q&A?"

I groan. "But then I'll have to read comments."

Neil grabs my laptop again. "I'll vet some good ones for you."

"Thanks," I say, leaning back on my elbows. I've barely done anything, so I don't know why I feel exhausted.

Aisha squeezes my arm. "Try and relax, okay? I know it doesn't seem like it right now, but maybe you could end up enjoying this? I mean, it's amazing you have so many people supporting you." She kisses me again. "Find any good questions, Neil?"

"Yep, now that I've sifted through the thirst comments," he says dryly as Aisha turns the camera back on. "So, when did you first learn to play guitar?"

We go through five questions then call it quits.

"There's about a million more here, so you won't have to worry about content for a while," Neil says, sliding my laptop over to me. "I can keep looking through later and pull out the best ones if you want."

"Thanks, man." I lean over and dap him up. "That would be great."

"I got you. I *will* be accepting dinner as payment, though." He jumps up and heads for the door. "I'm starved and whatever your mom's whipping up down there smells delicious."

Aisha wraps her arms around me before I can get up to follow him. "That wasn't too bad, was it?"

"I guess not." I press my forehead to hers. "Aisha, I'm sorry again that people have been saying rude stuff to you online. Are you sure you're okay?"

She pulls away, looking straight into my eyes. "Thanks, Ollie. I'm all right—please stop worrying. Anyway, are *you* okay? We haven't really talked about your family's situation. I'm sure it must be stressful feeling like you have to help fix it."

I press my lips into a thin line and fight the urge to look away. I know she just wants to support me, but I don't see how rehashing it all would help. I'm already dealing with the situation by going on tour and getting my family the money they need. I don't want to think about it anymore. "I'm doing okay, I guess. Thanks for being here—I'll let you know if I need to talk."

She opens her mouth like she wants to ask me more but then bites down on her lip. Grabbing my hand, she pulls me to my feet. "Okay. Come on. Let's go before Neil eats everything."

11

It's first thing on a Tuesday morning and I'm somehow both groggy and full of nerves as I head into the pretour rehearsal. Without work or school, the last few weeks have blended together in a haze of sleeping in late. The rehearsal space is a small, modern theater housed inside what used to be an industrial warehouse.

Recording videos has gotten a little easier and the label's been happy with them. But I've been feeling super stuck on the album. Instead of getting inspired by music like I usually do, all I can think about is not being able to create anything as good as the artists I admire. I've been listening to more of the artists Kamran recommended—the way they write about their spirituality and finding their true selves seems so effortless—but the more I've listened, the further I've felt from ever being able to express myself so clearly.

The only song I've been able to work on is the one I'd been writing for Aisha. The closer I get to leaving town, the more urgent it's felt to get the lyrics and melody down. I already recorded and sent it to Middle Path to be part of my set, but I haven't worked up the nerve to play it for her yet.

"Hey, Ollie." Jesse smiles when he sees me walk into the theater's auditorium. He's standing alone onstage. "It's really good to see you!"

His smile is just as immobilizing as when I met him in the RMA elevator. He looks genuinely psyched that I'm here.

I smile dopily back. "It's great to see you too." My voice comes out too quiet and I clear my throat.

When I reach the stage, he leans in and hugs me, enveloping me in the sharp scent of soap and aftershave. It's a short, friendly hug, but how it makes me feel is far from just friendly.

Stop. I thought I'd be prepared to see him since we've been talking and texting a lot to work on tour prep. But seeing him in person is a different story.

"Awesome looping kit," I say, gesturing at the equipment in front of us. We both have simple set ups and neither of us performs with a band. But off to the side, I notice some fancy electric and bass guitars, a shiny full drum set and a high-end keyboard. "This is killer."

"Some people from the label brought all the instruments in a little while ago in case you wanted to record samples to loop for your set. I got here pretty early so I've just been testing stuff out."

"This is your kit, though?" I say, gesturing at the looping equipment again. "I've always wanted one like this."

"Yeah, I was able to upgrade from my older pedals recently. Wanna hear how it sounds?"

I nod, grinning as he signals a sound guy in the back of the auditorium. His first track starts, a crystal clear, heavy rock bassline followed by some traditional Indigenous drums. He picks up a gorgeous silver electric guitar and starts playing on top, the sound of a full band and his stunning vocals filling the small theater.

I can't take my eyes off him as he expertly works his way through the track, adjusting loops on the fly while playing guitar.

My face hurts from smiling when he finishes. "Wow, that sounded . . ." I shake my head, at a loss for words. "That was *so* good."

"Thanks. Okay, let's go all the way through the set list in order of the way we prepped. You can start."

My heart thumps out a nervous up-tempo beat. "Uh, sounds good. I have my kit, but I'd have to disconnect yours . . ."

"You can try mine if you want."

"Really? Okay, awesome." I'm practically giddy as I move to the controls. I try to ignore when his shoulder briefly brushes mine before he moves away to give me room to set up.

I connect my acoustic guitar and rerecord some of my loops then get some mellow drumbeats and basslines going. It doesn't take that long since my songs are much simpler than Jesse's. He uses instruments and beats in such a masterful way it makes my head spin.

"Okay, I think I'm good to go," I say once I've rerecorded everything. I look up to find Jesse watching me closely. Burning heat immediately rises to my face. "What?"

He shakes his head. "Nothing. Just took me a while to get used to that new kit. You're a natural."

My cheeks get even warmer and I look down at my guitar, hoping my face isn't red. I glance over at the sound guy. "Ready!"

The speakers start up, my new and improved backing tracks boom through the empty theater. I can't get over how good they sound on this professional equipment. I take a slow, deliberate breath, the cool, recycled air filling my lungs as I start strumming and singing over the track. I try to hit my cues and switch my loops as smoothly as Jesse did.

We rehearse all day, and I'm so distracted by getting to play on such amazing equipment with someone so ridiculously talented that I forget the nerves I came in with. Since we only have the space for today, we want to make sure our sets are as tight as possible. We even stick around after the sound guy heads out for the evening, tweaking our equipment and smoothing out our vocal levels.

Late into the evening when we're sure we have everything down, Jesse starts improvising a new song, spontaneously recording and adding more tracks to the mix—different rhythms and instrumentals blending together seamlessly.

I shake my head, unable to tear my eyes away from him. I've never seen someone improvise an entire song so quickly.

"You're incredible," I blurt out.

He stops to look at me and I rush on. "I mean, how do you do that?"

He smiles. "Come here, I'll show you."

I do my best to calm my heart rate as I go to stand next to him. A tiny, tenuous shock runs through me when he hands the mic over, our fingers brushing.

Relax.

"What should I do?" I ask. He's already laying down a new drumbeat.

"Just start singing whatever comes to you," he says. "Go ahead."

"Um . . ." My throat goes dry. "I don't know."

"No pressure, we're just having fun." He's smiling at me again and I force myself to look away, focusing on putting the mic back in the stand. I pick up the electric guitar he was using earlier and start strumming some hesitant notes over his beat. I hum a little into the mic. "Yeah, that's it!"

I don't sound nearly as good as him, but I try to find my own rhythm. Slowly, a verse starts to form, and I repeat it a couple of times, enjoying the feel of the guitar in my hands. When I glance at Jesse again, he's giving me a patient, encouraging look that miraculously settles the nerves bubbling up inside me.

I look out at the empty seats and picture a full house as I play. The theater is about the size of my school's auditorium. I try to imagine Aisha sitting with Neil, Ebi, and all our theater friends cheering me on, but their faces won't quite materialize. A wistful heaviness tugs at me—it's going to be so weird not having any of them there.

I'm pulled back to the present by Jesse's hand on my shoulder. Another tiny jolt goes through me as I find him studying my eyes with concern. "You okay?"

I stop playing. "Yeah, I'm fine."

"Are you sure?" Something about the way he asks makes me feel like he's not just being polite. Like he really wants to know what's up.

"Just thinking about being away from home soon, I guess," I say with a shrug.

He nods. "Ah, gotcha."

"Not that I'm not excited about the tour," I add quickly.

"No, I get it. I'm sure it'll be a big change." He bites his lip and looks elsewhere for a second. "Takes a bit to get used to."

"Yeah," I reply, not sure what else to say.

He looks a little sad for a second but then he smiles again, bright as ever. "Anyway, I think we're gonna have a ton of fun on tour if today has been any indication."

I can't help smiling back at him. "One hundred percent. I can't believe how fast the day went."

As if on cue, two-thirds of the lights shut off, leaving only the stage lit up.

Jesse glances up and laughs, running a hand through his short hair. It's grown out a little from the buzzcut he had the last time I saw him. "Guess it's closing time." He starts packing up his equipment.

"Did you want to grab some dinner?" Jesse asks a few minutes later, as we step outside. His expression is easy and playful but something about it makes me short of breath. "I bet we could find something still open."

Everything in me wants to say yes, but I'm exhausted. "That sounds great. I should probably head home, though."

Disappointment is clear in his eyes, but he shrugs casually. "Okay, no worries. See you in Montreal!"

He smiles again and it takes me a second to tear my eyes away from him.

"See you then." I wave and walk off quickly, just in case he tries to hug me again. A weird mix of relief and regret courses through me.

I hate that the day ended on an off-note. Truthfully, part of me was scared of just how much I wanted to keep hanging out. The thought of spending so much more time with Jesse on tour is equal parts exciting and terrifying because, despite my best efforts, I can't seem to control how I feel around him.

I genuinely don't think I've ever been this physically attracted to someone besides Aisha. Usually I'm able to completely shut down any inkling of attraction toward anyone else . . . especially anyone who's a guy. But with Jesse, it's like this unavoidable, kinetic energy sparking inside me that's impossible to control.

But you have to ignore it. I heave out an exhale that billows into a white mist as I hunch my shoulders against the wind.

As I walk, I pull out my phone and write down some of the lyrics I improvised earlier. I feel my mouth turning into a small smile as I recall the freedom of getting back into my creative zone for the first time in weeks. Maybe, with Jesse's help, I *can* do this. It's going to be hard being away from everyone I love, but maybe it'll be worth it. Not just to help my parents out, but for me. Maybe I'll finally get a chance to experience something I've been scared to even dream about.

12

All of a sudden, it's the night before I leave on tour. I've been trying to make some progress on the album since the rehearsal with Jesse, but I've mostly been blocked again. The latest entries in my writing notebook are full of nonsensical, scribbled-out stanzas. Writing usually helps me make sense of my thoughts, but the pressure to make something good has been getting to me.

I spend most of the day trying to pack, and then I head over to school to meet Aisha and Neil. It's Ebi and Khadija's opening night performance of *Rocky Horror*.

As I walk toward the auditorium, a weird, unsettling feeling hits me. I've only been away a couple weeks, but it already feels like I don't belong here anymore. I can't imagine how much stranger it'll feel to come back once the tour ends. The thought of having to slog through classes again after getting a taste of freedom makes my heart sink.

When I open the auditorium door and spot Aisha smiling over

at me from the third row, everything I was just worrying about stops mattering. I'd take boring-ass classes any day as long as I get to be with Aisha. Being away from her has been getting harder and harder to think about the closer I get to leaving. A sharp, squeezing pain blooms in my chest at the thought of having to say goodbye to her tonight.

"Hey," Neil says from Aisha's other side as I sit down next to her. "You're cutting it close—the show's about to start."

Aisha pulls a party hat out of her bag and snaps it over my head before handing me a noisemaker.

I scratch at the hat's tight elastic. "Guess we're doing the whole props thing?"

Aisha beams at me, squeezing my hand. "I'm so excited! Neil and I have only seen *Rocky Horror* at home—we've never been to one of the sing-alongs at a movie theater or anything like this. Have you?"

"Same. I'm glad I was able to make it tonight."

I can't help thinking of the performance I won't be here for—her fall showcase. It will be the first time I'll miss one of her dance performances since I met her. She had a really bad dissociative episode at the fall showcase last year, and then the winter showcase was when she fell and got a concussion.

"So why do you look so worried then?" she asks, frowning slightly.

I blink. "Sorry—no reason."

Aisha raises an eyebrow and I remind myself I'm trying to open up with her more.

I take in a breath and continue, "I mean, I was just thinking about how I wish I could be here for your showcase."

Aisha sighs. "I'll be fine, I promise. Neil and my dad will be there."

I nod and do my best to smile again as the lights go down.

The audience quiets for a moment, but not for long. Almost everyone sings along over the cast's booming voices, quoting the most well-known lines throughout the show. The whole room gets on their feet for the entirety of the last number, and when the final curtain falls the sound in the auditorium becomes absolutely deafening. It's almost overwhelming, and I can't help wondering if the crowd will be like this tomorrow night.

Neil, Aisha, and I head backstage to congratulate Ebi and Khadija, dodging theater kids in an array of red corsets, torn fishnets, glittering formal jackets, and long, white lab coats. Neil spots them by a costume rack and leads us over, but Aisha takes hold of my arm and stops walking before we reach them. She turns to look at me, her face solemn.

"What's up?" I ask slowly. "Are you feeling okay?"

"I just wanted to check in with you about tonight."

I freeze, my heart stopping for a long second before thudding out a rib-bruising beat. I told Aisha this morning that my parents are visiting my uncle and aunt for the night. My mom talked to my uncle, and they're going to try to get Dad to take the loan he turned down earlier. Aisha said she might be able to come hang out after the show, but she hasn't confirmed anything yet.

"Um, sure."

"So, Ebi's hosting an opening night party at his place. If you feel comfortable, I was hoping you'd wanna come check it out with me and Neil?"

"Oh . . ." I try not to show my disappointment. I was really hoping to spend some time alone with Aisha tonight, to play her the song I wrote about how much I love her. I want her to hear it before I leave—even if tonight doesn't end up being "the night." But I don't want to be a buzzkill. At least we'll still get to spend a little more time together, even if we're around other people. "Okay."

Aisha gives me a skeptical look. "Are you sure? I know it's not really your thing, but we could just stay for a few minutes."

"Just a few minutes?" I nod and let out a breath. "I'm cool with that. And then, maybe we could hang out at my place?"

"We can definitely go to your place afterward," she says quietly.

I study her for a long moment and when she stares back unblinkingly my heartbeat resumes its punishing rhythm.

Does she want to have sex tonight? I feel like from the way she's looking at me that might be what she's thinking.

When I stay silent, she leans in and kisses me for an impossibly long moment. The backstage chatter fades to nothing as I wrap my arms around her.

Finally, she pulls back and laughs at my dazed expression. "Oh, and one last thing about Ebi's party. Let's say, hypothetically, if there were about ten minutes where everyone would be paying attention to you . . . Would that be okay with you?"

I stare blankly at her for a moment before it clicks. "Did you guys get me a going-away present or something? You didn't have to do that."

"I can't confirm or deny." She takes my arm again, pulling me toward where Neil's talking to Ebi and Khadija. "But if you think it'll be too stressful then don't worry about it."

I shake my head quickly. "No, it's fine. I mean, it won't be too stressful for me."

It's nice that she checked in with me first. That shouldn't make me feel like a loser, but it is sort of pathetic, especially considering I'm about to go on tour with one of the coolest musicians in the world.

It's only a matter of time until Jesse discovers just how deeply socially inept I am.

"You guys were spectacular!" Aisha squeals at Ebi and Khadija when we reach them.

"Congrats—you both were great tonight," I chime in, but Khadija starts talking to Aisha at the same time, so I don't think anyone hears me.

"Thanks, Ollie," Ebi says, evidently having heard. "It's good to see you—we've missed you at school! I'm having a get-together at my place tonight, you in?"

"For sure," I say, smiling like this is new information. "Sounds fun!"

Neil shoots me a sly look that lets me know he's clued in that Aisha already told me about the surprise. "Sweet, time to party!"

A wave of apprehension hits me. Not just because I'm so painfully awkward but because of all the times the words "Neil" and "party" have turned out to be a truly disastrous combo. One of the most notable times being when Neil threw me a surprise birthday party last year and ended up getting so wasted that he passed out in the bathroom. Maybe it wouldn't have been quite so awful if it hadn't been so soon after his end-of-summer bender when I couldn't wake him up and had to call 911. Thankfully it wasn't that serious when we found him on my birthday.

And after Aisha and I put Neil to bed that night, we had our first kiss. But that only lasted a minute before I ruined it when I panicked and bailed.

You didn't ruin it. Everything turned out fine when I explained to Aisha what happened. But that doesn't change the fact that I really hurt Aisha when I left that night. And I'm terrified about freaking out and disappointing her like that again.

I remind myself how much we've been through since then and that whatever happens, we'll work through it.

I need to worry less about Neil, too. Despite those awful experiences last year, I haven't seen anything that would make me think his recovery isn't going as well as he says it is.

I shake off my unease as the conversation moves on, and eventually we head to the bus stop in front of the school. As Ebi and Neil talk to some other kids on their way to the party, Aisha slips her hand through mine. She gives me a cute little smile then tunes into what Khadija's saying.

"This is a dry party, by the way," Ebi yells as the bus pulls up. "I'm too exhausted to deal with anyone puking at my place."

A couple boos and groans ring out, but mostly everyone laughs as we all board the bus.

"You don't have to look *so* relieved," Neil says with a snort before lowering his voice. "You know I'd be fine either way."

"I know," I say quickly. "It must be annoying when everyone else is drinking, though."

He shrugs. "It's been getting easier."

I nod and bite at my lip, considering whether I should tell him about the song I wrote about how proud I am of his recovery. I wrote it at the start of the school year, before my writer's block struck. I debated recording it and adding it to my set list, but I wanted to check in with him first and couldn't work up the nerve before the label's deadline. It could still be a track on my album though—especially now that I'm struggling to come up with new material. But by the time I open my mouth to mention it, Neil's turned away again.

"Hey, Ollie."

I look across the aisle to find Ebi leaning over his seat to talk to me. "What's up?"

"Not much. How's prepping for the tour been?" he asks. We've been texting a little and talking occasionally in the contributor group.

"Good. The rehearsal went pretty well . . ." I start thinking about Jesse and decide to change the subject. "Anyway, I'm gonna try and send a pitch for the blog soon. Maybe an album review."

I'm still not sure I'll think of anything as good as the pieces Kamran and the other contributors have been pitching. Everyone who's posted has mentioned at least one personal element that makes their piece more compelling than a dry write-up that anyone could put together. I'm having trouble coming up with an angle that's personal enough to be interesting but still feels comfortably detached from anything that could identify me.

He smiles. "Awesome! By the way, do you have any tour stops near Regina?"

"Yep, I'll be there in a couple weeks. Why?"

"Dev's out there—maybe you could hit them up at their studio if you have some time. I wish I could get out there myself, but my parents would never let me go on my own." He lets out an annoyed sigh.

"That sucks."

Ebi shakes his head. "It's whatever. At least they let me go to the festival with you guys. Anyway, if you end up going, maybe you could get some coverage for the blog?"

"What kind of coverage? No guarantees or anything—I'm not sure if I'll have time between shows."

"For sure, I totally get it," he says easily. "I know you'll probably be hanging with lots of cool people in the industry, so if you're comfortable doing any Q&As that would be sick. If you tell whoever you're interviewing that you're using a pen name you could probably still do it anonymously."

I nod, even though I can't imagine being invited to hang out with any cool industry people besides Jesse. But who knows. "Okay. I'll keep you posted."

*
*

At Ebi's place, I find myself standing mostly silent next to Aisha as she talks to Khadija, her friend Beth, and some other girls about the show. I'm trying to contribute to the conversation, but I keep missing the brief openings when no one else happens to be talking.

The lights in the living room flicker and everyone quiets down for a moment.

Aisha whispers, "Heads up, it's surprise time."

I nod, though I hardly register her words, entirely distracted by her warm breath on my ear. In the near darkness, I feel her lips meet my skin. She kisses behind my ear before trailing down my jaw. I shiver as she pulls away, her face glowing, lit only by candlelight.

When I finally manage to tear my eyes away from hers, I notice Neil and Ebi approaching with a sheet cake that reads "Bon Voyage Ollie!"

Everyone starts cheering and congratulating me, and I'm so overstimulated I don't know what to do or where to look.

Ebi puts the cake down on the coffee table, then yells to me over the noise, "Hey, can I give you a hug?"

I nod and he pulls me in, patting my back. "Congrats, Ollie! I hope you have a blast on tour. You're gonna do great."

"Thanks, Ebi," I say as Neil and Aisha throw their arms around our shoulders, joining us in a big group hug.

Khadija squeezes between Ebi and me. "Remember what I said about not forgetting about us when you're famous."

"I'll do my best," I quip as we all separate, and everyone laughs.

My face flushes—I didn't realize anyone besides Khadija was listening. The whole room is staring at me and no one's talking. After an excruciating second Neil clears his throat. He's holding a big piece of paper out to me.

"Oh, sorry." I reach for it, realizing it's an oversized homemade card.

Neil grins. "Everybody signed it."

"It's nothing big, but we hope you like it," Aisha says, rubbing my arm.

I nod, my throat clogging up as I scan all the encouraging messages.

"Thanks everyone." I manage to steady my voice and speak up, addressing the whole room. "I really appreciate this. I'm, uh . . ." My voice wavers for a second, but I push through it. "The last show of the tour will be downtown at The Vinyl Underground—you guys are all welcome to come!"

The room explodes in excitement, and conversations finally start up again. Aisha squeezes my hand before pulling away and grabbing some paper plates to help Ebi with the cake.

"You work at The Vinyl Underground, right?" Khadija asks me. "Do you think you could get us in for free? And possibly introduce me to Jesse Jacobs?"

Neil and Beth burst out laughing.

"God, you're obsessed with that man," Beth says. "Ollie, don't do it. For Jesse's safety. You can introduce *me*, though. I'll be chill."

"*Sure* you will, Beth," Neil drawls, shaking his head.

Khadija rolls her eyes and sighs. "I had to try. Jesse Jacobs is so freaking hot, I would literally let him run me over with an eighteen-wheeler. Ollie, you're so lucky you get to spend every day with him for three months."

I mean, she's not wrong. I am pretty lucky. But I stare at my feet, hating that now I'm thinking about Jesse when I should be thinking about my amazing girlfriend.

You don't deserve her. Burning shame consumes me for a second, but I push Jesse out of my mind.

"Look, you weirded him out," Beth mutters at Khadija. "He's not gonna want to get us tickets now."

"No, it's fine." I force out a laugh as Aisha hands me a slice of cake. "I can get you guys tickets, no problem."

"*Yes!!!*" They both scream, jumping up and down.

Neil snorts in amusement and Aisha chuckles as she digs into her cake. I let out a silent sigh of relief that she's not just picking at it.

"This is so good," she says through a mouthful. "After this we can head out if you want."

"Okay," I say, leaning into her frosting-coated lips. She lets out a small, surprised sound before pulling me closer. She slides her hand up the back of my neck and into my hair. When I finally remember to pull away, I'm unable to stop the ridiculous smile spreading across my face. "Sounds like a plan."

13

"Sorry about the mess," I say to Aisha when we get back to my place. There's a huge pile of clothes next to the open suitcase on my bedroom floor.

"No worries," Aisha says. "Not quite packed yet?"

"Not sure what to bring. All my stuff kinda sucks," I mutter as I sink to the floor and start haphazardly folding a few thrifted band tees.

"There's nothing wrong with your clothes. But if you feel that way, you won't mind if I borrow this." Aisha plops down beside me and grabs one of my hoodies.

I snatch it back from her. "How about you return one of the *three* you've already taken hostage and we'll talk."

She narrows her eyes but can't keep a straight face, breaking into an adorable grin. "Okay, fine."

We stare at each other for a long beat and I'm acutely aware of just how silent my house is with my parents gone for the night.

I look away, clearing my throat as I busy myself folding again. "So, what time do you have to get home?"

Aisha picks up a pair of my jeans and starts to help me pack. "I, uh, told my dad I'd be sleeping over at Khadija's place."

My pulse springs into my throat, but I keep stuffing clothes into my suitcase. "But you're not really going to Khadija's, though?"

From the corner of my eye, I see her looking at me. I can't make myself turn to meet her gaze.

"Right. Do you mind if I stay over?"

I nod, my heart still going at a breakneck speed as my brain races to catch up. Okay, so I wasn't imagining it earlier. I'm pretty sure she does want it to happen tonight.

"I don't have to if you don't want—"

"I do want," I cut in, my voice a little too loud. I swallow and manage to speak at a normal volume. "I mean, of course I want you to stay over."

"Okay . . ." she says slowly, searching my eyes. "What's wrong then?"

I shake my head. "Nothing's wrong. It's just . . . What about your dad? Are you sure he bought that you'll be at Khadija's? You know, considering it's my last night here?"

"I told him you left yesterday," Aisha says, wincing. "I kinda felt bad for lying, but . . . I knew he was going to be annoying, and I really wanted to spend some time with you before you leave."

I feel weirdly choked up all of a sudden. "How about I just don't leave?" I say quietly as I take hold of her hand.

She laughs a little, resting her head on my shoulder. "I'm really gonna miss you, you know."

"Me too," I breathe against her temple. I squeeze my eyes shut and try to keep it together.

I don't know what's wrong with me. This shouldn't feel like such a big deal. It's only a few months, and we'll still be able to talk and video chat.

I try to shake away the heaviness that's settled in my stomach as she pulls away and studies me again. "So how are you feeling about the tour?"

"A bit scared," I admit. "I'm still not sure if I can handle performing every night."

"I know it's gonna be a lot, but you can do this, Ollie. I know it." She sounds so certain that I almost start to believe it.

I shake my head. "I could barely handle you guys surprising me earlier even though you gave me a heads-up," I mutter.

"You handled it fine. I think you're just super in your head right now."

"Yeah, you're right. My therapist told me to try and focus on one thing at a time instead of obsessing about messing things up in the future."

"Okay, so what's one thing you can focus on right now?"

"Well . . ." I cram a few more shirts in my suitcase and shut it. "Packing's done."

She nods and then we're just staring at each other again, my pulse kicking back up to dangerous speeds.

"Aisha . . ." I do my best to collect myself. I guess it's now or never. "I wrote something for you. Do you want to hear it?"

She breaks into a big grin. "Yeah, of course!"

"Okay, cool." I grab my guitar from beside my desk, take in a full breath, and start playing.

As I sing, my nerves start to subside. Her eyes hold me so steadily that I forget myself; in this moment, there's only her.

I swallow down the knot forming in my throat and blink hard when I'm finished. "It's called 'Until the Stars Burn.' I hope you liked it because it's going to be part of my tour set."

Aisha's looking at me with glazed eyes. "That night at the festival . . . That's what you said, wasn't it? N'habek hataa i t'harkou lil njoum. I'll love you until the stars burn."

I gawk at her, the weight of her words stunning me. It didn't sound like she was just repeating it. It sounded like she meant it.

She winces. "Did I say it wrong?"

I shake my head before leaning in and resting my forehead against hers. "No, that was perfect."

She lets out a breath, and the warmth of it feathers across my face.

"I can't believe you looked that up. I hope it doesn't sound, I don't know . . ." My face warms. "Too intense."

She pulls back to look in my eyes. "Yeah, it is intense. But that's exactly how I feel about you, too," she whispers before her lips collide with mine.

*

A while later, Aisha pulls away from me, sitting up on her side. "I wanted to tell you something."

"What is it?" I ask as I catch my breath.

"Ollie . . . I'm on the pill now."

"Oh." That's all I'm able to get out for a long moment. "I, uh, I still have condoms if you want to . . ."

She nods, kissing me hard again before her hands start inching their way down my body. The moment where I would usually panic comes and goes and I can barely believe that this is about to happen.

Eventually, there's nothing left between us. I blindly reach for my bedside table as I kiss my way down her throat.

"Sorry, just give me a sec," Aisha gasps out, pushing me away. She sits up and wraps her arms tight around her knees.

"You okay?" I ask softly as I brush her hair back from her face. "Hey, what's wrong?"

"Nothing," she says, but her voice wavers. "I just . . . I just started thinking too much." She forces out a laugh. "Guess I'm the one being too in my head now."

"Thinking too much about what?"

"About, like, what if I make weird noises or accidentally fart when we're having sex, and then afterward you're grossed out or you just lose interest in me, and then you forget about me while you're gone and fall in love with a groupie and never talk to me again?" she blurts out.

"That's . . . oddly specific," I say, trying to process. A sharp pang of guilt hits me as I think of the way I felt around Jesse at our rehearsal. *That doesn't mean anything. I still love Aisha.*

She lets out a loud sigh. "Oli, I'm being serious."

I shake my head. "Aisha, groupies aren't even a thing anymore."

"*Oh my God, shut up!* You know what I mean! There's like a million girls that want you. It's actually ridiculous."

"None of that matters." I pull her into my arms, and she buries her face in my shoulder. "You're the only one I want. You know that."

She wraps her arms tighter around me.

"I know," she says. "But I can't stop thinking about how you'll be gone tomorrow. And I think that doing this tonight would make it harder for me to deal with missing you."

My eyes soften. "Aisha . . ." I swallow hard. A heavy ache settles in my stomach at the thought of being away from her in just a few hours. "Don't worry, I get it. Do you wanna wait until I'm back?"

She nods as she lies back down. I settle next to her, and she rests her head on my chest. We stay like that for a long while and I do my best to commit every part of this moment to memory. How impossibly soft her skin is. How beautiful she looks as her eyes start to flutter closed.

Even though we decided to wait, I feel like something did change between us tonight. I didn't think it was possible for me to love her more than I already do, but I couldn't have imagined just how overwhelming tonight would be. I feel so much closer to her than I ever have.

I run my fingers through her hair as her breathing starts to slow. I'm exhausted, but I fight to keep my eyes open just to take her in for a little longer.

It's scary how permanent it felt when she told me she loved me. How I can tell she feels the exact same out-of-control way about me as I do about her. I can't imagine ever loving anyone else as much as I love her.

I hate that she was worried, even for a second, that I would forget about her on tour. She said it didn't bother her, but I know it must be impossible not to let all the weird comments get to her sometimes.

Guilt pinches at me again when Jesse pops into my head. No matter what I've been feeling when I'm around him, I would never forget about Aisha. She's always been there for me; her faith that I can get through this makes me feel like it's actually possible.

As much as I just want to curl up under my covers and hide away with Aisha forever, that's not an option. I already gave my mom my first advance installment, which should help for a while. But the only way to get the rest of it is to actually do this.

My throat tightens as I picture myself alone onstage in Montreal tomorrow night. I rub my face and realize my hands are trembling. I slowly fill my lungs to capacity, but my pulse continues to race. Jesus, if even the *thought* of it is getting to me like this, I don't want to think about how badly I'll be shitting myself at the show.

All the ways I could bomb run through my mind. I make myself focus only on the even sound of Aisha's breathing. I finally start to calm down as my breath slows to match hers. Closing my eyes, I soak in every last bit of this moment, letting go of all my terrified projections of tomorrow.

14

I start awake when the front door slams so hard the house shakes. From downstairs, I hear Mom raising her voice to a level I've rarely heard her reach. I sit up quickly as Aisha begins to stir beside me.

"What was that?" she yawns out.

"My parents are back." I jump out of bed and grab my jeans. I can hear Dad yelling now. "I guess trying to convince my dad to take my uncle's loan didn't go too well."

Aisha winces sympathetically as she gets up and gets dressed. "I can go out your window if you want."

I nod then gather her in my arms. "I'll call you when I get to Montreal, okay?"

She gives me a small, sad smile before kissing me. Even though I hear footsteps coming up the stairs, I can't make myself care, wrapping my arms around her even tighter.

We finally break away from each other when there's a knock on my door. "Olia? Are you up yet?" Mom calls out.

Aisha opens my window and mouths, "*Love you, bye,*" disappearing as she climbs out and descends the big oak tree in my backyard. Mom knocks again and I finally move toward my door, taking a deep breath before pulling it open.

"Hey," I say carefully, taking in her red face and wet eyes. "Things didn't go well with Dad?"

She sighs. "I don't know what I expected."

"I'm sorry," I say.

"It's all right. We should be okay for a few more months, at least until you get home. Thanks again for your help, Olia."

I give her a hug as I process that the money I gave her a few weeks ago will only go as far as the end of the year. Honestly, I'm thankful Dad didn't flat-out refuse my offer, too. He just didn't acknowledge it.

"Let me make you some breakfast," Mom says, and I nod before shutting my door again with a sigh.

After a quick shower, I pick up my suitcase and guitar and take a last look around my room. I take in my band posters, my vinyl collection overflowing from the stacked wooden crates set up by my record player. The plaid love seat falling apart under my window, overlooking the red and orange leaves of the tree outside. The perfectly worn Persian rug that takes up most of the dark hardwood floor. This room is the one place I feel truly at ease in the world. I finally turn and head for the door, reminding myself that getting through the next few months is the only way this room will stay mine.

Downstairs, I don't protest when Mom stacks my plate with way too much baghrir. I eat every bit I can manage to stuff in my mouth. Dad hasn't come down yet, and I don't think he's going to come out to say goodbye.

I shrug my irritation away, smiling at Mom across the kitchen table. "That was great, but I have to get to the train station now."

"Do you need a ride?" she asks, taking my empty plate from me.

"That's okay, Soph's picking me up," I say, just as I glance out the window and see her station wagon pulling into the driveway.

"Have a safe trip." She gathers me in a bone-crushing hug. "And try not to worry too much. Everything's going to be okay."

"Thanks, Mom," I say into her shoulder, wishing I could believe her. "Love you."

I grab my stuff and head outside. After throwing my things in the backseat, I jump in the front beside Sophie.

"Thanks again for the ride," I say as she pulls out of the driveway. "You didn't have to."

It's out of her way to pick me up now that she's downtown for school. I was tempted to tell her I could just take the bus when she offered, but we haven't seen that much of each other lately and I felt bad about how I've been dodging her.

"Don't mention it," she says easily. I lean back in my seat as classic rock murmurs on the radio. "I might as well get some final use out of this car. I'm hoping to sell it soon."

I frown at her. "But you just got it."

She shrugs. "I'm gonna need some extra cash to cover my classes and textbooks next semester. Gas is so expensive right now anyway."

My stomach turns over. "Sorry I can't help out. I already gave Mom my first advance payment for the mortgage."

Sophie glances at me again. "Yeah, Mom told me. That's so great of you."

"Not that Dad even cares," I blurt out before biting my tongue.

"Dad's so annoying sometimes." She shakes her head. "I'm sure he appreciates it just as much as Mom, even if he didn't say anything."

"Whatever. Mom just told me he refused to take Uncle's loan again."

Sophie groans. "Great. Look, promise me that you won't worry too much about money stuff while you're gone, okay? Just try and have a good time. You deserve it—this is going to be such a wonderful experience for you!"

"I'll try." It's beyond frustrating that what should be the most thrilling time of my life is going to be muddied by my brain's constant need to sabotage me. I sigh. "Anyway, I hope Aisha's gonna be okay. Same with Neil. He's been doing good for a while, but . . ."

"I'll keep an eye on him," she says quickly, and when I look over at her she clears her throat. "I mean, I'll keep an eye on *them*. I'm sure they'll both be fine, though."

"Right . . . Neil told me you guys have been talking?" He'd said they'd just been worried about me, but I'm not an idiot.

"Uh . . ." Her face turns pink. "A little, I guess."

"Uh-huh. Soph, come on."

Her eyes flicker to mine for a moment, guilt written across her face. "Oh God, did he tell you?"

I raise my eyebrows. "Oh, there's something to tell me?"

Sophie swears under her breath. "I, uh, kissed him at the festival."

I blink at her. I knew something was going on, but I didn't expect that. "At the festival when?"

She winces. "That first night, after you guys went to bed. I'm really sorry."

I give her a confused look. "Sorry for what?"

"You aren't mad?"

"Why would I be mad? Soph, it's fine, I don't care. I just want you to be happy, okay? But Neil's . . . Well, you know what he's like. He never seems that serious about girls. And you're, like, actually into him, aren't you?"

"I'm not *that* into him," she says, her voice squeaky and high-pitched.

I just stare at her, and she lets out a loud breath. "Okay, so maybe I used to be pretty into him, but not anymore. I do care about him, but he's still in high school and I'm busy with my classes and everything. So yeah, it wasn't a big deal. It was more like a goodbye thing."

"Okay," I say. "You know I just don't want you to get hurt or anything."

"That's so sweet of you," she says, sounding choked up. "Especially since I've been such a shitty sister."

"No, you haven't." I brace myself for what she's about to bring up next.

"I'm so sorry, Ollie. I'm so, so sorry about what happened."

"Hey, stop," I cut her off, staring out at the dull gray sky. "I told you, I'm okay now. And I'm sorry I haven't wanted to talk about it. I know you just wanna help."

She takes a shaky breath. "It just makes me so fucking mad that he hurt you. And that he got away with it and now he's just out there." She flashes me a worried look. "I didn't mean . . . Ollie, I completely get why you didn't want to report him."

I can't say it hasn't crossed my mind that Thomas might have hurt other people since he assaulted me. But it took me over a year to even admit to my therapist what happened. Going to the police would have been impossible. On top of that, even before we were about to lose the house, it's not like we could afford a lawyer. Thomas's family has money so it would have been pointless and humiliating.

We fall into silence, the radio the only sound in the car.

"So, what venue are you playing in Montreal tonight?" Sophie asks after a while.

"Club Bibliothèque," I say. "Midnight Cavalcade's played there a few times so that's kinda cool. It's a tiny place, but yeah, still freaking out. Hopefully I don't *completely* screw it up."

"Did you bring your anxiety meds?" she asks.

"Yeah. I only take them for emergencies though." I used to take them more when I first started therapy, but now I only use them if I feel close to passing out. They work really well, but I don't feel like myself when I take them. Plus, they're super addictive, so I have to be careful about not relying on them too much.

"Don't you have another kind you take daily?"

"Uh, yeah. I did." I'm surprised she's asking me about this; we don't talk about my anxiety very often. "The SSRIs made me sleepy all the time, so I stopped those a while back."

She nods. "Okay, well, if you ever feel really bad I'm glad you can take something. Ollie, look, I get that Mom and Dad don't exactly understand how difficult this is going to be for you with your anxiety. I know you want to help them out, but if it turns out this is too much, it's totally okay if you need to come home."

I fiddle with the volume button on the radio, turning it down a smidge as I collect my thoughts. On one hand, I'm glad she gets how stressful this is going to be. But on the other, it scares me that she thinks there's a chance I can't do this.

"Don't worry. Whatever happens, I'll figure out a way to get through the tour," I finally say, keeping my voice steady. I can't give myself any room to fold on this. Even though things aren't the best with my dad, I still don't want to let my mom and Soph down.

She nods, her eyes teary as we pull up to the train station. "I know you will. Call me if you need anything," she says, giving me a quick hug before wiping her face and grinning at me. "Now go kick some ass, okay?"

15

Last night with Aisha loops in my mind before I conk out for most of the train ride from Toronto to Montreal's downtown core. Figuring out the transit system isn't too difficult, and I eventually get off a bus across the street from a small but fancy hotel. Thankfully, Middle Path is footing the bill for our accommodations on tour, along with our food.

Sound check is in an hour so I don't have much time to check in, meet up with Jesse, and head down to the venue. I hustle toward the hotel's front entrance, huddling against the early evening chill.

"That's not going to work for me."

I untuck my chin from my jacket collar and look around at the sound of Jesse's voice. I spot him in the hotel parking lot, standing in front of an old, pale-blue van talking to two men in their forties in dark bomber jackets and dress pants. None of them are smiling.

"Hey Jesse, everything good?" I ask as I head over, and they all turn to me.

One of the older guys, the taller one with dark hair, fixes me with a hard look that makes me slow down.

"That's the other talent," his shorter, stockier buddy says, nodding at me briefly.

I nod back before glancing at Jesse again.

He rubs at the back of his neck and shoots me a tight smile. "Hey Ollie. This is Greg and Tim. Middle Path hired them as security for the tour, apparently."

"Oh." I look between them and Jesse again. Seems like it's just as much a surprise to him as it is to me. "Nice to meet you."

"They just told me Pierre and the team want us to use a rental van and put mine in storage," Jesse continues tonelessly, looking down at his phone. "I'm trying to get in touch with Pierre right now."

"The storage place closes soon so we have to get a move on," Greg says.

Jesse shakes his head then pulls open the van door. He hops in the driver's seat and glances at me. "Ollie, can I talk to you for a minute?"

"Uh, sure." I get in the passenger side, avoiding Greg and Tim's annoyed gazes.

I slide the door shut, taking in the neat, sparse space with a couple rows of fold-down seats and some storage in the back. Jesse looks up from his phone, his face grim.

"God, this really sucks," he mutters.

"Pierre didn't give you a heads-up about this?" I ask. I didn't see anything about security in the contract and I didn't think about it until right now either.

"Not really. He said Helen was supposed to call." He stops short when his phone starts ringing. "It's her." He picks up her video call and her face appears.

"Hey, Jesse! I'm just in a meeting, is everything okay?" Helen asks.

He doesn't waste time with pleasantries. "I told you that I don't need security. And I thought we agreed I could use my van."

I glance out the window to see Tim on his phone and Greg smoking a cigarette as he paces around the empty parking space next to us. In the next space over is a large black SUV I'm assuming is theirs.

"Sorry about the confusion, but this is the safest option. We don't want you to worry about getting followed while you're traveling," Helen says. "Oh, hi Ollie," she adds when she spots me leaning in to see Jesse's screen. I nod hesitantly. I guess it does make sense considering how popular Jesse has become lately. I can't imagine how weird it must be for him.

Jesse doesn't say anything, so Helen continues. "Greg and Tim will give you your space. And I promise the rental van is great! It's a newer model and has more room—"

"My van's fine, though," Jesse insists.

"I'm sure it is! But the rental has tinted windows and reinforced glass. Not to mention you probably don't want the media or anyone else tracking your license plate."

I blink, wondering if people would actually be creepy enough to do that. How intense are Jesse's fans and the press going to be?

Jesse is quiet for another long minute. "Okay. I guess you're right," he finally concedes.

"Perfect! I'll let you go or you're going to be late. Let's touch base after the show," Helen says, hanging up unceremoniously.

Jesse leans back in his seat and closes his eyes. "Shit."

"You okay?" I ask carefully.

"Yeah," he sighs out. "I've just kind of been denying it's gotten to this point. Most fans are chill when they spot me, but sometimes not so much."

"Is that why you cut your hair?" I ask. He turns to study me, and my face instantly warms. "Sorry I didn't mean to—it's not really any of my business."

"It's okay." He bites his lip, uncertainty crossing his face for half a second before disappearing under his calm and collected exterior. "It was partly why I cut it, I guess. It's been getting weird, having to dodge people following me and stuff. But it's not like I want some off-duty pigs tailing me everywhere either."

I open my mouth, but I don't know what to say. The security guys do have that unsettling cop vibe that I don't think anyone enjoys, but Jesse seems particularly uncomfortable with it. If he's been getting followed, though, Helen's probably right that having them around is for the best.

"It's fine. We should get going," Jesse says after a beat.

I wince at myself as we get out of the van.

I don't have time to check in, so I take all my stuff with me when Tim drives us over to the venue. Greg took Jesse's van to the storage place and is going to meet us at the club later. Tim tells us it's only about fifteen minutes away so at least we won't miss sound check altogether.

I look up from my phone when I hear screaming. We're coming up on the little shoebox of a club and the line at the door extends over a block. There must be at least three times as many people outside as the space's maximum capacity. The sight of the crowd makes my throat tighten painfully. People point at our car and wave as we pass even though the windows are completely tinted.

I look over at Jesse. "Do you think they oversold tickets?" I ask, managing to keep my voice calm.

He smiles tightly and shakes his head. "A lot of people just want to try and meet us before we go in."

Tim chuckles, his eyes carefully scanning the massive line. "Sorry, not happening. The crowd's way too big for you to take pictures or sign anything. We're going in the back entrance."

I'm sure lots of people will be disappointed they won't get to meet Jesse—or me, I guess—but I can't help the relief that washes over me as Tim takes a back alley up to the club's loading dock. He tells us to stay put then gets out of the car and walks up to a guy waiting at the back door.

"How you feeling?" Jesse asks.

"I'm fine." I do my best to relax my shoulders. I've been making myself breathe as deeply as possible for the last few minutes. I slowly count to four in my head for every inhale and exhale, just like Nadine taught me. It's not doing anything to help my stomach, though—nausea almost overwhelms me.

"You sure?" I feel him looking at me, but I avoid his gaze.

Tim approaches the car again. "Straight inside. Don't go out again, even for a smoke break," he says. "I'll be standing out here and Greg will take the front entrance with the club's security."

Jesse and I nod before shuffling toward the guy at the door. He's a pale, haggard-looking man in his thirties. He's wearing an unimpressed expression but fixes his face into an overly enthused smile as we approach.

"*Bienvenue!* I'm the stage manager, Emile. Follow me."

"Sorry we're late," I say, following him down a dim, narrow staircase covered in old show flyers and graffiti.

He doesn't respond. I can feel Jesse looking at me again, but I keep my eyes on my feet as my stomach twists even more. After working at a venue, I know that people talk. I don't want to get a reputation as a spoiled kid who doesn't respect the crew's time.

Emile leads us to a closet-sized greenroom where I drop my bags off before we continue to a small backstage area. "Denis will lead you through the sound check. Great to meet you," he says with forced cheer before he takes off.

Denis, a shorter guy in his midtwenties, doesn't bother to hide his annoyance as we follow him out onto the stage. "We have to open the doors in fifteen minutes so there's no time to go through your full songs. We'll just set up your equipment and check the levels."

When it's time for our sound check, I force myself to focus on my breath again and step up to the mic stand, wiping my clammy hands on my pants. I catch my cue and sing out the first verse of "On Repeat."

Even though I make myself project, my voice is almost drowned out by the bass. The track stops short, and Denis cues the start of my next song, "Slow Down." This one is about managing my anxiety—pretty ironic since I'm having a lot of trouble with that right now. The bass is still way too loud.

I turn to look at him. "Um . . . could you . . ." Sweat is already starting to drip down the back of my neck, the hot stage lights aimed right at me.

"What is it?" he snips.

I almost shut down and say nothing, but I'll sound like shit if I don't tell him what the problem is.

"Can you turn the bass down like five notches?" I ask, managing to keep my voice steady.

He nods and gets the levels adjusted before my second track restarts. I block everything out and wait for my cue. The bass still sounds crunchy, but I can hear myself fine when I start singing, my voice ringing out clearly in the soon-to-be packed room. I can already hear the crowd, the noise vibrating through the ceiling as they start letting people inside for coat check. I squeeze my eyes shut against my blurring vision as I finish up the verse.

The track stops short and it's time for my third and final song, "Until the Stars Burn." It takes everything in me not to puke, but I get through the first verse and then it's Jesse's turn to run through his set.

As I step away from the mic stand, Jesse leans in close so I can hear him over his opening notes. "Hey, you don't look so great. Are you sure you're okay?"

I nod, ignoring my heart hammering even harder now. "Yeah, I'm just gonna grab some water."

I book it offstage and stumble down the narrow hallway to the greenroom. I pick up one of the water bottles lined up on the table in front of the mirror. I'm shaking so badly that I have to pry it open with my teeth. Jesse's voice rings out as he rehearses the last part of his set. My trembling fingers go numb. I slide down the wall to the dusty floor, trying in vain to get oxygen into my body.

For a terrifying moment, I think I'm genuinely going to die. Like right here, right this second. My vision is beginning to darken, but I somehow manage to crawl over to my bag. I get the side pocket open and root around for my meds. I pop a couple in my mouth and choke down another sip of water.

After a couple minutes, I'm able to stand again and my breathing slowly returns to normal. I'm soaked in sweat, so I change into another T-shirt. I wipe my face on a towel, then I stare at myself in the small, lit-up mirror. A chill passes through me. My face is eerily expressionless, like nothing happened. The door to the greenroom opens and I spin around to find Jesse.

"Everything good?" he asks, looking me up and down with concern. "You're on in two, but I can let them know if you need—"

"I'm cool." I lift the corners of my mouth even though I don't feel anything. The meds have stopped me from freaking out, but they've also blotted out anything even close to a normal reaction to this situation. Zero anticipation or excitement. Not that I was feeling much of that before since I've been so preoccupied with worrying. "I'm ready."

16

My ears are ringing so badly the hum blocks out a good portion of the screaming as we reach the backstage area. When I peek out, I see Emile onstage, shouting at the top of his lungs.

"You're here on a very special night! We're *honored* to have Jesse Jacobs here for the opening stop of his debut tour! But first up, give a warm welcome to viral sensation Ollie Cheriet!"

Emile turns to me, big fake grin plastered on his face again. Jesse gives me a light punch on the shoulder before I blindly step out onstage. The screaming somehow gets louder and I try not to wince. Emile nods curtly as he heads offstage.

Stepping up to the mic, I get a good look at the audience. There's around two hundred people packed into the small space, jumping up and down and clutching their friends. Some are reaching toward me. Some are even holding up signs that say my name.

I shake my head. It's as if I'm in the middle of a dream. One I think I've had before but can't quite remember, the details soft and fuzzy. I bite hard at my tongue, but instead of waking up, the copper taste of blood tinges my mouth.

You're awake. This is real.

I raise the corners of my mouth reflexively again and grab a firm hold of the mic in the stand. My hands are steady now, but I still don't risk free-handing it. I glance up at the sound booth and the guy signals thirty seconds at me. I guess I have some time to say hello.

"I can't really believe this is happening . . . but thank you all for coming out tonight!" I blurt out in French.

"*Oh my God! His French is so good!*" they shriek. "*We love you!*"

My first notes start, and I count a few inhales and exhales before I start singing "On Repeat." Thankfully the levels are still okay and I can hear myself fine, even though the audience is singing along.

I've been scanning the crowd without staring at anyone for too long, but I lock eyes with a girl around my age. She immediately burst into tears and starts screaming so loudly it genuinely scares me. I quickly avert my gaze and keep singing, getting through the last verse.

The song ends and the audience explodes in cheering. The surrealness starts to hit me again, everything seeming strange and uncanny. The crowd's reaction feels entirely divorced from my performance. This type of praise isn't something I deserve, isn't something I feel I've earned yet.

I push the thought aside as I move into "Slow Down." I avoid looking at anyone else for too long again, and I'm doing okay until my eyes land on a familiar-looking tall, blond guy near the back—his face twisted into an unpleasant smirk. He turns to say something to his friend, and they start laughing.

My heart stops altogether, and I squeeze my eyes shut. *It's not him. There's no way he's here.* Even as I internally shut down, my body keeps doing its job, getting air into my lungs. My voice still rings out clearly over the mic. I open my eyes and my shoulders relax half an inch when I glance over again and confirm that the guy isn't Thomas.

I go through the rest of the song on autopilot and when it's over, the cheering is notably quieter. It's not a big deal. "On Repeat" is the song everyone knows so it makes sense people won't be as into my other two. *Or maybe it's because you're acting like a robot.*

"Until the Stars Burn" starts up, and I block out the thought. Closing my eyes tight, I put all of my energy into the emotion behind the music and lyrics. I try to remember how it felt to sing this for Aisha in my room last night, but that moment feels scarily far away.

When I finish, the crowd is deafening again, just as loud as they were after my first song. I wave then turn to head offstage.

My eyes catch Jesse's as he flashes me a blinding smile.

"Great job," he says. There's a hint of surprise on his face, which makes total sense considering how badly I freaked out earlier.

"Thanks," I get out, but he's gone, taking his place at the mic. The crowd absolutely loses it now—the room is literally shaking as I lean back against the grimy backstage wall. My eyes start to sting and I wipe an arm over them, suddenly realizing I'm drenched in sweat again.

My phone buzzes. I pull it out of my back pocket and see a couple of missed calls from Aisha. Shit, I meant to call her earlier. I shoot off a quick text letting her know I'll call her back at the hotel.

The entire room cheers as Jesse's first song ends. He's grinning and waving at the crowd. It's almost comical how at ease he is compared to me. He grabs the mic off the stand and launches into his second song. The entire place is transfixed as he makes use of the whole stage, his gaze seeming to connect with everyone in the audience.

You should definitely be taking notes. I flip to my phone's camera and hit record. Jesse throws his hands up over his head and starts clapping, the whole room joining in as the chorus of his second song hits. He dances through it, jumping up and down as he loses himself in the music. The energy in the room reaches hysterical heights.

I've seen hundreds of live shows, but I don't think I've ever seen a performer have an effect quite like this. He sings and dances with complete abandon, the crowd losing all their inhibitions with him. Their roar crescendos as his second song ends.

"Having fun?" Jesse screams over the noise, laughing when the shrieking starts up again. He wipes a hand across his forehead then tugs off his T-shirt.

"You're so fucking hot!" a high-pitched voice screams out before being drowned out by even more screeching.

Jesse starts singing, looking unfazed as he takes total command of the stage, perfectly in his element.

He suddenly turns to glance at me. Blood rushes to my face. I stop recording and pocket my phone.

Relax, it's not a big deal. Helen mentioned I should try and get some performance footage anyway. I was just doing what she asked. As far as taking notes . . . I can't imagine ever feeling remotely as confident as Jesse does onstage. It's probably something that just comes naturally to him.

I watch Jesse go through the rest of his set, and slowly the effects of my meds start to wane. When it's over he waves goodbye to the crowd and jogs offstage.

"Man, it's boiling in here!" he yells over the still-deafening noise. He wipes his balled-up T-shirt over his face.

"Yeah. They definitely need to update their stage lights," I mutter, hoping none of the stagehands hear me. I focus on a guy on the crew heading onstage instead of Jesse standing shirtless in front of me. "Uh, are they already packing up? Aren't you gonna do an encore?"

"No encore tonight," a voice says sternly, and I spin around to find Tim frowning at us. "The crowd outside is getting out of control. We have to leave now."

Tim strides back down the hall before we can respond. I register that he's got our bags slung across his wide shoulders. I frown at Jesse, and he shrugs.

"Okay . . . Guess we're going," he says.

"'Out of control'? How bad do you think it is?" I ask as we head toward the back exit. Tim's standing beside Greg along with a few of the club's security guys talking into walkie-talkies.

Jesse shrugs again, but his jaw tightens.

"All right, listen up," Tim says. "Greg's going out first. Stick as close as you can behind him. I'll bring up the rear. The club's team will keep the crowd at bay. Absolutely no stopping. Straight in the car, as fast as you can. Got it?"

I nod, focused on the alarming, muffled roar of voices outside. Even through the closed steel door, it's *so loud*.

I sneak a glance at Jesse and find him nodding as he pulls his shirt back on. "Got it. Ready."

Tim opens the door, and my pounding pulse picks up so much speed it hurts, like my heart is going to burst out of my chest.

Over the explosion of noise, I hear a supersonic screech. *"Oh my God, it's them!"*

Every eye in the seething mass of people is wild and wide as they catch sight of us. Hundreds of hands reach toward me before being brushed away by the security team.

"Move!" Tim barks at me and I pick up my pace. The barriers they had set up have been breached by the crowd. The alleyway is so packed with bodies it's taking us forever just to get the few feet to the car. From my left side, a surge of people hits us in a wave of flailing limbs. One of the security guys beside me stumbles. He careens into me so hard it knocks the wind out of me. My feet tangle together as I struggle for breath. Jesse grabs hold of my arm, keeping me upright. I try to thank him, but I can't hear myself over the unrelenting boom of my heartbeat.

Finally, we're at the car and Tim pushes me inside. I scramble across the backseat as Jesse tumbles in after me.

"You okay?" he pants.

"I'm totally fine," I get out as my heart rate finally drops back to normal.

"You can't lose your balance in a crowd like that." His face is more serious than I've ever seen it. "If you fall when there's that many people, you could . . ." He trails off, swallowing hard.

"He's right," Greg says, turning around in the passenger seat with a grim expression. "Never lose your footing in a crowd-crush situation. If you go down and get trampled, it's over."

I nod, not mentioning that I couldn't help it since it was one of the club's security guys who bumped into me. When I glance at Jesse again, he looks a little ill. He rubs a hand over his face, sinking lower in his seat.

I wonder if he's ever fallen and gotten hurt in a crowd or seen it happen to other people. It's never happened at work. We don't let people in above capacity, and we've never had this many people without tickets show up.

I glance out the front window as Tim inches the car forward. The club's security is slowly getting the crowd to part so we can drive out of the alley. The screams are mostly muffled, but hands tap loudly against the windows, faces pressing against the glass, trying to see inside. It's like we're zoo animals. I stare at my feet, feeling claustrophobic. I try to breathe through it, the meds still dampening the full intensity of my anxiety.

When we finally make it back to the hotel parking lot, there's a new shiny black van in the spot Jesse's had been. It's wider and taller than his van, just barely fitting into the space.

Jesse glances at it warily. "Can I have the keys for the rental?" he asks Greg.

"Sure." Greg reaches into his pocket, then stops and frowns. "Wait, how old are you?"

"Nineteen," Jesse says unhappily, realizing what's coming next.

"The rental place said drivers have to be twenty-five or older," Greg continues. He tosses the keys to Tim instead of Jesse. "We'll take turns driving you while one of us follows in the SUV."

Jesse rubs his face again, nodding mutely.

It's silent for an awkward beat. "Did you check in already?" I finally ask, hoisting my bags onto my shoulders.

Jesse shakes his head, heading toward the hotel entrance without saying anything to Greg and Tim.

"Uh, guess we'll see you later?" I say to the guys.

Tim nods. "We'll be taking shifts in the lobby if you need us."

Are they going to be downstairs guarding the door all night? Seems a bit much, but what do I know?

I find Jesse at the front desk.

A thin older guy looks up from rapidly typing as I approach. "My deepest apologies, but it seems we accidentally overbooked. There's only one room left, a suite with two queens."

"That's fine," Jesse says without hesitation. He glances at me and frowns when he sees my frozen face. "Or if you want your own space, we can figure something else out. I could—"

"I'm cool sharing a room," I say quickly. I'm going to have to get used to being in tight quarters with him. We'll have to crash in the van for some of the small-town stops with no hotels in the area.

The guy gives us our key cards and we take the elevator to the top floor. On the ride up, I can't help thinking about first meeting Jesse in the RMA building elevator. How his brilliantly warm eyes held mine, all my nerves about the meeting slipping away for a brief moment—

"Christ, I need a shower," Jesse says, bringing me out of my daze as the elevator door opens. "Do you mind if I use the bathroom first?"

"Go for it." I clear my throat, psyching myself up to speak again. "By the way, I didn't get a chance to say it earlier, but your set was amazing tonight."

He smiles for the first time since we left the club.

"Thanks. Yours, too."

In the room, Jesse flips the lights on, revealing an all-white suite with a giant window overlooking a beautiful view of the lit-up Montreal skyline.

"This is sick!" Jesse throws his bags on the floor next to one of the beds and collapses face first onto the ultrasoft-looking comforter, sighing deeply.

I drop my bags next to the other bed and rub the back of my neck. "Yeah, this is really nice."

Jesse pulls himself upright with a groan. "Okay, I'm gonna hit the shower." He heads for the bathroom, shutting the door behind him.

I let out a shaky breath as I perch at the end of my bed. My mind replays the night's events, still not quite believing all of it happened.

I take out my phone and call Aisha. It rings a couple of times then goes to voicemail. Not surprising since it's late and she has dance rehearsals before school tomorrow. I leave her a quick message then lie down, resting my eyes for a second. I think again about how different playing "Until the Stars Burn" felt tonight compared to playing it for Aisha last night. How already that seems strangely long ago—the distance between us widening by the second.

I jerk awake at the sound of the door. Blinking, I spot Jesse emerging from the bathroom in his boxers. I freeze, just staring at him.

"Sorry to wake you up. Do you want me to turn off the light?"

"Um . . . s-sure." I quickly lie back down, facing away from him, my pulse rushing in my ears. I shut my eyes, but I'm still seeing him, the sharp lines of his body and his damp skin burned into my retinas. I'm glad he turned off the lights because I'm sure I'm turning red—my face is boiling.

"We're supposed to call Helen to debrief, but maybe we can do it before we hit the road tomorrow? I'm exhausted, too," he says. I hear the quiet squeak of springs as he gets into his bed.

"Sounds good," I mutter, keeping my eyes tightly shut. "Night."

"Ollie?" he asks after a quiet minute.

"Yeah?"

"Are you sure you're good? I mean, tonight was way more intense than I thought it would be."

"I'm okay," I say, slowly opening my eyes in the near-darkness. "I guess I'll get used to this soon."

"I don't know if it's possible to get used to it," Jesse says softly.

"What do you mean?"

For a moment, there's only the sound of his breathing.

"I don't know. This is all fresh for me, too. My only other major show was at Niagara Fest this summer. And even though it was a huge event, I wasn't a headliner or anything. It didn't feel as overwhelming as tonight."

"That makes sense. You know, I was going to see you there," I find myself saying. I bite my tongue and wince. It smarts from when I bit it onstage earlier. "I mean, not to see you, specifically. But uh, yeah, I was there."

"You were?" I hear him shift in the darkness. "I don't remember seeing you at my set."

I let out a small laugh. "You didn't know me then, why would you remember?"

"I think I probably would have," he says through a yawn.

"Oh." My face heats up for no good reason. "Well, my girlfriend wasn't feeling great so we left early. I didn't make it to your set."

"That sucks. Was she okay?"

"Yeah, she's good now," I say, worrying my bottom lip between my teeth. I'm remembering the sad smile she gave me before she left my place this morning.

Jesse doesn't say anything else and after a minute I hear the soft sound of snoring. I roll over again, half-considering getting up and taking a shower . . . but this bed is way too comfortable. When I close my eyes, my mind whirs through the night's events. The meds have finally worn off, and a swirling mix of emotions pushes to the surface. Feeling this overwhelmed the first night on the road makes my fears about getting through this swell inside me. Finally, though, my exhaustion drowns everything out, and I drift into a dead sleep.

17

I groan against the first rays of sunlight piercing through the giant hotel window before dragging myself out of bed and closing the curtains. Jesse's still asleep, his muffled snoring breaking through the comforter he's buried beneath. My bed is still neatly made; I was too tired to even get under the covers last night.

I head to the washroom for a quick shower, taking a fresh change of clothes with me.

Jesse still hasn't moved when I emerge fully clothed a few minutes later. When I check my phone, there are even more notifications going off than usual. I open my feed, and my heart stops—my name and Jesse's are trending.

What the hell? I almost can't work up the nerve to look more closely. All things considered, I don't think I did *that* badly onstage last night . . . but maybe I'm deluding myself and everyone is talking about how shitty of a singer I am, that Jesse should never have chosen me to open for him.

I finally tap on my name and the first thing that pops up is a shaky video of Jesse and me leaving the club. The sight of the seething crowd makes me lightheaded all over again—there are hundreds of people packed into the tiny alley. A few people start to trip, creating a massive domino effect that ends in the security guard slamming into me. The camera zooms in on me just as I'm about to topple over and Jesse grabs hold of my arm. The shot stays on our faces as I thank Jesse before we continue toward the car.

That's it? I don't get why this is trending, to be honest. Sure, it was scary in the moment, but I'm not sure if me tripping qualifies as breaking news. I can't stop myself from scrolling through the comments and immediately regret it.

In several of the replies there's a shorter clip slowed down to half speed. It's the moment Jesse catches my arm. The comments are all zeroing in on the brief second when Jesse glances at my mouth as I thank him for steadying me. It's obvious he was trying to read my lips over the noise, but a lot of people are trying to make it into something else.

But what if . . . Something equal parts hopeful and shameful ignites inside me. I've been telling myself that whatever I've been feeling toward him is completely one-sided. That I've been misinterpreting the tension between us. But the fact that so many people think otherwise makes me start to question whether or not that's true.

I know I should just close the app, but for some reason I don't. I keep scrolling through the weird thread. There are claims that the video confirms Jesse is into guys. He's never spoken publicly about his sexuality or been romantically linked with anyone. There aren't any clues in his music since his lyrics are mainly about social issues.

I feel gross for thinking about this, for even reading that invasive thread. I'd be beyond uncomfortable if thousands of people were trying to figure out the same thing about me. My stomach churns—loads of people must already be speculating about me, especially now that this stupid video is going around.

My phone rings and my heart starts pounding again. I wonder if Aisha saw that video and the comments on it. My stomach twists at the thought of her worrying that there's something to the rumors.

I pick up the phone and see that it's Helen on a video call.

"Morning, Ollie," she says. "Are you about ready to go? You guys have to be on the road soon."

"Yeah, I'm ready. Jesse's not up yet though. Jesse, wake up!"

"Oh." Helen's eyebrows raise almost imperceptibly. "He slept in your room?"

"Uh . . ." I don't know why I feel tongue-tied, like I've done something wrong. "Yeah, the hotel overbooked," I stutter out.

Jesse finally starts to get up, rubbing his eyes. "Is that Helen?"

I nod, my mind racing, wondering if she's going to ask us about the video.

"So, we need to talk about last night," she says and my heart sinks. "We didn't anticipate such a huge crowd. To be safe, we'll be adding two more staff to the security team."

Jesse frowns. "I don't think we need—"

"The venue's security last night was not up to par, to be frank," Helen pushes on. "We can't let outside security put either of you at risk again."

Jesse shoots me a confused look. "What do you mean?"

"There's a video online of one of the club's security guards almost knocking Ollie down while you were leaving the show," Helen says.

I keep my eyes glued to my feet.

"Oh. Ollie, you didn't mention that was what happened."

I shrug. "It was an accident, I'm sure he didn't mean to—"

"Accident or not, we just want to make sure you're safe. I have to get going, but here's a quick rundown of today's schedule. You'll be in the car all day, but at two in the afternoon you have a phone interview with an indie radio station. Ollie, you didn't post a vlog yesterday, so we need you to catch up on that. If you could make some short-form content, that would be great, too."

"Short-form content?" I ask warily.

"Yes, we need longer videos for YouTube, but we're also hoping to increase your engagement with your target demographic on short-form-focused apps. I'll email you later with the details and some quick media-training pointers. Gotta go."

She hangs up and I let out a heavy sigh.

Jesse stretches as he gets out of bed. "God, she's a lot first thing in the morning. Let me get dressed and we'll get out of here, okay?"

*
*

We manage to make it out of the room by nine and pile into the rental van. Tim's driving us again, while Greg and two new security guys follow behind us in the SUV and another new van.

I spend the morning sprawled out in the back row, trying to finish editing the video I missed yesterday. My phone dings and I see it's a message from Kamran in the group chat.

KamranTheSufi: UGHH, why couldn't the Jesse Jacobs tour have any US stops??? I'm DYING to see him and Ollie Cheriet perform. The footage from their show last night looked AMAZING!!!

I smile at that. I felt like such a mess, but Kamran has great musical taste, so it's nice to hear he liked the show.

My smile drops when another message pops up.

SuzieKay17: I know right! Did you see how they got swarmed after? That was wild.

KamranTheSufi: It was an all-ages show, so it was probably a bunch of deranged fourteen-year-olds desperate for pics. So cringe.

SuzieKay17: For real. I get that younger kids get excited, but acting that way and then trying to out him online? Yuck. This is why we can't have nice things.

Kamran hearts her message and I do too. My stomach starts to settle. They're right. Tweens who don't know any better are most likely responsible for the majority of the gossip. That doesn't exactly make the situation better—their actions still have consequences. But I'm glad there are some people pushing back, even in a private chat.

I finally get back to editing. Jesse promptly went back to sleep when we started driving, but he wakes up and glances back at me squinting at my screen.

"How's the video coming along?" he asks.

"Almost done," I say. "I can't believe you slept through how bumpy the ride's been." We've been on the highway for a couple hours now and Tim's been gunning it.

Jesse chuckles. "Used to it, I guess. I had to hitchhike sometimes before I saved up for my van and started living on the road."

"You live out of your van full-time?" When he said he was from Vancouver, I just assumed he had a place there.

He nods. "Yeah, for, like, the last four years. I know it probably sounds terrible, but I actually like it. Just being able to go wherever, whenever I want. Or wanted. Guess that's a thing of the past."

"I'm sorry about the whole situation with security and—"

"It's not your fault," he cuts in, shrugging. "It's not anyone's fault, really. This is just how things are now. I have to get used to it. Anyway, it's almost two, are you ready for the interview?"

"I think so. Helen sent along all these notes on being careful not to swear or say anything offensive. Which I'm not that worried about. I'm more concerned about not being able to answer their questions and sounding like an idiot," I blurt out, my face warming. He probably can't relate.

"It's okay if you don't want to answer some questions," Jesse assures me. "Usually if they start asking about stuff that's too personal, I try to change the subject back to music."

I nod as I close my laptop and take a deep breath. He says it like it's the easiest thing in the world . . . and for him it probably is. I've seen one or two of his interviews and he seemed unfazed when the interviewers asked inappropriate questions.

"I wish they sent the questions beforehand," I mutter. Jesse's confident ease is so far removed from how I'm feeling right now.

"That would be great, wouldn't it? It's just a local radio station so it shouldn't be anything too intense," Jesse says.

"And it's going to be live?" I ask.

Jesse nods as his phone starts ringing. "You ready?"

"I guess."

He picks up and puts the phone on speaker.

"Thanks for coming on today and welcome to QKWT Indie North! Kate and Dave here. We're so happy you have some time to talk to us today!" Kate says.

"No problem, thanks for having us," Jesse says breezily.

"Just a little introduction for our listeners, we have Jesse Jacobs and Ollie Cheriet joining us," Dave says. "So, you guys are embarking on a cross-country tour, and you had your first show at Club Bibliothèque in Montreal last night. How was it?"

"It was a really fun time," Jesse says. "The crowd was so high-energy—it was a perfect way to start the tour."

"How about you, Ollie?" Kate asks. "How did it feel performing in front of a crowd like that for the first time?"

"Uh, it was great," I say leaning over the seat so I'm closer to Jesse's phone. "It was surreal to see people holding signs and singing the lyrics to my songs."

"After 'On Repeat' going so viral, I'm sure this must be a whirlwind experience for you."

"Yeah, definitely," I say. There's a pause, where I guess they're expecting me to say more, but I can't think of anything.

"So, Jesse," Dave jumps in. "Your rise to fame has been almost as quick as Ollie's. Your album's already gone platinum and there's been some buzz about upcoming award nominations. How are you feeling about all of this happening so fast?"

"Like Ollie said, this has all been surreal. I'm just glad that so many people are connecting with my music."

"You have such a unique sound," Dave says. "Very distinctly Canadian since you incorporate traditional Indigenous instruments in your background tracks. Can you tell us about your musical inspirations?"

"The Halluci Nation, even though they have more of an electronic sound than my stuff. When I was younger, there weren't any mainstream musical acts I could relate to on a cultural level. But playing traditional music was always a big part of my community experience growing up. It's a big part of keeping cultural knowledge alive."

"And you grew up in a Squamish Nation reserve in Vancouver, is that right?" Kate asks.

I catch Jesse's jaw tighten and he pauses for a second. "That's right."

"How has your family reacted to all your success? I'm sure they must be thrilled to have you bringing your culture to an international audience," Kate says.

"Uh-huh," is all Jesse says, and there's another awkward pause.

I shoot Jesse a curious look, but he seems zoned out. I know he said he didn't like to talk about personal stuff in interviews, but I didn't realize he meant he didn't talk about his family at all. Maybe he doesn't get along with them? I open my mouth, trying to think of something to say to change the subject, but come up blank.

"So, Ollie," Dave says, filling the dead air again. "We'd love to hear about that moment when Jesse shared your video."

"Uh, sure. It was a total surprise. I was already a fan of his music, so I was shocked he found my tiny channel."

"Sometimes I like to look up videos of people doing covers of my songs, just to see how they interpret and translate them into something that's totally their own," Jesse says, finally speaking again. My shoulders relax as he continues, "When I came across one of Ollie's covers I was blown away. And his original music really spoke to me, too. I'm glad I was able to help get it out to more people."

"That was a big risk, taking a chance on him, introducing him to your label, and having him open for your tour," Kate says. "And Ollie, you must be very thankful."

"Yeah, I'm basically forever in his debt. Seriously, I'm beyond grateful." I shoot Jesse a small smile and he smiles back.

"*Aww,*" Kate says. Her tone makes me tense up again. "That's so *sweet.* I'm sure you guys have bonded *a lot* already, even though you just started the tour."

"Uh, yeah." Jesse stops smiling at that, his face closing off as he picks up on her weird tone. "It's been cool getting to know each other so far."

"We saw you guys had a scare last night when the crowd outside your show got too intense," Kate continues, and my entire body stiffens. "Looked like you were *really* worried about Ollie."

Jesse's brow furrows. She's not technically saying anything that strange, but there's something off about the way she says it. I know she's trying to get the scoop about the video, but I don't think Jesse's seen it yet.

"Yep. Crowds like that can be dangerous for sure," Jesse says, his tone cool.

"Okay . . . We'll let you boys go now," Dave says. "Thanks again for calling in, we hope you have a great rest of your tour!"

Jesse rolls his eyes at me after ending the call. "What was up with her?"

"I don't know. She was kind of annoying." I shrug, avoiding his gaze. If he hasn't seen the video yet, there's no way I'm going to be the one to tell him about it. "But, uh, are you good though? Sorry I couldn't think of anything to say when she asked about your family . . ."

"That's okay. I kind of froze up there." He sinks down in his seat again with a sigh.

I can't decide if I should ask if his family is only off-limits for interviews or if it's a sore subject in general. I bite my lip, deciding against it. "At least it's over," I say as I open my laptop again.

"God, I'm starved," Jesse says. "I'm gonna check with Tim if we're stopping for food soon."

I nod, eyes on my screen. Soph told me to try and enjoy myself on tour, and I really wish I could relax enough to do that. But when I'm not freaking about yet another high-stress situation, I'm missing Aisha. What should have been such an amazing moment—performing my first show—was muted by my meds. I think back to what I said in the interview about being beyond grateful for this experience. Deep down I am . . . but it sucks that I haven't been able to feel it yet.

18

I wake up early the next morning after crashing hard when we got into Thunder Bay around two a.m. I check my phone, not daring to look at my feed. I have a good-morning text from Aisha. We talked on the phone while we were driving last night. I could tell she was exhausted from practicing for her showcase, and I know she's already up and at rehearsals this morning too. I hope she's not pushing herself too hard again.

There's a text from Neil too. He's never been a consistent texter, so I appreciate him taking the time to check in. I tell him things have been pretty hectic, but overall I'm doing okay. Then I ask him how rehearsals with Aisha have been before I finally put my phone down. I should probably touch base with Sophie and my mom, but my stomach is grumbling so I get up to find some food.

We get back on the road before noon, headed toward our next show in Winnipeg. Jesse leaves me alone for most of the drive. I attempted to make conversation over breakfast, but he didn't seem into it. There's been this awkward vibe since yesterday, like he doesn't even want to look at me. As I watch rocky terrain and miles of evergreens give way to canola fields, I can't help wondering if I did something . . . or if he finally saw the video. Is he freaked out that so many people are assuming he's into me?

We arrive at our hotel a few hours ahead of sound check. I kill time trying to film another Q&A for my channel. It's not my favorite activity, but at least it distracts me from worrying about Jesse . . . and about tonight. We'll be playing in a four-hundred-seat concert theater downtown, about twice the size of our first show.

In the late afternoon, I hear a knock at my door.

"Hey," Jesse says, half-smiling at me when I open the door. "I was gonna grab something to eat if you wanna come."

"Sounds good." I smile back, relieved he seems like he wants to be around me again. Maybe I was overthinking his silences. "Just let me grab my phone."

I head back over to my nightstand and hear Jesse's voice behind me as he steps into my room. "What have you been up to?"

"Just working on a video," I say, glancing at my open laptop.

"Oh, I can let you finish up."

"Okay, cool. I'm almost done, I can meet you downstairs in a few." I take a seat on the carpet at the foot of my bed.

"Or I can wait for you." Instead of turning toward the door he comes over and sits down next to me. "Do you need any help?"

"Uh sure, that'd be great." Since Jesse's a natural at this kind of thing, I might as well see if he wants to be on camera. Maybe I can get some pointers from him. "Would you mind answering some questions for a Q&A? I know we just had that interview yesterday, but—"

"Sounds good to me," he says, seeming genuinely relaxed. "Ask away."

I start recording and ask him about his favorite bands and the best shows he's seen live. Somehow, talking to Jesse feels way less nerve-wracking than being on camera alone. Unsurprisingly, he has great taste. It's kind of fascinating to hear about what's inspired his music.

"I wish I could write like you." I wince at myself. "I mean, I feel like my songs are so one-dimensional."

He looks at me sideways. "That's not true. You're a great song-writer."

I shake my head. My stuff seems so juvenile in comparison to his. "I have no idea how I'm going to write this album. It was really great jamming together at rehearsal, but other than that I've been incredibly stuck lately."

"Well, let's keep working on the song you started at rehearsal then," he says. "I think you should have enough for the Q&A. We've been going for nearly an hour."

"Oh." I look at my phone in surprise. It feels like we've only been talking for fifteen minutes. "Okay, sure."

I stop recording then grab my guitar and start playing quietly, building up through the verse. He listens intently, nodding along. I stop when I get to the chorus, not sure where it's going next.

"Keep going," he says.

"I'm not so quick at improvising like you are," I admit, staring down at my guitar. Usually, I figure things out in my head first. Well, that's what I do when my head isn't a mess.

"You're overthinking it. Just play," he urges me on.

He's right. All my fear about not getting it right has been immo-bilizing. I close my eyes, letting out an intentional exhale before continuing, singing out the short chorus I've been working on. I focus on shutting out all my fears of failure. After a minute, my brain switches off and I feel fully present. My instincts take over as my fingers fly across the strings. I'm surprised at how much emotion pours out of me—all the pressure to help my family and the uncertainty of whether I'm even cut out for this channeling into the melody.

After I'm done, I open my eyes and we're staring right at each other. I'm suddenly aware of how close we're sitting, his knee almost touching mine. Jesse seems to realize at the same time and immedi-ately looks away. He sits back, putting some space between us.

Yep, he's definitely seen the video.

Clearing my throat, I put my guitar down and peek at Jesse again. His expression is unreadable now.

"That sounded so genuine," he says quietly.

"Thanks," I mumble. "I don't have much for lyrics yet . . . but I was trying to get across the feeling of not knowing which step to take next. Like the path is constantly shifting but you still have to move forward."

"And maybe feeling like you're trapped?"

I nod slowly. I hadn't consciously been thinking that, but he's right. "And trying to let go of everything in the way of me figuring out my next move. Trying to quiet my mind enough so I can trust my intu-ition."

He smiles a little. "Seems like your lyrics aren't so one-dimensional after all," he teases.

I let out a laugh. "Yeah, I guess."

Jesse jumps up from the carpet. "Well, I think you're on the right track. We can work on it some more tomorrow if you want."

I bite down on a smile, trying not to look too hyped about it.

*
*

Jesse and I grab lunch in the hotel restaurant and then we meet up with the security team and head to the venue early. We're here even before the sound check crew so we have some time to explore the mostly vacant theater.

I film a mini-tour of the backstage area while I walk around with Jesse, checking out all the signatures and photos on the walls. Broken Social Scene did a show here years ago, which is pretty cool. I'm trying to keep calm about tonight, but the closer we get to sound check, the more my nerves build.

Finally, the crew arrives, and we head out onstage for rehearsal. The sound guy cues my first song and I step up to my mark. I look out, taking in the hundreds of velvet maroon seats, and my stomach plummets to my feet.

"Ready?" Jesse calls out from the edge of the stage.

I nod as my opening notes come over the speakers. The sound quality is way better than our first show and I can hear myself clearly as I begin singing, but I have to fight the urge to stare at the stage floor. When the song ends, Jesse jumps up and claps.

"You're doing great," he says as my second track begins.

I give a brief nod then start singing again, bringing my attention back to the empty seats. The stage lights aren't as hot as last time, but I'm already sweating like crazy by the time I start my third song.

You're doing fine, relax. The thought does nothing to squash my rising nerves.

When I'm done, I step back so Jesse can take his spot at the mic. He frowns when he sees my face. "You cool?"

Avoiding his gaze, I rush offstage. I find my way to my dressing room and collapse on a dingy couch. I put my face in my hands as my breath begins to shorten.

Christ. Is it going to be like this every single show? I grab my phone out of my pocket and stick my headphones in, turning on a meditation that Nadine recommended for when I'm about to have an attack. I close my eyes and after a few minutes, my breathing calms down.

My eyes fly open when there's knocking at my door. "Ollie? Hey, are you okay?" Jesse asks.

"I'm fine!" I call out, even as my heart starts to race again. *Shit.* I don't want him to regret inviting me. I don't want him to think I can't handle this.

"Are you sure? Can I come in?"

"No! I mean, I'll be out soon, okay?"

There's no response and I let out a long, trembling breath. God, I have to get it together. There's still another twenty minutes until I go on, so I have some time to get some more practice in. I should have stuck around to watch Jesse's rehearsal. I need to figure out how he's so at ease when he's performing. I consider asking him about it, but it's too embarrassing, admitting that I have no clue what I'm doing.

It wasn't embarrassing when I worked on my song with him earlier. But I don't want to have to rely on him for everything. I can get through this myself. Getting up, I turn off the meditation and switch to a recording of "On Repeat." I sing along to the track, concentrating on hitting all my notes. I practice not shutting my eyes and smiling out at an imaginary audience. I can already hear the murmur of the real audience outside. My heart picks up its pace again. A painful pressure builds in my chest, forcing me to stop singing.

I can't do this. I head over to my bag and take out my anxiety meds. I stare at the bottle for a second, letting out a sigh.

I wish I didn't need them. Even though they helped me get through my first show, I still hate the weird, removed feeling they gave me. Like I was watching what should have been the best night of my life as if it were happening to someone else. But if meds are what it takes to get me through this, I guess enjoying myself can take a backseat.

The sound of the audience gets louder, and my throat starts to constrict. Cursing under my breath, I pop a couple pills in my mouth then head out of the room.

Jesse nods at me when I get backstage. I know he wants to ask me if I'm doing okay again, but he stops himself.

"I'm good to go," I say, my voice steady thanks to the meds already kicking in.

"Okay. Good luck, man."

There's no theater manager to introduce me this time; the crew cues me up and I step out onstage. I squint at the audience, the oscillating stage lights blinding me for a second before my eyes adjust.

Every single seat in the theater is filled. Just like in Montreal, there are people holding signs and girls wearing T-shirts with my name on them. A far-off, dreamlike sensation hits me like a wave, nearly drowning out the cheering and screams. I scan the audience with a distant, plastered-on smile, glancing around the room as I sing without focusing too much on anyone.

"Thank you!" I scream at the top of my lungs when my last song ends. "Now make some noise for Jesse Jacobs!"

I give a final wave as Jesse walks on. He smiles at me, then turns his attention on the audience, immediately drawing them in. I stand in the wings, pulling my phone out and pressing record as he whips the crowd into a frenzy. I don't think I could ever get tired of seeing him perform. His presence fills the entire theater, the audience hanging on his every note—me included.

When his set ends, he heads offstage to thundering screams and applause. I put my phone away as he approaches.

"Awesome set," I yell above the noise. I lean into him so he can hear me, careful not to get too close. "I hope you don't mind if I use some shots from tonight and the first show for my vlogs."

"Yeah, of course," he shouts back. The way he smiles at me is exhilarating, his endless energy somehow pushing past the dulling effect of my meds.

He sobers a little, searching my eyes. I quickly look away, realizing I've been staring at him too long.

"I'm gonna do the encore and then we can head over to the VIP area, okay?"

Shit. I completely blanked on the fact that our first meet and greet is happening tonight. It was on our schedule, but I was too nervous about the actual performance to remember to worry about this. Even though I only sang three songs, I'm completely drained.

After Jesse finishes his encore, security leads us through a series of winding hallways until we reach a large backroom. There's lots of merch and a long table set up with water bottles and permanent markers. The murmur of excited voices rings out from beyond a set of closed doors guarded by security.

"Remember, no more than five minutes per person. Pictures are fine but stay on your side of the table," Tim tells us.

"Got it." Jesse picks up a marker and absently spins it between his fingers. There are some chairs, but he doesn't sit down. Neither do I. "And what about hugs? Just over the table?"

Tim nods. "That's right. Signal me or Greg if there are any clingers."

Jesse nods and then Tim takes off to talk to the guys by the doors.

I shoot Jesse a worried look. "Clingers?"

He smiles tightly. "Don't worry. If anyone freaks out, just stay calm and ask them to move back. They should chill out after a second."

I open my mouth to respond, but a chorus of shrieks rings out as security opens the doors. Normally, my heart would start pounding at the sound, but I'm still in a medicated mirage of calm that prevents me from panicking, my vacant stage smile returning.

Security gets the fans to form an orderly line and I try to take cues from Jesse on how to act like this is a normal situation. Sometimes we host small meet and greets at work, and I've attended lots of them on my own, so it's not like I don't know how this works. But being on the other side is totally different.

Most people are friendly and relaxed, but a few younger fans start crying or shaking when they meet Jesse. Thankfully no one is quite so overwhelmed when they meet me. Some don't even acknowledge that I'm there and walk off as soon as they get their picture with Jesse, which is perfectly fine with me.

Then two girls ask for a photo with both of us. I hold my breath with a big dumb grin on my face as Jesse throws a firm arm around my shoulder. As he leans down to get in frame with the girls, his cheek brushes mine for half a second. I stay as still as possible, pretending like I didn't notice, but it's all I can think about as the fan snaps the picture.

"Thank you!" the girls call out. The moment the words leave their mouths I straighten, taking a step back. Thankfully there's already another group of girls talking to Jesse so he's too busy to see me freezing up. I wipe my sweaty forehead, feeling my meds starting to wear off.

"Hey Ollie!"

A girl about my age is standing in front of me. She looks like she might have a South Asian background, or maybe North African like me. I instantly relax at her expression, thankful she doesn't have that weird, manic glint in her eyes that some of the other girls have had.

"Hey!" I say as she hands me a poster to sign. "Thanks for coming out, nice to meet you. What's your name?"

"Radhika," she says. "I can spell it if you—"

"It's R-A-D-H-I-K-A, right?" The name sounds familiar. "Are you Radhika725 on YouTube?"

She nods and my smile grows bigger. "You're one of the first people to ever comment on my videos!"

She smiles back as I finish signing her poster. "It's so cool to meet in person. You were great tonight! You've grown so much as an artist from when you first started posting your stuff."

"Thanks so much, Radhika," I say, trying not to get choked up. I remember her comment on my first video last year saying that it inspired her to disclose to her partner that she was a survivor of sexual assault. She said she wasn't sure how they'd react, but hearing my song helped her work up the courage. I don't usually reply to comments, but hers was so sweet I had to thank her. I've replied to a couple more of her comments since then too. "You've really helped me feel more comfortable posting stuff since the beginning."

She just nods, looking a little teary. "Can I give you a hug?"

"Yeah, of course," I say and she gives me a quick one.

She wipes her eyes as she pulls back. "I'm glad so many people get to hear your stuff now. If you ever need a moderator for your channel just shoot me a message. I'd be happy to help."

"That would be great!"

After we take a picture together, she leaves, and then a squealing group of younger girls comes up to me. I manage to get through the rest of the meet and greet and have a few more conversations with fans that don't feel forced.

When we finish, security leads us outside and back into the van. Jesse and I are both talked out. Still, today went better than I thought it would. I feel a twinge of regret that I wasn't able to fully absorb how special the night was, but I push it aside. What matters is that I got through it. Hopefully once I've been doing this for a little longer I won't have to rely on my meds as much.

19

Way too early in the morning, I find myself sitting in a TV studio in a checked-out daze that's a mixture of lack of sleep and the effects of my medication. The last week and a half has been a blur, traveling from small town to small town throughought Manitoba's interior before heading west to Saskatchewan. Thankfully there haven't been any major hiccups. This morning we arrived in Regina before the sun was up. Tonight will be one of our biggest shows of the tour yet. I've never taken my meds this early, but there was no point in even pretending I would be able to get through my first on-camera interview without them. Especially with how badly I slept in the back of the van.

It's going to be a jam-packed day. If I can just get through it, then I can relax for a tiny bit. We have a couple rest days here over the weekend. I'm considering dropping by Dev's studio but haven't gotten a chance to let them know I'm in town yet. I've checked in with the contributor group chat a couple of times since I saw Kamran and Suzi talking about the video of Jesse and me in Montreal. I've been chatting more with them and some other contributors too.

It feels a bit weird that I've been talking to people who are basically strangers more than I've been talking to everyone back home. I call Aisha whenever I have a spare moment, but I've already fallen behind on check-ins with Sophie, my parents, and Neil. Trying to keep up with them all feels draining in a way that talking about music with the contributor group doesn't. Honestly, it's been a nice break from all the stress.

"Look up for a second?"

I check back in to find a woman in her midtwenties standing in front of me with a makeup brush pointed at my face.

"Oh, I don't need—"

"Relax, we're just going to get rid of a little shine here," she says, swiping the brush across my forehead. By shine she must mean the sweat already forming on my brow.

After she's done powdering me up, she whips out a small black tube. "And maybe just a touch of—"

I turn my face away, putting my hand up to stop her. "I'm really okay, but thanks."

"All right," she says with a sigh. "Your eyelashes are gorgeous—I just wanted to make them pop even more. But if you're sure . . ."

"I'm sure," I say firmly, and her hopeful look dies. She moves on to Jesse.

I wince, wondering if that came out too rude. I didn't really mind that much, but if my dad saw me on TV wearing that stuff he'd freak.

I consider apologizing, but she's already too busy laughing at something Jesse says as she works on his face. He's just as professionally friendly as he was at the meet and greet, putting everyone at ease. Besides his discomfort about us getting close for pictures, he's been the same way with me. Friendly but slightly distant—other than that moment in my hotel room and a few other fleeting times since then. Which I shouldn't even be thinking about. He's just been trying to be nice by helping me out with my songs.

My mind flashes guiltily to Aisha. Her fall showcase is tomorrow so I know she'll probably be too busy with last-minute rehearsals to talk later.

"Morning, boys!" A tall, redheaded woman is standing in front of us now. "I'm Lara, welcome to the show."

Jesse and I stand to shake her hand then sit back down on the couch, Lara taking the host seat across from us.

"So is this your first TV interview?" she asks.

I nod before Jesse responds, "I've done a few already. Super excited for this, though, thanks so much for inviting us today."

"Of course, we're so happy to have you! You guys have *a lot* of fans here in Regina, as you can see." She glances out the wall-to-wall studio window where there's a huge crowd pressed up against the glass. They cheer when we look their way, getting louder when Jesse waves.

I wave too, relieved it's a closed set for our segment. If I don't look out the window during the interview, maybe I can pretend like it's just us, like it's not as much pressure. But it's hard to ignore the giant cameras that will be broadcasting this live across the city in less than a minute.

Lara turns the wattage of her smile up a few more notches as she stares into the camera, introducing Jesse and me.

As usual, Jesse looks perfectly relaxed, but I don't know what to do with myself. I put my hands on my knees, hoping my sweaty palms don't stain my pants.

After Lara goes through all Jesse's accolades and mentions my viral video, she turns to shine her huge pearly smile at us.

"So, we polled our fans on what to do for today's segment, and they wanted you two to play a fun little game, if you're up for it?"

"Sure, let's do it!" Jesse grins.

I nod mutely. I was barely ready to try and coherently answer a few questions, let alone whatever this is going to be.

"Okay!" Lara picks some cards off a small table beside her and hands a stack to each of us. "Don't worry. There aren't any complicated rules or anything." She winks at me. "All you have to do is read out some funny online comments from your fans and try not to laugh. Whoever manages to read all the comments without laughing wins. Jesse, why don't you go first?"

"JollieOTP posted . . ." He squints at the cue card in front of him, his mouth turning downward briefly before his face returns to neutral.

"Jollie" is the ship name our fans made up for our nonexistent romantic relationship. Jesse clears his throat and continues. "They wrote, 'I need Jesse Jacobs to throw me out a window, light me on fire, and then hose me—'" He stops short and raises his eyebrows, shaking his head. "Uh, yeah, definitely can't say *that* on morning television."

Lara laughs lightly. "Oh, sorry, I forgot to mention, you can just skip over any profanity. Ollie, you're up now."

"Uh . . ." I read my card and see it's a sexual comment about me that's grosser than Jesse's was. Even the username is filthy.

I shoot Lara a panicked glance. "I really don't think I should read this."

"Oh, come on, is it that spicy?" Lara laughs again, but it sounds forced. "Okay, why don't you read another one."

I flip to the next card, which is somehow even worse. "Um . . ."

"It's okay, don't be shy. Go ahead," Lara urges when I fall silent.

I can't manage to get a single word out of my mouth. I just stare down at my cards, completely frozen.

"Aww, you're blushing," Lara teases. "That's adorable!"

Even with my meds, this feels excruciating. I wish I could just spontaneously blink out of existence. I can feel Jesse staring at me, but I can't make myself look at him. From the corner of my eye, I see him put his cards down.

"Do you mind if we switch things up?" Jesse asks Lara. "We'd love to talk more about the tour."

"Oh. Yes, for sure," Lara says. When I finally manage to look up, I see her smile falter. It returns full blast as she seamlessly shifts into questions about the tour, which Jesse answers while I nod along silently for the remaining five minutes.

"Sorry about that," Lara says when it's over. "My team vetted the comments. I didn't mean to make you uncomfortable."

"No worries," I say quickly, forcing a smile onto my face.

"Thanks for taking over," I mutter at Jesse as we leave the stage.

"It's cool," he says with a sigh, looking at his phone. "Helen's calling."

He picks up as we get back to the greenroom and her face appears on screen.

"Hey guys, everything okay?"

"Yeah, sorry I messed up," I blurt out. "The host said she didn't know the comments were going to be that inappropriate."

"That's all right. Jesse, good job with changing topics. Ollie, I know this is a lot to get a handle on, but try to go with the flow more. We need you to stay fully engaged for interviews. That's part of the deal."

My face heats up. "Got it."

"Well, it's not really his fault," Jesse jumps in. "It would be great if we could get a better sense of what to expect before we go into interviews. And if you could ask reporters to stick to questions about the music."

Helen's quiet for a moment, her face carefully composed. "You guys wanted to have your own space. That's why I'm not traveling with you and overseeing every aspect of the tour. I have other responsibilities here at the label, so I'm not going to be available to vet every single question for every interview you have scheduled. You contractually agreed to do interviews, but you're not obligated to answer any questions you don't feel comfortable with. Jesse, like I said, you did great asking them to move on. So if anything else comes up, just keep the conversation moving. Does that work for you?"

I nod but cringe internally. I know she's mostly talking to me, since I was the one who froze.

"I'll do what I can to let interviewers know you'd like them to stick to music questions. But you guys are gonna have to think on your feet if they throw any curveballs, okay?" Helen finally smiles. "Anyway, Ollie, great work with your videos! Your Q&A together did extremely well. Keep it up with the concert footage too—we're getting good numbers. If you could go live on your socials that would help as well."

"Will do," I say quickly. "I can do a live stream before the show tonight." I'll message Radhika today to see if she can help me out.

"Perfect. Touch base later," she says, clicking off.

Jesse frowns at me as Greg and Tim lead us to the van. "This sucks.

It's not your fault you got caught off guard like that."

I shrug. "I mean, everything she just said was in the interview pointers she sent. I'll keep it together next time."

In the van, I take some slow breaths as Helen's disapproving face appears in my mind's eye. The words "contractually obligated" echo in my head. This is what I signed up for. My family's future depends on me getting through the tour. And this might be my only shot at making music a long-term thing for myself. It's nice that Jesse stood up for me, but I have to get better at this. Even if it's terrifying.

*
*

Back at the hotel, Jesse agrees to pitch in for the live stream. Thankfully, Radhika responds right away when I message her. She helps me get everything ready on my channel while I try to psych myself up. Going live feels like way more pressure than recording myself and being able to edit out any fumbles.

But as soon as I start talking to Jesse, my nerves fade and I almost forget we're on camera. We answer some fan questions that Radhika picks out of the chat for us and then we end up talking about music again.

"I saw your record collection video," Jesse says. "I would absolutely *kill* for a collection like that."

He's been watching my videos? Duh—that's how he discovered my stuff.

I guess he couldn't really have a big collection of his own while he was living on the road. I don't ask in case he doesn't want to talk about that on camera. "I'm lucky since I get a discount at the record store where I work."

"I would have loved to work at a record store growing up," he says. "Back in high school, me and my friends would trek out to our favorite little record shop in downtown Vancouver. The owner let us hang around for hours, just playing stuff in the listening booth, even though we usually couldn't buy anything."

I smile, happy he felt comfortable sharing that. "That sounds fun."

He nods, looking lost in his memories for a second. "Anyway, do you want to work on that song from yesterday again?"

"Uh, now?" I glance at my laptop to see people already spamming their excitement about hearing new music in the chat.

"If you want to," Jesse says. "No pressure if you don't feel like it."

"Um . . ." I told myself after the interview that it's time to get out of my comfort zone. But I don't think I'm quite ready to share a song I'm still struggling with in front of so many people. "Maybe next time. I can play something else though."

I grab my guitar, focusing on the familiar feel of the worn wood, my fingers tracing the strings. I start to play an older song that's a lot closer to being done. Instead of thinking about the thousands of people watching, I concentrate on Jesse's encouraging presence. I focus on the chords, gaining confidence as I sing. It's mostly about being back at home, hanging out with my mom and Soph in the living room after dinner, laughing and listening to records. I let myself travel back there as the melody pours out of me. My meds from this morning have worn off, and a warm, relaxed feeling envelops me.

"That was really sweet," Jesse says, smiling when I finish. He scrolls through the chat. "Looks like everyone loved it. They're asking if you want to play it again."

I glance at my notes one last time then nod and take it from the top.

I go through the entire song with no hesitation, the notes feeling completely natural.

Jesse high-fives me when I'm done. "So good! We should probably wrap it up now though—we have sound check soon."

I check the time, seeing that it has flown by again. I look at my screen. "Okay guys, we have to go. Hopefully we'll see some of you at the show later!"

I close my laptop and turn to Jesse. "Thanks for helping me out with this."

"No worries, that was fun," he says as he jumps up. "And we'll have lots of free time this weekend to work on stuff. I'll meet you downstairs."

I can't help the smile that takes over my face. Letting myself step out of my comfort zone actually paid off. I open my phone and message my mom and Sophie, finally responding to their last texts to let them know I'm doing okay. I don't message my dad; I know my mom will tell him I checked in with her. I haven't felt up for talking to him while I've been on tour, considering how he acted before I left. But working on the song has made me realize how much I've been missing being back home with Mom and Sophie.

I sigh. Now I just have to figure out how to get through the show tonight. We're playing our biggest venue yet, a two-thousand-seat theater. No pressure.

20

I down a few more of my anxiety meds before meeting Jesse to head over to the venue. It was nice to feel the emotion behind what I was singing during the live stream, but I'm not ready to relive the panic I felt at the Montreal and Winnipeg shows. I'll never be able to get out of my comfort zone if I'm paralyzed by fear.

My heart's beating a mile a minute as we pull up to the theater and see a huge line of fans outside. With the meds kicking in, I don't physically tense up, but I feel a bit lightheaded when I step out of the van. This is more than I've ever taken in a day. We continue on to the loading dock entrance and my muscles stay relaxed.

When we get to our greenroom door, I stop in my tracks.

Serafina and Victor from Midnight Cavalcade are lounging casually around the room.

"Hey Jesse!" Serafina says, jumping up and giving him a big hug.

"Hey! What are you guys doing here?" Jesse asks, hugging Victor next. I can't help but notice that it lasts a little longer than his hug with Serafina. "It's great to see you!"

I'm still frozen in the doorway, but I make myself move, entering the room and closing the door behind me.

I try not to look too starstruck, even though I'm internally losing my mind. I can't believe I'm standing in the same room as Victor and Serafina. I've been listening to them for years. I technically shared space with them when they played at The Vinyl Underground, but I was just a part of the crew—I never got a chance to speak to them.

Serafina shrugs, her pink and purple sisterlocks bouncing against her shoulders. "The label flew me out to be a surprise guest tonight." She turns to me with a smile. "Hey Ollie, it's great to meet you!"

I nod awkwardly, a dazed grin on my face. "You too. Big fan," I blurt out like an idiot.

"We're fans of yours, too," Victor says. "That's why I insisted on tagging along with Sera."

I just nod again, in total disbelief. There's no way this is real life. Regret and relief swirl inside me. I hate that I feel emotionally distant for such a cool moment, but I'm glad I'm still able to outwardly function.

Feeling mostly out-of-body, I shake out my tingling hands before I head out onstage for sound check.

I go through the motions of rehearsing, trying not to think about my favorite musicians watching me from the wings. When I finish, Jesse takes my place to rehearse his set while I meet Serafina and Victor at the side of the stage.

Serafina smiles reassuringly and Victor gives me a pat on the back.

"Excited?" Serafina asks. "I'm guessing this is your biggest venue so far?"

I nod and try to form a coherent sentence. "Yeah. It is."

I know she catches the nerves in my voice. "Don't worry, you're gonna do great! This is Victor's hometown, so he'll find a good place to get food after and celebrate."

Victor goes on to tell us about some of his favorite haunts in the city, but I'm half tuning out because this is still too bizarre to actually be happening. Maybe it's the meds, but I somehow manage to appear calm, responding whenever they ask me questions. After Jesse finishes rehearsing, we head back to the dressing room.

I keep my hands and mouth busy, downing a bag of chips and a few granola bars I find on the table, while Jesse tells me about meeting Serafina and Victor at Niagara. I'm surprised he only met them this summer—it seems like he's known them for years. Victor seems especially taken with him, hooked on his every word. I let Jesse do most of the talking and manage not to fanboy too much, only asking a couple questions about Midnight's upcoming album. Then it's time for me to head onstage.

Sweat pours down my back, but thankfully the meds keep my heart rate under control, and I hold it together throughout my set. Absolutely no part of this feels real as I stare out at the sea of screaming faces. I finish "Until the Stars Burn" to thundering applause, then I introduce Jesse and head offstage again.

"You killed it!" Serafina says.

"You're just as great live, man," Victor says. "Congrats, the crowd loved it!"

I grin, even though none of this is remotely sinking in. I take out my phone as Jesse starts.

"Do you guys mind being on camera? I'm going live for Jesse's set."

"Yeah, that's cool." Serafina steps into frame, waving at the camera.

Victor does the same. Within thirty seconds there are thousands of people tuned into the live as I turn the camera on Jesse. His set is just as electrifying as ever. I'm so captivated that I forget about Serafina and Victor for a moment.

When Serafina joins Jesse onstage for his final song, the crowd completely loses it. I turn off the live, engrossed in their performance, a heartrending, slowed-down version of one of Jesse's latest singles.

"She's the greatest, isn't she?" Victor says from beside me, his eyes on Serafina.

It's cool to see there isn't any animosity between them, even though she left the band—contrary to all the fan rumors floating around since she went solo. I think about all the rumors about Jesse and me, how distant he seemed right after that video of us at the Montreal show went around. But things have been less and less awkward between us since then. Maybe Jesse and I can rise as far above all the online gossip as Victor and Serafina seem to be. God willing, I'll get more used to being around Jesse, and whatever I've been feeling toward him will be a thing of the past soon, too.

"Do you guys want to come out for the encore?" Jesse asks Victor and me after he and Serafina finish the set.

I open my mouth, but nothing comes out. This night just keeps getting less and less believable. I never in a million years would have imagined I'd get a chance to share a stage with any of them.

Victor grins at me and I finally manage a nod.

"Sounds good!" Victor says. "Sera, do you want to do 'First Good-bye?'"

"Sure." She loops her arm through mine. "You know it, right?"

I know the lyrics to every song on all four of their albums. "I'm familiar," I say as casually as I can.

Jesse heads back out onstage first, followed by Serafina, then he introduces Victor and me to ear-splitting screams. I know the reaction is mostly for Victor, but it's still completely overwhelming to take in the kind of welcome he's used to. As he says hello, I realize I must have sweat out the effects of my meds. I'm starting to feel more present than I did onstage alone earlier.

There are only two mics set up. Serafina and Victor share one and Jesse and I have to huddle together at his mic stand. For once he isn't careful to keep his distance—he's too wrapped up in the song. He closes his eyes while hitting a stunning note just a breath away from me, and I have to remind myself to keep singing.

Tearing my gaze away, I look out at the audience. Everyone has their arms raised with their phones in the air, moving in a slow, lit-up wave. I glance over at Victor and Serafina as their voices crescendo in gorgeous harmony. Taking a deep breath, I try to tuck every little detail away in my brain. Suddenly it's all sinking in, how big this moment is. A wave of gratitude hits me and my eyes start to sting. What I used to be scared to even dream for myself is happening, right here, right now. And I'm finally feeling it—letting myself be immersed in it.

I start a little when Jesse puts an arm around my shoulder, giving me a light shake.

He's smiling, but his eyes are glazed too, and I know he's feeling exactly what I am right now. Just beyond appreciative of this moment.

The song ends and he pulls away, shouting good night to the crowd one last time.

✻

Back in the greenroom, there's a bottle of champagne waiting for us from the venue staff.

Victor grabs it out of the ice bucket. "I guess Sera and I are going to have to confiscate this since you guys are underage."

Jesse shrugs as he grabs a towel and wipes his face. "I'm not underage, but go for it. I don't really drink."

"I don't either," I chime in, chugging from a bottle of water. I'm feeling less lightheaded than I was earlier, but I definitely don't think it's a good idea to add alcohol to my system. I don't drink much anyway, especially since Neil's recovery and everything that happened last year.

"I was just kidding," Victor says with a laugh. "You deserve to celebrate!" He pulls the cork out with a loud pop.

Serafina lets out a surprised scream as we all jump back. Champagne explodes from the bottle.

Victor quickly aims it at his mouth before it spills all over the floor. "Well, there goes half the bottle. Are you guys up for just a toast then?"

"Sure," Jesse says, passing around champagne flutes. Victor fills them up.

"Cheers," Serafina says as she holds up her flute. "To Jesse and Ollie. You guys were marvelous tonight. That was so much fun!"

We clink glasses. I don't want to be a buzzkill and figure a tiny sip won't hurt. The moment it hits my throat I start to feel way too warm and floaty.

Shit.

"Oh no! Are you a lightweight?" Serafina says, giggling as she pinches my face, which I'm sure is already bright red.

I laugh too loudly as I pull away from her, shaking my head. I carefully set the rest of the glass down and pick up the water bottle again. "I just need to get some more food in me."

"I know just the place," Victor says.

*

The crowd outside the venue isn't as bad as that first night in Montreal, but it's still intense as we navigate our way to the van. Serafina and Victor have their own security joining us, so we're well protected from overenthusiastic fans.

Once we're safely packed inside, Victor gives the driver instructions to the restaurant. My phone starts to buzz and I see that it's Aisha calling. I want to talk to her but know I won't be able to hear her over the noise from the crowd, Victor shouting directions, and Jesse and Serafina's high-volume conversation.

I quickly text her.

Ollie: *Sorry, can't talk right now.*

Aisha: *Ollie, I just saw a clip of you on stage with Serafina and Victor AHHH OMG!!! Call me back later so you can tell me all about it, okay? Even if it's late. I'm dying to hear what they're like!*

I promise to touch base when I can.

"Who are you texting?" Serafina asks beside me.

"My girlfriend," I say, my cheeks starting to hurt from smiling so much. "She's freaking out—she's a big fan of you guys, too. We saw you at Niagara Fest this summer and we went to your show in Toronto for our first date last year."

"*Aww!* That's so cute," she says before Victor taps her on the shoulder to show her something on his phone.

Jesse leans in on my other side, speaking quietly. "Are you okay?"

I take a deep breath and try to calm my heartbeat. I've been talking faster than normal.

"Yeah," I assure him. "I just should have eaten more earlier, like I said."

He says nothing, just studying me for a moment, and I try not to fidget under his gaze.

"Okay. If you're sure," he says slowly. "Just let me know when you wanna head back to the hotel. It's been a long day."

"I'm fine."

He nods then turns to Victor and Serafina.

My stomach twists uncomfortably. What if he wants me to go back to the hotel because I'm embarrassing him? I do my best to shake off the feeling. He probably doesn't want me to leave. And Serafina and Victor seem to want me here, too, so I should just try to relax.

When we get to the restaurant, there's a huge crowd and photographers outside flashing cameras right in our faces. We have to fight our way through with security again. Once we're inside, it's almost eerily quiet. It's some type of exclusive members-only place with fancy artwork on the walls and low lighting. The staff lead us to a private room where we order a ton of food and lounge in a giant booth, stuffing our faces.

After I get a couple of tiny, fancy burgers in me, I feel less woozy and I'm able to speak normally again. Serafina and Victor share stories from their years touring together and I can tell that they miss it. I'm curious about why Serafina split from the band, but there's no way I'd feel comfortable asking. They've never shared it publicly.

"Do you guys think you'd ever be in a band?" Victor asks, looking at Jesse and me. "You sounded great together tonight."

"I was in a band in high school, but it didn't work out too well," Jesse says. "I think I'm usually better off doing my own thing."

"What kind of stuff did you guys play?" I ask him.

"Well, that was the problem," he says with a chuckle. "We couldn't agree on a sound—we were all over the place sonically."

"Yeah, it's hard finding people who have the same vision," Serafina says. "It's a special thing when you can find it. And that vision can change as people grow and move into different stages of their life."

I can't help but think she's alluding to leaving Midnight Cavalcade. Her sound has shifted since she went solo.

"And as you evolve, your fans do, too. It's hard figuring out if you're heading in the same direction as your audience," she continues. "It can be confusing—like, should you try to please old fans or just do what feels right, even if it's not what your base is used to?"

"You're never going to please everyone, no matter what direction you go in," Victor says with a sigh. "Me and the guys have found that we just have to stay true to what feels right for us instead of trying to guess what other people want, you know?"

Jesse nods. "I think you both have done a great job with that."

Serafina smiles at him. "Thank you! I get in my head about stuff like that sometimes and, honestly, it can really slow down my creative process."

It's reassuring to hear that someone as talented as Serafina has gone through tough creative periods as well.

"What are you working on right now?" Victor asks her.

"Well, I'm stuck on the last half of my next album," she says. "I have this demo that I've been playing around with for a while, but nothing's been clicking. Do you wanna hear?"

She plays the demo on her phone and Victor offers some suggestions, which somehow turns into them improvising on the spot. Jesse and I join in, singing along. By the time I look at my phone, it's after two in the morning, way too late to call Aisha. I push away the twinge of guilt. I can call her back tomorrow; I'm sure she'll understand.

Serafina jots down some lyrics on her phone. "Thanks, guys. I'm starting to get excited about this album again!"

"Ollie's working on a couple of great songs right now, too," Jesse says.

"Oh yeah? Let's hear one," Victor urges.

Oh God. After what Serafina just shared, I can't say no. "Uh, sure."

I haven't made any more progress on the one I played for Jesse alone the other day, but I'm feeling pretty good about the song I played on stream about listening to music after dinner with Soph and Mom.

I push my nerves aside and take a deep breath. "It's called 'Records on the Living Room Floor.'"

Thankfully Jesse joins me when I start to sing, so it's not quite as scary, singing a cappella in front of my idols.

They both seem to genuinely like it, and Victor gives me a couple of helpful pointers on the melody. I still can't believe this is happening, but I'm definitely not complaining.

"So how are you guys feeling about the rest of tour?" Serafina asks when I'm done. "What are you most looking forward to?"

"The label was able to help me out with providing free tickets to some Indigenous youth organizations near my hometown and a few other cities, so that's cool. A little nerve-wracking though, since I might see some people from home who I haven't seen in a while."

Victor looks at him closely, his face solemn. "Yeah. Things with friends and family can sometimes get weird when you blow up. It's still difficult for me to deal with that sometimes."

Jesse nods, but his gaze looks far off for a moment. "I haven't been back to my hometown for a few years, even before all of this. So, it's gonna be extra weird."

"That sucks," I tell him. I didn't realize he hadn't been back home at all since he started living on the road. I'm a little surprised he's sharing, but I'm glad he wants to talk about it at all since he's been so close-lipped about stuff like this. "Sounds like a tough situation."

He shrugs. "It's fine. Even if it's weird with a few people, it's worth it to donate tickets to some kids who might not have been able to get them."

"That's great," Serafina says. "I've been trying to figure out some ways to give back, too." She goes on to tell us about the initiative she's starting for Black youth interested in pursuing music professionally. It's sounds really cool, but I find myself starting to nod off as the late hour hits me.

"You okay?" I open my eyes to find Serafina frowning at me. "Do you think it's time to turn in?"

I stifle a yawn. "Yeah, Jesse and I should probably get back to our hotel soon."

I glance over to see Jesse completely absorbed in a quiet conversation with Victor, their heads bowed together.

An uncomfortable pit forms in my stomach. I'd completely forgotten about their lingering hug in our greenroom earlier, but now I'm wondering if there was something more to it. I know that Victor is out as queer—he used to date Midnight Cavalcade's drummer.

What difference does it make? It's none of my business.

"Hey guys," Serafina says, getting their attention. "Ollie says he's ready to hit the hay."

"Oh." Jesse glances at me and then back to Victor again. "Is this place closing soon?"

"It's open twenty-four hours. But if you two want to get going, that's cool."

Jesse's face falls a little and I interject quickly, "I'm good to go back on my own."

"Are you sure?" Jesse looks at me carefully.

"It's really okay." The pit in my stomach grows bigger as I stand and start to say my goodbyes.

"See you in the morning," Jesse says. He pulls me in for a hug, and I hate how my heart immediately kicks up into double time. "Later." By the time the word is out of my mouth, he's already turned his attention to Victor again.

Back in my room, I keep replaying every extraordinary moment of the night. But then my mind strays back to Victor and Jesse at the restaurant in their own little world. It was nice to learn more about Jesse, but he probably only shared that stuff because Victor is so easy to talk to. Part of me wishes it could have been me who made him feel like he could open up.

Then again, it's not like I've been that open with Jesse. He's been so great at trying to help me feel comfortable with shows and interviews and I haven't been that great at receiving his help. It's just not that easy to admit how terrifying a lot of this has been for me. But maybe tonight wasn't just a magical fluke. Maybe I'm actually getting better at this tour thing. And maybe one day soon I'll get better at letting myself open up, too.

21

My head is a horrible, pounding mess when I wake up the next morning to my phone ringing. I roll over, bury my face in my pillow, and pray that it stops. When it doesn't, I groan and blindly reach for it on my nightstand.

"Hello?" I croak out.

"Ollie, we need to talk."

Helen's serious tone makes me sit up. "What's up?" I ask, rubbing at my burning eyes.

"Were you drinking last night?"

"Uh . . ." My mind reels, wondering how she could know that. It feels like I have a massive hangover and I know it's the toxic combo of my meds and that sip of champagne. "Not really. We did a toast, but that was it."

"Okay. There were some media outlets reporting that you looked drunk when you went out to dinner. Honestly, we aren't sticklers about what you do in private, but appearing publicly intoxicated is not a good look for us, especially since you're underage."

"I wasn't, I swear," I say, shaking my throbbing head. I don't feel comfortable telling her about my meds, especially since I already mentioned the champagne. I can only imagine what she and the label would say.

"Okay, all good then. The press is always trying to get a juicy headline." Her tone lightens. "Just be careful not to give them any ammunition, all right?"

"I understand," I say, wincing. This is the second time she's reprimanded me in two days. I need to get my shit together.

"Anyway," she says briskly, "have you talked to Jesse this morning?"

"Not yet. Why?"

"He just told me Victor invited you guys to record at his home studio over the weekend. This is actually great timing—the team would like you to add some new songs to your set. It would be ideal if you could record a few tracks and send them over by Monday morning so we can have them ready for your show that evening."

That's in forty-eight hours. "Uh, sure. I think I can do that."

"Perfect! Jesse's already at Victor's so you should get ready. Security's waiting downstairs to take you over there."

When she hangs up, I throw my phone on the bed and put my head in my hands. Jesse's already at Victor's place? I wonder if he came to the hotel at all or if he spent the night there.

My head continues to throb. God, I can't believe I was so stupid, taking so many pills and then drinking. That's literally the number one rule of taking this medication. I had no idea a sip would hit me like that, but still. Headache or not, I have to get it together. I'm suddenly on a tight deadline.

After a quick shower, I pick up my phone again and see I have unread messages from basically everyone I know, asking me if I'm okay. I send my mom, Sophie, and Neil quick replies telling them that I'm fine then listen to the message Aisha left this morning.

"Hey. I tried to stay up last night in case you called, but I fell asleep," she says with a yawn. My stomach twinges with regret again. "My showcase is tonight, so I'm not going to have time to talk today. But don't worry about all the dumb gossip online, okay? Don't even read it. I know it's all made-up crap. I'll call you tomorrow. I love you."

Oh no. What dumb gossip is she talking about? It sounds worse than people speculating about me being drunk. Even though Aisha said not to read it, I can't help but check. I scroll past a few articles with pictures of me looking red-faced and smiling dopily outside the restaurant. Then I see some clips from Jesse's encore, mostly zoomed in on Jesse and me singing together.

It's impossible not to read the comments. Lots of people are saying Jesse is looking at me like he's into me, just like that stupid clip from after our first show.

The difference is, now people are saying they think I'm into him, too. And the worst part is that they're pointing out moments when I did look at him a little too longingly.

My face erupts in unbearable heat and I screw my eyes shut. Aisha said she knows it's all bullshit, but *I* know some of it isn't. Why did I spend so much time thinking about whether anything's going on with Jesse and Victor instead of calling her back last night? I leave her a quick voicemail thanking her for checking in and wishing her luck on her performance.

Jesse's a great guy and I'm glad we're becoming friends, but that's it. That's all it can ever be, and I need to start acting like it so this stupid gossip doesn't get any worse.

My throat starts to close as I realize that Aisha's not the only one who's seen this. My mom and Sophie kept their messages vague, but I have a bad feeling my dad might have seen the articles, too. Hopefully not the ones about Jesse and me. I know he'd be a lot more upset about that than me drinking.

I bury the thought as deep as I can before I pack up and head out the door.

On the drive over to Victor's house, I close my eyes against the bright sun piercing its way through the tinted window.

When my phone rings, I ignore it for a few seconds then finally check the screen and answer.

"Hey, Ebi." I try to keep my tone upbeat. "What's up, man?"

"Not too much," he says carefully. "Just wanted to check in. How's it going?"

"Okay, I guess." I rub at my burning eyes.

"I saw everything online this morning. It must be a lot dealing with everyone talking shit and trying to get into your business."

I take in a calming breath. "It's fine, I'm okay."

Ebi's quiet for a second. "Look. I can't imagine what it's like to have the entire internet prying into stuff that you might not be ready to talk about."

"Yeah . . ." I sigh. "It's been a lot to handle lately."

"I get it," Ebi says. "I know it might not seem that way because I was mostly out when I started at Huntley, but first telling my crew in ninth grade . . . it wasn't easy. Even with the people in my life I knew would be cool with it, you know?"

I nod, even though he can't see me. I guess it was pretty silly of me to assume that Ebi's always been this confident with himself, that he's never been where I am.

"Yeah," I finally get out. "Thanks for sharing that."

His voice isn't light and joking for once. "And you know I got you, right? I got your back no matter what."

I swallow down the lump in my throat. "I know. And thanks for, you know . . . not telling anyone about me before I'm, like, ready." I expect panic to hit, but a refreshing sense of release fills me instead.

"Of course. Are you sure you're good, though?"

"Yeah, I'm just trying to focus on writing. Victor from Midnight Cavalcade invited me over to his studio to get some recording done this weekend. I'm headed there now."

"Hold up, are you for real? See? I told you that you'd meet lots of cool people on tour! You *have* to tell me how it goes. Like every detail."

"Definitely. But I'm not sure if I'll be able to make it to Dev's studio. I have to finish some tracks for the label by Monday morning."

"No worries. Do you think you might be able to do a quick Q&A with Victor while you're there? Maybe you could ask him about some of his queer musical influences? No pressure if not," Ebi says gently.

"Uh . . ." I trail off, shutting my eyes again as my insides start to squirm. I remind myself that I can use a pen name—being a contributor won't add fuel to the rumors. "I'll try."

What if Victor just wants to have a chill weekend without being bombarded with fan questions? I really do want to be part of the blog, though. The group has been a much-needed distraction from all the stress of the tour. Ebi, Dev, Kamran, and the rest of the group are so open and creative, it makes me feel like I could work up the nerve to put myself out there too. Even if it's in this small, not-so-scary way.

"Again, no pressure. And just let me know if you want to talk. About the blog or anything else, okay?"

"Will do," I say as the van pulls up to a tall gate, a long driveway visible beyond. We must be here. "Thanks again, Ebi. I gotta go."

I let out a long breath when I hang up, noticing my headache has finally subsided. I was terrified when I came out to Nadine and then to Aisha, even though they were both super supportive. But with Ebi knowing what was up and helping me skim over the hard part of actually saying it . . . it somehow felt normal instead of impossible. It's like a tiny bit of the pressure bearing down on me has been lifted.

The gate opens and we drive up to a huge house. It's only one story, but the rectangular glass structure is sprawling.

When I get out, the front door opens and Serafina walks over to meet me, grinning.

"Hey!" She gives me a hug then leads me into the house. "The guys are still in the studio, come on."

I glance around as I follow her, trying to not give away that this is the fanciest house I've ever been in. It's sparsely decorated, but the few things that are on display look like they are to be admired from afar and not touched. We enter a large white-and-gray marbled kitchen, and Serafina stops at the island in front of a charcuterie spread and some drinks.

"Can you help me with this?" she asks. "This is all Victor has— we'll order some actual food soon. We've been holed up in the studio since super early this morning."

I grab a tray as she leads the way back out of the kitchen. "Did you guys even sleep?" If she was with them the whole time then nothing probably happened between—

I cut the thought short, remembering I promised myself to stop thinking about Jesse like that.

Serafina laughs. "Barely. You know how it is when you get in the zone. Made some really good progress on my album. Hopefully we can keep it going for yours!"

"Sounds awesome." I find myself smiling at her excitement. Jamming at the restaurant was really fun, and I can't believe that now they want to hang out for the whole weekend. I already feel less nervous than last night, even though I didn't take any meds today.

Serafina opens the patio door out to a perfectly manicured back-yard with a long rectangular pool. Just beyond it is a small pool house—well, small in comparison to the actual house. Serafina leads me toward it.

"Look who's finally here!" she says, stepping inside. "And I brought some refreshments."

"Hey Ollie!" Victor beams at me. He's sitting next to Jesse at a big desk with a ton of screens. The place is outfitted like a professional studio with high-end production gear.

"This is amazing," I can't help but blurt out as my eyes travel from the equipment to all the shiny instruments—guitars, basses, and even a small piano in the corner. "Thanks for inviting me."

"It's great, isn't it?" Jesse takes his headphones off and looks over at me. There's no guardedness in his expression. He looks a little tired, but other than that he seems relaxed and happy.

He's probably been too busy to have seen the photos of me ogling him during his encore. Embarrassment boils up again, but I push it down, reminding myself that I'm putting any weirdness with Jesse behind me.

I nod and do my best to smile genuinely back at him, then quickly move my gaze back to the display of guitars.

Victor points to the guitar I'm currently eyeing. "Go ahead. Check it out."

I pick up the guitar, marveling at the craftsmanship. I take my time moving from instrument to instrument, knowing I'll probably never play anything as nice as these again.

"Are you classically trained?" Victor asks a bit later while I mess around on the piano.

I chuckle. "Uh, no, not really. I'm in the music program at my arts school."

Victor raises his eyebrows. "Art school. That must be cool. Growing up, my family didn't even have money for lessons for me."

I nod. "I'm lucky it's a public program. My family didn't have much money for me to take lessons, either."

Just like last night, it feels so strange to be hanging out with my favorite musicians. I glance over at Jesse and Serafina, who are both listening to headphones at the computer. Victor follows my gaze. "I think we're pretty much done with Sera's recordings. We can start working on yours if you're ready."

"Not really sure where to start," I say under my breath, my shoulders tightening.

"That song you shared last night was so sweet," Serafina says, taking off her headphones. "'Records on the Living Room Floor'? Why don't you get in the booth, and we'll get your vocals first?"

"Sounds good," I say with more confidence than I feel. I get up from the piano and head over to the small recording booth. I adjust the microphone and then notice Jesse, Victor, and Serafina all staring at me. Again, I remind myself how comfortable they made me feel when I shared the same song with them at the restaurant, and I start to relax.

Victor counts me down and I start singing. I close my eyes and concentrate on hitting my notes, blocking everything else out. When I finish, they're all grinning at me, and my stomach unknots.

"Good?" I ask as I step out of the booth.

"Perfect! I think we may have got it on the first try," Victor says. "You cool with laying down guitar next?"

We fly through recording the guitar, bass, and drum parts, and then Victor lets me get my hands on his amazing production software so we can start mixing. It barely takes me an hour to finish layering. Sometimes when I'm in the zone back at home, I can lay a track this fast, but it hasn't happened in a while. Getting into a creative flow has been so difficult for me lately. Being around all this talent must be helping. We play the finished product through the crystal clear speakers.

"This sounds incredible, man!" Jesse says, holding his hand up to high-five me.

"Thanks." I smile, bringing my hand up to meet his. My heart rate doesn't spike at all from the brief contact, and I consider that a win. Maybe this no-feelings thing won't be quite as difficult as I thought it would. "Helen said she still needs a few more songs to add to my set for Monday, though."

"Easy," Jesse says confidently.

I nod, biting my lip. I've been making good time so far, but what if I can't keep up the momentum?

"Don't look so worried," Serafina says. "We'll figure it out. Do you have a theme for the album?"

"Well . . ." I think it over for a long moment. "I've always kind of used music as, like, a coping mechanism in tough times. As a way to sort through what I'm feeling. But I want to explore the idea of what making music *could* be for me. Evolving from a way of coping into something more . . . I don't know."

"Maybe something more fun?" Jesse suggests.

I nod slowly. "Yeah. I think so." The concept of unalome comes to mind again, my unique path to finding peace. I still don't know exactly how to describe it. "I guess . . . just enjoying making music for the sake of making it and truly being in the moment without always thinking about heavier stuff."

"I love that," Victor says from across the room where he's messing around on bass. "I could hear some of it on the first track. Do you have any other lyrics in that vein?"

I pick some lines out of a few half-written songs in my notebook. As I'm reading them over, I realize what I've been trying to work through. It's not just about being fully present all the time. It's about not feeling like I need to force myself to stay in the moment—about letting go and accepting the ebb and flow of that awareness.

We go from there, recording vocals and then working on the instrument parts again. I can't believe how easily we're all able to riff off each other, how smoothly things click into place. A couple hours later I realize I haven't had any anxiety all day. It's just like when I used to make music back in my bedroom, but about a million times better. Jamming with the musicians I used to listen to on repeat.

We record and mix the second track, which I decide to call "Only Now." It perfectly encapsulates what I was going for, and it's one of the most upbeat songs I've ever made.

After that, I finish the lyrics for the song I was working on with Jesse, everything flowing just as smoothly as the first two songs. When I record the vocals, I put my all into it, channeling the pressure and expectations I've felt trapped by into my voice. When I finish, I open my eyes to find Jesse staring at me. His eyes are unreadable, but there's something simmering behind them. Breaking his gaze, I duck out of the sound booth.

"How was that?" I ask, glancing at Victor, who has his eyes glued to the computer.

"Smashed it," he says. "Let me just finish adjusting the levels."

"You sounded amazing," Jesse says earnestly.

I shake my head, my face flushing as I take a seat next to him, and I curse my body for betraying me. So much for this not being difficult. "Uh, thanks. Where'd Sera go?"

Jesse looks around. "Oh. I don't know, she was here a second ago."

Just then, the door to the studio opens and she walks back in carrying take-out bags.

"You're the best!" Victor gets up to help with the food. "We were wondering where you disappeared to."

She laughs. "I was gone for like five minutes. You're one to talk after you two disappeared for hours while I was recording in the wee hours of the morning."

Victor laughs. "I told you, we lost track of time, I'm sorry!"

Lost track of time doing what? They keep talking, but I'm tuning out, my mind immediately going places it shouldn't again. *It's none of my business.* I force myself to snap out of it and notice Jesse studying me, his face unreadable again. And I highly doubt that I'm managing to be as inscrutable as he is.

Looking away, I jump up to grab some food.

After I get some sushi in me, I get back to mixing the last song we recorded, so totally in the zone that I'm not really paying attention to what everyone else is saying as they sit on the shag carpet and finish their food.

"You sure you don't want any more, Ollie?" Victor asks. "It's almost done."

"I'm good," I say, still focused on the computer.

"You should take a break," Serafina says with a yawn. "You recorded three songs already and we'll have lots more time tomorrow. That all-nighter is finally catching up with me."

"Your room's all ready for you," Victor says.

"Thanks, Vic." She hugs him. "Make sure you get some rest too, guys. Night!"

Jesse and Victor talk quietly for a while and, instead of being completely immersed in my work like I was earlier, I strain to hear what they're talking about. I can't make much out.

"Think I might turn in too," Jesse says eventually, raising his voice as he stands up.

I nod at him then turn back to the screen. "Night."

Victor jumps up, too. "Come on. I'll show you where the guest rooms are."

They both head out and I'm left alone in the studio listening to my track even as my mind is elsewhere. If Victor's only showing him where the guest rooms are now, they must have stayed up the entire night. Maybe they just disappeared together to talk . . . or maybe they went to Victor's room instead. I groan, turning the volume up to block out my thoughts.

Victor comes back about ten minutes later.

"How's it going?" he asks, taking the seat next to me at the computer.

"Pretty good," I say truthfully. Despite my mind wandering, I've still been making progress. "Tell me what you think." I play the third song over the speakers.

When it's over, Victor grins. "I think this album is going to be a hit!"

I shake my head in disbelief—I feel like he really means it. "Thanks, Victor."

"Of course. Honestly, this weekend has made me excited about recording with the band again. I haven't felt like this in a while. I've been mulling over the idea of pitching the guys a concept album, but it's really different from a lot of our old stuff. Hearing the way you're using a theme to tell a bigger story has been so inspiring."

It's hard to believe that anything I've done could have inspired him. "I mean, right back at you. I've been in a rut for a while, so thanks again for all this. I feel like I'm finally getting back into the creative flow."

He smiles. "You're welcome, anytime. I'm glad I could help."

I nod, still kind of in disbelief. "So, uh, what's your concept album idea?"

"I was thinking of having an ongoing thread about these fictional characters inspired by Gabriel García Márquez's works. It's kind of out there and abstract, but I've always loved his books and I feel like reimagining the themes would be a good way to put some personal stuff into the album without it being super obvious. It makes it feel safer, not basing stuff so directly on my real experiences."

"That sounds incredibly cool. And yeah, I get what you mean about creating some distance between you and your work." I take a deep breath. "How do you deal with that? I mean, fans making assumptions about your personal life all the time?"

Victor smiles, but his eyes are sad. "It's tough, tuning everything out. And when we first blew up, it was a lot harder."

He shoots me a sympathetic look and I glance away. Of course he knows why I'm asking, considering what "On Repeat" alludes to with Thomas, but it still feels awkward.

"Um, yeah. Anyway, I'd love to hear what you've been working on. I mean, if you feel comfortable."

He studies me for another second. "Sure." He picks up a guitar and starts playing. It's a departure from Midnight's past discography, but it's a breathtaking song that leaves me wanting more. "Wow. That was just . . . wow," is all I can manage when the song's over.

Victor looks at me skeptically. "You really liked it?"

"I loved it! Seriously." I start asking him a little bit more about his inspirations and he gets into his favorite artists from his childhood in Colombia.

Since he seems comfortable answering my questions already, I work up the courage to ask him about the interview. "Do you, uh, mind if I ask you a couple questions on the record? I'm doing a piece for my friend's music magazine."

"Sure," he says. "What magazine is it?"

I tell him and his eyes light up in recognition. "I think I've heard of them. They're a queer indie mag with a studio space here in Regina, right?"

"Yeah, exactly." I look away and fiddle unnecessarily with the equipment but resist the urge to give some type of qualifier for why I'm involved, to separate myself from the word "queer."

For as long as I can remember there's been this awful disconnect inside me. I'm one hundred percent accepting of queer people, but when it comes to me . . . it just hasn't felt like it's okay. Like . . . deep down, I don't just feel guilty for having a crush on Jesse because I feel like I'm betraying Aisha. It's mixed in with the guilt I feel for liking a guy at all. I know that's related to my dad's messed-up way of looking at things, and I hate how hard it is to get his voice out of my head.

"That's awesome, Ollie." The sincerity in Victor's voice interrupts my thoughts. When I make myself look at him again, I'm taken aback by his expression.

He doesn't say anything else, but I just feel really . . . seen. In a good way. Like who I am is actually all right. More than all right, maybe it makes me something special.

I clear my throat. "Yeah, so, I told my friends running it that I'd try to get an interview and possibly check out their studio space this weekend."

"I'd love to check it out too," Victor says. "Since you're flying through your tracks already, let's stop by tomorrow afternoon after you're finished."

"Okay, awesome." Dev will be psyched. "So you're okay with an interview then? It won't take that long, I promise."

"Totally fine, ask away."

We talk for a while and Victor's presence slowly puts me at ease as I jot down his answers. He tells me more about his influences, the queer artists that helped him get through rough times when his family wasn't as accepting as he'd hoped they'd be.

I think about my own family—my dad in particular. All my unnamed worries about him not accepting me for who I am swirl in my head then shift into coherent words, the beginnings of a new song coming together.

"You okay?" Victor asks.

I snap back to the present. "Yeah, sorry. Something just came to me for a song."

He smiles. "Wow, you're really on a roll! I'm getting pretty tired, so I'll leave you to it. Do you have enough for the interview?"

I nod. "Thanks again for being down for this."

"Don't mention it. There's a spare guest room around the corner and fifth door on your right for when you come in later. Good night."

"Night," I say distractedly, turning to a blank page in my notebook. I scribble down the lyrics before they float away.

It's a relief to get down some of the stuff that's been stuck in my head about my relationship with my dad. Hearing Victor talk about not feeling supported by his family and getting through that gives me hope that things could work out eventually for me too.

I can't imagine ever coming out to my dad . . . but talking to my mom and Soph seems like it could be within the realm of possibility. It was such a relief talking with Ebi today, and maybe I could have that with them, too. Same with Neil. I know he would be just as great as Ebi was about it, but there's a part of me that's still so uncomfortable with the idea of saying it out loud. That same part of me that just isn't comfortable with me being bi, period.

I don't think I'm ready to put this song out into the world, but starting it helped me clear my head. I turn back to mixing and another hour flies by. My eyes start getting heavy, and when I can't concentrate anymore, I stretch out on a couch in the studio, too tired to go find the guest room.

22

I start awake and squint against the first rays of sunlight lighting up the darkened studio. The door opens and I sit up as Jesse comes in.

"Morning." He shoots me an apologetic smile. "Just went for a swim and then I figured I'd check to see if you got any shut-eye. Sorry to wake you."

"That's okay," I say groggily, rubbing my eyes like I can wipe away the sight of him in swim trunks, a towel draped over his bare shoulders. "I got some sleep."

I look anywhere but at him as he sits right beside me on the couch, so close his damp arm brushes mine. I take in a breath and the smell of chlorine and soap fills my nose. He's talking again; I think he's asking me about what we should have for breakfast. I'm having trouble concentrating on what he's saying—most of my attention is taken up by wondering why he's sitting so close to me. I can feel him looking right at me, but I still avoid his gaze.

Eventually he sighs. "Ollie . . . You know nothing happened between me and Victor, right?"

I bite my lip to keep my mouth from dropping open.

"Sorry, what?" I ask after a moment. Is it that obvious that I'm jealous? Even though I've told myself countless times that I don't have any right to be.

"I said there's nothing going on between me and Victor."

I finally look up at him. He's studying me so closely that everything in me wants to look away, but I can't. There's something in his eyes that I haven't seen before, and I don't want it to disappear.

I'm frozen as a silent, heavy something settles around us. Finally, I move to turn away again, but his hand finds the side of my face, turning me back toward him.

That's when I realize that I must still be asleep, because now he's kissing me. Like *really* kissing me, and I'm kissing him back. I must be dreaming, but it's absolutely wild how vivid it feels. How real he feels.

I can't be awake. I would never do this because . . . because . . .

Aisha. It takes way too long for her name to materialize. *I'm in love with Aisha.* The thought doesn't stop Jesse from occupying the exact same space in my head that she does, his presence overwhelming me.

He's gently pushing me back down onto the couch, and I don't stop him because this isn't real. I keep telling myself that, even as I feel the warm whisper of his breath against my neck. For once, I stop chastising myself. I close my eyes, fully losing myself in the feeling of his skin against mine—

Cold concrete rushes up to meet my face, the scene changing all at once. The pain is all-consuming, but I can't get enough air into my lungs to scream. Jesse's hands aren't gentle anymore because they're not his hands. I struggle with all my might, but I can't get free.

"Stop moving." Thomas's voice rumbles in my ear and bile rises in my throat.

I jolt upright in a cold sweat, waking up. I jump about a mile again when I realize there's someone in the room with me, their hand gripping my shoulder.

"Are you okay?" It's Jesse. For real this time. He's fully clothed and looking at me like I've lost it.

I scoot away from him on the couch. I'm still breathing too hard to respond so I just nod, rubbing a hand over my sweaty face.

"You were yelling. Bad dream?"

"Um. Yeah, I guess," I mutter. My face feels like it's going to burst into flames. "Sorry."

"No worries. You sure you're okay?" When I finally glance at him, I have to look away immediately, unable to take his pitying expression.

"I'm fine now. I, uh, gotta go to the bathroom," I blurt before I bolt from the room.

The house is silent when I step inside. I wash my face and then stare blankly into the sink drain.

I used to wonder a lot—especially right after it happened—why Thomas did what he did. Why he wasn't content with just breaking my bones. He always read as straight to me, but after going to therapy for a while I realized it wasn't about that. He's the kind of person who humiliates people to feel better about himself.

As many horrible thoughts as I've had about Thomas, I've thought just as many if not more horrible things about myself. All the stuff that I've talked about so many times with Nadine still never really goes away. Like if I wasn't the way that I am then it never would have happened. I know that doesn't make any sense, but it still *feels* that way, no matter how much time has passed.

I try to bring back the warm, welcoming glow of Victor's acceptance last night and of Ebi being there for me. I try to remember how freeing it felt to get down some lyrics about my fears about my dad. How hopeful I was that I could mend the awful disconnect inside me. But right now it feels just as big as ever.

Get it together. I shake my head and look up from the sink, meeting my own eyes dead-on in the mirror. I recite some affirmations from therapy until they start to feel like they might be true. I really need to set up a call with Nadine soon.

Nothing's wrong with me. I'm not a bad person for being attracted to guys. For being attracted to Jesse; for having that dream about him. Admitting that to myself isn't betraying Aisha. It doesn't make me love her any less. If I stop pushing it down . . . maybe it will finally pass. Maybe this infatuation will finally go away.

I groan, suddenly remembering I forgot to check in with Aisha after her showcase. I grab my phone out of my pocket and call her, even though it's super early.

"Hey," I say, closing my eyes when I get her voicemail. The tinny recording of her voice makes me ache for the real thing. "I hope the showcase went well. I'm sure you were great. Thanks again for your message yesterday. I appreciate you understanding about . . . about everything." I take in a shaky breath. It's not even close to everything. How could I possibly explain all the things that have been going on with me and all the conflicting emotions I've barely been able to sort through in my own head? "I miss you. Call me later, okay?"

When I get back to the studio, Jesse's sitting at the computer.

He gives me a hesitant smile. "Hey."

"Hey." I nod and manage a smile back. "I'm good."

"Okay." He doesn't push me to talk about it more, thankfully. "I was just checking out what you've done; it's sounding really polished already. Great job."

I take a seat next to him and shrug. "With this equipment, it doesn't take much."

We spend the next hour working on some final tweaks. By the time Victor and Serafina come in with breakfast, I'm just about done mixing. I blast the speakers while we eat so Victor and Sera can listen to what I've been working on. We're all on our feet as "Only Now" plays, our waffles abandoned as we dance around the room.

Serafina grins and gives me a hug when it ends. "That one's such a bop! All of them are fantastic, honestly."

Victor and Jesse start saying complimentary things too and I'm able to thank them without putting myself down. I'm actually really happy with the songs. These three plus the three songs in my original set are sounding like a solid first half to the album.

I head over to the computer again and open up my email. "So I guess I'll just send the finished tracks along to Helen and that's it."

"I can make mimosas to celebrate," Sera suggests.

"Thanks, but I'll have to pass on that," I say quickly. I need to stick with the no-drinking plan. I've been doing so well without my meds too, and I want to keep that going as long as I can.

"Okay, just an orange juice for Ollie. Victor? Jesse?"

"I'm good with water," Jesse says.

"Me too," Victor chimes in. "But we do have to do something fun to celebrate. How about we head over to your friend's studio now?"

"Ooh, what studio?" Serafina asks.

Victor fills her in as I press send on my email to Helen. I rub the back of my stiff neck as I slowly push my breath out, trying to quell the nerves suddenly rising in me.

"How you feeling?" Jesse asks. "I mean about the tracks," he adds.

"I'm happy with them," I say honestly. "Hopefully Helen and the team like them too."

He gives me a pat on the shoulder. Thankfully, I just feel reassurance and nothing more. "I think they'll love them. Come on, let's go."

*
*

I text Dev that I'm headed over with some guests in tow and they let me know it'll be low-key at the studio because they're working on their own today. Still, I feel like I probably should have mentioned we would be rolling in like a Secret Service convoy.

The unit is cozy, with high windows and walls plastered in cool DIY art collages, posters, and note-covered whiteboards. I introduce everyone and Victor recognizes Dev from when their band opened for Midnight Cavalcade a few years ago. Serafina had recently left the band. Dev and Victor animatedly tell me, Jesse, and Serafina all about the surprise show; apparently it was one for the books. Afterward, Dev shows us around and lets us check out some completed submissions for the print issue.

I start skimming Kamran's article about queer Islamic poetry inspiring his music. The last part of the article details how their work helped Kamran come to terms with being gay. I stop skimming and carefully read each word of that section. I've heard about a few ancient

Islamic poets' work celebrating same-sex love, but I've never looked into it in detail.

"Find something interesting?" Dev asks, and I jump. Jesse, Sera, and Victor are looking at some art across the room.

I nod and try to shake the feeling that I've been caught reading something I shouldn't. "Um, yeah. Kamran posted about working on this a while ago. It's a great piece."

Dev smiles. "I loved that one too. I think it's really cool that even though he felt isolated from his family, he was able to find poetry that was affirming for him culturally and inspired his own art. Growing up in an environment like that, it really resonated with me."

I want to say I feel the same way, but the words stick in my throat.

Dev looks at me sideways for a long second and I force myself not to look away. I know they get that I related to Kamran's piece too.

"I really appreciate you coming down here, with everything you have going on."

"No worries," I respond, relieved at the subject change. "Thanks for not blowing my cover in the contributor group."

"Don't mention it." Dev smiles again, softer this time. "How's your piece coming along?"

"I interviewed Victor yesterday and that went well. I'm just trying to, um, think of a personal lens."

"What did you guys talk about?" Dev asks.

"Ebi suggested I ask him about his queer musical influences. So . . . mainly that." I glance over at Victor, Sera, and Jesse still chatting quietly across the room.

"Got it. So maybe your personal lens could be your own musical influences and how Victor and Midnight tie into that? Maybe you could even pull from Kamran's theme of searching for self-acceptance?"

I make myself focus on Dev again and they give me another long look.

Yeah, they one hundred percent know what's going on with me. But they're not being pushy or trying to pry.

"I was kind of thinking something along those lines," I admit. But thinking about it and having the courage to write it are two different things. Even if no one besides Dev and Ebi will know that I'm the author.

"Feel free to run a draft by me. I'm sure Kamran would love to read it over for you too." Dev lowers their voice. "Anyway, I'm trying to be chill, but this has been beyond incredible. I thought famous people were supposed to be assholes, but they're all so lovely. I mean, I knew Victor was nice, but still."

I laugh a little. "I know, I'm right there with you. Everything's felt so surreal lately. Jesse's been really great at helping me get through this."

"I'm glad to hear that. I'm really thrilled for you. Even though you totally missed out on being our bassist," they tease.

It seems so long ago that Dev asked me about trying out for their band, how I'd yearned to be touring like they were. It's impossible to process where I am now.

We hang out until we have to get on the road again. It's weirdly sad saying goodbye to everyone even though we basically just met. Victor and Serafina give me their numbers, which feels so odd, especially when they say to call anytime. I'm pretty sure they mean it, though. I turn away from Jesse and Victor when they hug goodbye so I won't be able to mull over how long it lasted or if they said anything to each other in hushed voices. It would be stupid to focus on that when I'm honestly just grateful that Victor welcomed me into his home and helped create such a comfortable space for me to make music.

23

Later, back in the van, the high of the weekend is pretty much gone as I squint at my computer, trying to keep my eyes open to finish editing a video. Jesse's passed out in the row in front of me, his head resting against the window. I find myself staring at his sleeping form a little too long, my gaze moving to his lips as my dream from last night pops into my head again.

There's nothing wrong with just thinking about it. The thought doesn't do anything to dispel the shame rising inside me as I turn my attention back to my screen.

I have to stop repressing every time I think about him in that way if I want it to start going away. I just need to accept that my feelings for him exist and let them pass. I try to keep editing, but Kamran's article runs through my mind again. After a few minutes, I give up on the video for the time being. I open my notebook to work on my piece for the blog. My pen flies across the page; everything I've been so confused about the last few days pouring out of me. I write about how frustrating it is trying to escape the endless loop of shame

I'm stuck in. Shame about the feelings I've been having and then more shame about feeling shame instead of just letting my feelings be without judging them. I don't think I'll end up putting a lot of it in the actual piece, but it's a relief to get it out of my head.

I'm so thankful for this weekend. That I'm finally back in the groove of making music again. I'd forgotten just how much it fueled me. In all my anxiety about the tour, I'd kind of lost sight of how amazing it is that I get to do what I love most in the world. And, by some miracle, to get paid for it. I'd always thought I'd have to compromise, to relegate my music to a hobby once I graduated.

I want to keep doing this. Not just to help my family, but for me. After this weekend, I know this is truly what I want to do.

My phone rings and I put my notebook down to take a look. School's not out yet, so I'm surprised to see it's Neil calling.

"Hey, man. What's up, is everything okay?"

"Yeah, everything's cool," Neil says. He sounds a little tired. "How about you, how's the tour treating you?"

"Are you sure you're good? Don't you have class right now?"

"Well, if you must know, I'm headed to a meeting with my sponsor so I got out of last period, thank God."

"Oh. Okay," I say cautiously. I'm glad to hear he's keeping up with his meetings.

"Before you ask, yes, everything's going good with my meetings," he drawls.

"Glad to know I'm so predictable," I chuckle. "How was the show-case? I haven't been able to reach Aisha yet."

"Honestly, it was pretty great. Nobody fucked up the choreo and the crowd seemed to like it. Weirdly enough, my dad even showed up."

"Really?" Neil and his dad don't get along very well.

"Yeah. I'm pretty sure Aisha's dad told him about it. After the show they were talking to me and Aisha about applying to dance programs. I'm sure my dad's taking some time from his eternally busy schedule to make sure I'm on track to graduate and move out," he scoffs.

It's weird thinking about next year. I'm not sure where I'll land yet or if it will be anywhere close to either of them. Even before the tour, I'd avoided thinking about it too much. I didn't want to be constantly dreading the inevitable.

"Anyway," Neil says when I don't respond. "Enough about me. How's life on the road?"

"Sorry. I was listening. I've just had a lot on my mind lately. I've been . . . I don't know, kind of all over the place mentally."

"What do you mean?"

I bite my lip, thinking about my last conversation with Ebi. I'm almost certain that Neil has my back in that same way. I don't feel prepared to tell him about everything I've been dealing with, but I do want to tell him something.

"I'm . . . I'm working on a piece for this music blog Ebi's a part of," I say.

"Oh yeah, I think he's mentioned it. What are you working on?"

"I interviewed Victor from Midnight—"

"That's sick, Ollie! I saw you performing with him and Sera the other night."

"Yeah, it was really great. It's just . . . for the interview, I'm working on a personal angle about, like, my own, um . . . identity. I'm writing under a pen name, but it's . . . it's just kind of out of my comfort zone."

"Ah." Neil's quiet for a second and my heart starts to pound in the silence. I'm pretty sure he knows what I mean. "Well, I'm not a big music nerd or anything, but I'm excited to read it. You know. Whenever you feel okay sharing it with me."

I find myself smiling as a warm surge of relief pumps through me. "Okay. Cool. Thanks, man. Wait, are you calling *me* a music nerd?"

"Anytime. And don't worry, it's a compliment. I got to get to my meeting, but don't be a stranger, okay? I'm around anytime you wanna talk."

I find myself smiling when we hang up, even as my eyes start to sting. That same lightness I felt when I talked to Ebi is hitting me again.

It's hard to describe how much it means to know without a doubt that Neil supports me. I wish I remembered to mention the song I wrote about us being there for each other, but I can ask him about it next time we talk.

I sigh. Even with a little more of the weight lifted just now, there's still the unknown of my family's response pushing down on me. Particularly my dad.

I open my notebook again, turning back to the lyrics I was working on about my relationship with him. I start writing, the words overlapping with some of the notes I was making for my interview on trying to find acceptance. I keep at it for a while, finally pausing to glance out at the last of the sunset painting the dark sky with faint streaks of pink, orange, and red. Closing my notebook, I lean my head against the window to take it all in, letting my mind go quiet.

*

A makeup person is powdering my sweaty face as I sit under TV studio lights next to Jesse a few hours later in Saskatoon. I tried Aisha after school let out, but I got her voicemail again. I hope she's all right. Neil said their showcase went well, but I really want to hear how she felt about it.

What if she's avoiding you? I shake the thought away. She said everything was okay in her last message. But what if she felt like she had to say that because she didn't want to worry me? What if she actually is freaked out about the gossip about Jesse and me?

Stop. I bring my focus back to the present. The makeup person starts penciling something onto my eyebrows and then my lash line. Taking a calming breath, I resist the urge to pull away, putting whatever my dad might think out of my mind.

After I tried Aisha, I texted Ebi in the dressing room, filling him in about the weekend like I promised. He was psyched to hear that I was able to get the interview and visit Dev. He offered to take a look at my interview, too. I made some progress earlier, but I'm not quite ready to share it with anyone. I still have a few more weeks until submissions are due.

I go through Helen's media pointers, practicing in my head. Considering I don't know what they're going to ask, I need as much practice as I can get. This program is a serious prime-time thing instead of a fluffy gossip segment like last time. Which was hard enough.

I look over at Jesse to find him watching me.

He nods reassuringly. "We've got this, okay?"

I nod back and then the host approaches to introduce himself. I already know who he is—Anthony Rodgers, a famous music journalist who's interviewed a ton of my favorite artists. I've never seen him ask any vapid who's-dating-who questions so we should be safe on that front. All I have to worry about is not sounding like a complete idiot.

Thankfully, Anthony has way more questions for Jesse than for me. It's basically like I'm sitting in on a conversation between them.

"Your music has an overall hopeful slant to it, even though you often get into very challenging issues, like injustices against Indigenous people. How did you find that balance of injecting some lightness into dark subject matter?" Anthony asks Jesse. "Were you trying to make your message more palatable?"

Jesse's mouth twists downward before his face smooths out again.

"No. I think it's just a natural coping mechanism. My community has dealt with so much horrific stuff both historically and on a day-to-day basis. So, whenever I mention it in my music, I highlight hope wherever I can."

Anthony nods then turns his attention to me. "Dark subject matter seems to be a theme in your music as well. Your first single 'On Repeat' touches on a very heavy topic—sexual assault."

I manage not to flinch, even as my ears start ringing. It takes everything in me to keep my face calm. This shouldn't be a surprising question since the lyrics obviously suggest that, but it still catches me off guard.

"A lot of survivors have expressed how much your song means to them," Anthony continues. "Especially male survivors who are much less likely to talk about their experiences. What made you feel comfortable talking about such a difficult issue publicly?"

"Well . . ." My mind races. I can feel Jesse's concerned look, but I keep my eyes on Anthony.

I'm not ready to talk about this. If I say that it's based on my own experiences I can only imagine how much press coverage that would get. Everyone would be talking about it, wondering what exactly happened to me. I can't deal with that kind of scrutiny on top of all the stuff going around about Jesse and me.

I finally answer. "Like you said, it's a tough topic for a lot of people to talk about. But it's something that affects everyone—survivors and their friends and families. And, um, even though it's not something that I have . . . that I have experience with personally, it's, um, something I'm passionate about raising awareness about. I'm really glad it's helped some people feel less alone."

I glance at Jesse as I finish speaking. There's a quick flash of pity in his eyes, just like when he woke me up from my dream. He knows I'm lying. I turn back to Anthony, nodding along to his response. At least Anthony seems to have bought what I said.

The interview continues, and Anthony focuses on Jesse again. A few minutes later, it's over. Anthony thanks us for coming and then we're directed offstage.

Helen calls us in the car on the way to our hotel, seeming pleased with how we did. She says the team was happy with my tracks too—thank God—and will be adding them to the set list for our show tomorrow night. After she hangs up, I put on my earphones and close my eyes, trying not to replay the interview—to no avail.

I feel like such a fraud for not telling the truth. But I can't imagine any reality where I would feel comfortable admitting that to the world. I think of Radhika and the other people I've heard from—I can't deny that my song has helped people, like Anthony said. But sometimes I feel like it doesn't really count because I'm not brave enough to share my own story. I push the thought away, reminding myself I don't owe that to anyone. But . . . Nadine has been right so far about opening up to more people in my life. Ebi, Neil, and Victor's support took such a big weight off when I shared a bit more about my identity. But all the guilt and shame I struggle with is so intertwined with what happened to me. What Thomas did. It's hard enough to untangle it all in my own mind, let alone talk about it with other people.

I find myself thinking about that night at the festival with Aisha. How patient and understanding she was when I couldn't bring myself to say anything. I wish I could go back to that moment, knowing what I do now. That it only makes it worse to hold it all in. That she's the one person who I'm sure won't judge me.

I still have no idea how to talk to her about so much of what I've been feeling since the tour started. But the possibility of talking to her about this feels less scary than it used to. I don't think it's something I could do over the phone, but I think I could try when I get back from the tour.

24

I'm still feeling weird about the interview the next day, but I avoid checking what people are saying online, reminding myself that it wouldn't be healthy for me. Thankfully we don't have any interviews or photo shoots today, so I have some time alone for a therapy session with Nadine.

"How is everything going anxiety-wise?" she asks when she calls.

I tell her I'm feeling a bit more confident after the show we did with Victor and Serafina, then I fill her in on the weekend at Victor's. "I finally felt like I was getting back into a flow state with my music," I say. "I hope that carries into our next shows since it can be hit-or-miss with breathing exercises and meditations."

"Back at home you had the additional support of your friends and family. How have you been dealing with not having that as much on tour?"

"It's been hard," I admit. I'm still constantly playing phone tag with

Aisha. I'm glad I caught up with Neil the other day, but I've only been getting back to my mom and Sophie sporadically. I feel bad that I've been avoiding catching up with them and hiding out in the contributor chat, but the intensity of tour life and all of the emotional turmoil that's come with it is just too much sometimes.

"How have things been with Jesse?" Nadine asks. As soon as she says his name, my pulse quickens. "Do you feel like you can talk to him when you need support?"

"Um, yeah." I take a slow, calming breath. Yet another thing I don't know how to talk to her about. But I can manage my feelings on my own. I just need to stop chastising myself all the time. "Jesse's been really welcoming and supportive so far. But I don't want to make him feel like it was a mistake to invite me."

"Have you told him about your anxiety?" she asks.

"I mean, it's obvious I get stage fright. But no, I haven't actually told him." I think of all the times he's asked me if I'm okay and how I always brush him off.

"Do you think you might feel comfortable talking to him about it directly?" she suggests gently.

"Maybe . . ." I say slowly. I can't imagine him being weird about it, but it's always scary telling people about my mental health stuff.

Not allowing people to support me has been an "ongoing theme" for me, as Nadine would say. I've been working on that lately with Ebi, Neil, and even the contributor group in a limited way. And I've still been thinking about opening up to Aisha about what happened with Thomas when I get back.

I should probably talk to Nadine about what happened in the Anthony Rodgers interview, but I already know she would say I shouldn't feel guilty for not being comfortable talking publicly about my assault. Thankfully, I'm finally starting to get that.

Nadine's speaking again, and I pull myself from my thoughts. "That's good to hear. Having someone there with you to talk through it could help a lot." She's said a variation of the same thing so many times to me, but it's finally feeling like it isn't such a distant goal.

After I hang up with Nadine, I walk down the hall to knock on Jesse's door. Might as well try out her advice instead of sitting around my room thinking about it.

When he opens it, I smile cautiously. "Hey. What's up?"

"Hey." He smiles back, glancing briefly at my ears. I'm wearing my unalome earrings. I haven't since the festival, but I've been trying to stop overthinking things and do what I want to do in the moment. When I put them on, I blocked out the nagging thoughts about my dad and focused on the acceptance I've felt from the people I've been able to open up to lately. "I'm okay. How are you feeling?"

"Fine," I say automatically. I take a steadying breath. "I'm gonna film a video if you want to join."

His smile spreads wider across his face, becoming brilliant. "For sure."

There's a quiet beat before he speaks again, his face sobering. "So . . . That Anthony Rodgers interview was intense. Sorry if that question about . . . the heavy stuff in 'On Repeat' was stressful," he says, seeming to choose his words carefully.

Heat rushes to my face, my heart pounding. I can't forget his pitying looks. Even though I want to try to talk to Aisha more about what happened . . . I'm not really prepared to get into any of it with Jesse right now. I know trying to talk to him about my stage anxiety is going to be hard enough as it is.

"Uh, it was fine. Anyway, are you good with live streaming our session today? Or I can just record it now and then edit and post it later."

He lets out a small sigh. "A live stream sounds cool."

We spend about an hour on live and I play some of the new songs I recorded over the weekend. The reception is great so I'm optimistic the songs will go over well for my set tonight.

After we finish up with the live, he glances at his phone. "We still have some time to kill before the show. There's this cool museum called Wanuskewin right by here if you wanna check it out."

"Yeah, I'm down." It'll be nice to go out and do something less scheduled again.

Jesse tries to get security to let us go on our own, but they insist on coming with us. Jesse finally gives in since Tim usually gives us our space instead of creepily lurking like some of the other guys on the team.

Wanuskewin is an Indigenous heritage museum and national park with lots of walking trails. We spot a small herd of bison grazing in the distance of the sprawling grasslands. As we head inside the big, asymmetrical glass building, Jesse tells me about an artist friend of his whose work is currently on exhibition. Tim enters a few feet behind us, sticking out like a sore thumb.

He nods at us, staying put by the door.

Jesse lets out a relieved sigh when we walk around the corner out of Tim's line of sight. His shoulder briefly brushes mine and a warm shiver runs through me. When I glance at him, he doesn't seem to notice; he's looking at the entrance of the gallery we're approaching. I step away, putting some space between us as casually as I can.

It's fine. Relax. The words are starting to become my mantra whenever I'm around him.

Jesse points out his friend's work, some beautiful black-and-white photos of the park outside. Afterward, we stop in front of a display of a massive rock covered in tiny markings.

"This was originally found on the grounds outside. These markings are petroglyphs," Jesse says, pointing at the symbols carved into the rock. "My friend told me last time I visited about how this whole park used to be an ancient gathering place for a ton of different Indigenous groups. These markings were used to share knowledge between groups. See that grid pattern? It represents a vision quest, like a spiritual experience."

"Cool," I say, stepping closer to get a better look. "It's wild to think about how long ago this was carved. How different life must have been and what spiritual experiences meant to them then."

"I imagine it wasn't so different from people's spiritual experiences nowadays. I think it's sort of universal, a loss of material self that reframes your perspective on what's most important to you. That's the thing about experiences like that—they kind of transcend time."

It suddenly clicks for me that that's how I feel when I'm listening to or making music, like I'm moving into a timeless state. "I know exactly what you mean."

"Yeah? I mean, I kind of figured from some of your lyrics that you might be into spirituality."

I nod, smiling slightly. "I kind of figured you might be into spirituality from your lyrics, too." That's a big part of the reason I was originally drawn to his music. I've been tempted to ask him about it, but I didn't know how exactly to bring it up before. I think again about Nadine encouraging me to open up, and I take in a breath. "A couple of years ago, my therapist recommended I start meditating for, um, my anxiety. That's how I first got into it."

I brace myself, waiting for his reaction.

He's quiet for a moment, then he smiles in understanding.

"That's great, Ollie," he says. "It's cool that you go to therapy."

The tension in my shoulders starts to loosen. "Yeah, it's been really helpful."

"I'm glad. And yeah, I wasn't much into medicine growing up, but since I've been on my own it's become a daily thing for me. Therapy, not so much. I've tried, but I haven't been able to find someone I feel comfortable talking to."

"Yeah, I know it can be difficult to keep trying, but it's worth it. What kind of medicine do you mean, though?" I ask. I'm guessing he's not talking about pharmaceutical stuff like my anxiety meds.

"Spirit medicine, it's a traditional thing. Like, if you've heard of a medicine wheel before, it involves taking care of both your physical and spiritual health."

"Ah okay, that makes a lot of sense. What do you do for medicine usually?"

"Writing and listening to music are big for me. Besides that, working out when I can, and I try to meditate and do some self-reflection too. It can be hard to keep up on the road sometimes."

"Got it," I say slowly. Even though I got into Jesse's music because of the spiritual elements, it's still strange to realize we have so much in common.

I can't relate to the working out thing though, besides long walks. I wonder when exactly he works out. I mean, it one hundred percent looks like he does, I've just never seen him do it. Maybe he hits the gym whenever we get a chance to crash at a hotel with one? I avoid gyms whenever possible so it's plausible I've just been oblivious. I hope he doesn't suggest I go with him. I barely made it through PE class. But if he wanted to meditate together, that could be cool. Working on music with him has kind of felt like that. Something about his energy helps me let go of everything and get in the zone.

"Ollie . . ." I pull myself back to the conversation as his face clouds over. "I've been meaning to say sorry for sharing your song with everyone before messaging you. It was just a spur-of-the-moment thing, but looking back . . . maybe I shouldn't have done it like that, especially now that I know about your anxiety."

"No, it's okay," I say quickly. "I'm glad you did." If he hadn't, none of this would have happened. I wouldn't be standing here right now.

His gaze turns skeptical. "This whole being in the public eye thing . . . it's a lot, and I feel like I just threw you into this without thinking through all the stuff you'd have to deal with. Like all the gossip about . . ." He looks away, his cheeks flushing.

Another jolt of warmth runs through me, but I try to keep my emotions off my face. This is the first time he's acknowledged what people have been saying about us online. I don't think I've ever seen him blush before, not even around Victor. I can't help but wonder if it's just because it's awkward and embarrassing or . . .

Jesse locks eyes with me again and I know I'm not doing a good job of masking my thoughts. I'm completely frozen as he studies me, then his face closes up and becomes frustratingly opaque again. Sunlight streams through the gallery windows, shifting his dark eyes into a stunning ochre. I tell myself there's nothing wrong with notic-

222 / MAYA AMEYAW

ing. Just like everything else in the gallery, looking is fine as long as I don't step beyond the velvet rope.

"Don't worry, I can handle it," I finally get out. "This experience, being here, is something I would have never thought was possible a few months ago. I'll always be grateful to you for this. I mean it." As stressful as the tour is, I'm eternally thankful that everything lined up for me to be able to help my family. And despite all the pressure, this really is a dream come true, getting to do what I've always loved doing most.

He smiles, his expression finally warming. "I'm glad you're here, Ollie. Let me know if there's anything I can do to help when you're feeling anxious before shows. Or anytime."

"I really appreciate that, Jesse." My shoulders start to relax as I turn back to the display. I try to forget about the palpable tension when I looked at him a little too long. He was cool with my anxiety stuff—that's what matters right now. Shutting people out when things get difficult has been my normal for so long, but yet again, actually letting myself be seen has made me feel so much lighter and more free than I dared to imagine.

*
*

When we get to the venue later, rehearsal goes well, but my nerves shoot up to dangerous levels before I'm supposed to go on. I'm pacing in our shared dressing room, trying to listen to a meditation.

I squeeze my eyes shut. God, I *hate* this. I feel like I'm doing everything Nadine recommended—reaching out for support, breathing exercises, mantras, and meditation. But sometimes, no matter what I do, nothing seems to work.

Just take your meds. The temptation starts to tug at me, my resolve wavering.

"Hey." Jesse's voice cuts through my earbuds. I remove them and turn my attention to him. He's sitting on the couch near the door. He's wearing several handmade earrings he bought at the museum earlier. I bought a pair too and finally put them on after some internal debate. They're big and colorful, more noticeable than my unalome ones. I'm kind of worried about them being too much, but when I catch a glimpse of them in the greenroom mirror, I'm reminded of Ebi's understanding and Victor's warmth. I try to focus on that feeling and not give in to the urge to play it safe.

"You doing okay?" he asks, bringing my attention back to the room.

Sighing, I shake my head and sit down beside him. "This meditation my therapist recommended isn't really doing the job."

"Do you want to meditate together?" he asks. "I feel like having another person usually helps me."

I nod and smile, super thankful he asked. We close our eyes. I've never meditated with anyone other than Aisha. We've only done it together a few times, when she was stressed and dissociating. It feels different with Jesse, though. I can sense how present he is, like it's a physical force growing around me. I fully relax, letting go of the last of my thoughts. I let myself become part of our shared stillness, my heartbeat slowing and my throat starting to loosen.

A knock at the door jolts my mind awake again a few minutes later. I glance over at Jesse as he slowly opens his eyes and smiles at me.

"Are you feeling okay to go on?" he asks.

I grin. "Yeah, let's do this."

We head over to the backstage area and my heart rate stays at a normal level, even as the sound of the crowd gets closer.

I walk out onstage and wave at the screaming audience. *Come on, you've got this. You know how to do this. Stay calm.* I hold onto the stillness I just felt with Jesse.

As I grab the mic, my hands start shaking, but I think it's more from adrenaline than from nerves.

"We love you, Ollie!" the crowd screams. For once, I'm taking it all in. All the love in the room that's meant for me. I feel like I'm about to burst with emotion and I channel it into my performance, surrendering fully to the present moment, the music moving through me effortlessly.

At the end of my set, the crowd roars so loud it makes my ears ring.

Jesse pulls me into a hug when I get offstage. I hug him back, forgetting to care about all the eyes always on us.

When we pull away from each other, he doesn't say anything, but I feel that he's proud of me. As he heads onstage, I let out a relieved breath. I got through a performance without any meds. Jesse had a lot to do with that. I can't deny how intimate it felt to meditate together, but I try to focus on the fact that his support helped me keep it together tonight. I can let both feelings exist. I just have to keep them in check and this crush will finally pass.

25

"Um, Ollie? Hi." A South Asian kid who looks about fourteen or fifteen stands in front of me at the meet and greet table. He smiles a little, but he's visibly nervous. "It's great to meet you."

"You too," I say as I take a T-shirt from him to sign. I'm still feeling pretty good after the success of the show, my nerves at a manageable level. "What's your name?"

"I'm Absi. I actually, uh, do music too. I've been watching your stuff on YouTube for a while," he says, his voice quiet.

I grin. "That's so awesome! What's the name of your channel?"

He blinks at me, seeming surprised at the question. "Oh. It's Acoustic Absi."

"Sweet, I'll check it out," I tell him as I hand the T-shirt back.

"You will?" He shakes his head. "You don't have to. My stuff isn't that good."

"I'm sure you're great! I'll definitely check it out, okay? Do you wanna do a picture together?"

"Oh yeah, I almost forgot to ask," he says as he pulls out his phone, his hands shaking.

"I can take it if you want," I offer. He shoots me a relieved smile and passes me his phone.

"Thanks again," Absi says when I hand the phone back. He's looking at his feet now. "There was, uh, something else I wanted to tell you, if that's okay."

"Sure," I say in a way that I hope is reassuring. He looks even more nervous now than when he first started talking to me. His voice grows quieter, and I have to lean in to hear him.

He goes on to tell me that my single meant a lot to him because of his own assault experience. He shares some details that are tough to hear. His story is like so many of the personal messages I've gotten from fans online, but this is the first time I'm hearing something so heavy in person. I'm thankful that I'm feeling calm enough to hold space for him. I know what it must be taking for him to be this vulnerable with me, and I really hope I'm communicating that to him even though I'm just listening.

"Everything okay here?" I suddenly hear Tim's voice behind me. "There are people waiting."

Absi's been speaking for a while, but I didn't want to interrupt.

I nod at Tim briefly. "Yeah, just another minute."

Tim nods and I focus on Absi again.

"Sorry for taking up so much of your time," he says. "I really appreciate you listening."

"Of course, thanks for sharing that with me. Can I give you a hug?" I ask him.

He nods and I throw an arm around his shoulder. "I'm glad you're doing better now. Just message me if you ever want to talk more. I'll subscribe to your channel, okay?"

He manages a small smile. "Thanks again, Ollie."

When a new group of fans approaches, I plaster a smile on my face again even as my stomach turns. I can't stop thinking about what Absi just told me. How could someone hurt such a sweet kid?

I flash back to the interview with Anthony Rodgers and my discomfort rises. I remind myself that I don't have to feel guilty about not being ready to publicly share my experience. I'm still trying to take things at my own pace, and I feel like I'm getting more comfortable with the idea of talking to Aisha about it when I get back. But the heavy ache of hearing Absi's story makes me think about the weight that I'd be putting on Aisha. She said she could handle hearing about it, but now I'm acutely aware how painful it might be for her.

*

"You're being quiet," Jesse says, back in the van later.

We're headed to a campground a few hours away from Saskatoon, where we plan to stay on the way to our next show in Calgary.

I sigh as I look out into the darkness. Even though I don't think I'm prepared to fully get into what Absi shared, maybe Jesse has some general advice for dealing with fans opening up like that. "Yeah. There was this kid at the meet and greet who ... he shared some really personal stuff with me. I'm glad he felt comfortable telling me, but it was a lot."

I try not to shrink away from Jesse's cautious gaze. I feel way too exposed, like he knows exactly why it was tough for me to hear Absi's story.

"I get it," he says quietly. "I know they just want to share how our music's helped them get through tough times, but it can be hard to process all of that in, like, a five-minute interaction. Sometimes I still have no idea how to react. But I've figured out that, mostly, you don't have to do anything besides listen and then take some time to yourself after."

I look over at him. "That makes a lot of sense. Thanks, man."

"Of course. And let me know if you ever want to talk through it when stuff like that happens."

I nod then put my earbuds in, my thoughts still buzzing. It's hard to think about fans sharing traumatic things with me on a regular basis. I remember what Victor said about dealing with fans' assumptions about his experiences and using characters to separate his personal life from that. Maybe that's something I could explore more in my own songwriting. I want to keep creating music that's meaningful and possibly even healing for people . . . and for me. But at the same time, I want to create some boundaries with what I'm putting out there.

In the meantime, I'm glad Jesse's here if I ever need help handling stuff like this. Maybe I'm finally getting the hang of this support thing. I flip from my playlist over to my draft for the blog, reading it over a few more times. When I press the button to send it to Kamran, I don't feel the twinge of fear I thought I would. I exhale, feeling my body relax as my thoughts are finally washed away by the calming music filling my ears.

*

When we arrive at the campsite, Tim agrees to camp at another site with the rest of the security team and leaves the van to Jesse and me for the night. We hang our feet out the back doors as we stare up at the breathtaking night sky.

"I don't think I've ever seen this many stars before," I say, breaking the comfortable silence between us.

"Yeah, away from the city it's kind of otherworldly, isn't it? It's views like this that make me feel like life is just too inexplicably beautiful to be a random accident, you know?"

"It really is incredible," I agree. "But there's also so much horrible shit that happens that makes it hard to think that there's some bigger plan or whatever. I don't know if that makes sense." I'm thinking about what Absi told me again and everything I went through with Thomas.

"It makes perfect sense," Jesse says with a sigh. "Even with all the heinous things happening, I try to take in every bit of good that I can. Like this moment is just as precious and amazing as us performing with Victor and Sera the other night. The big stuff and the small stuff. I hope in, like, fifty years I still remember all of it, how important it all is."

We fall into silence again and I can tell he's meditating. I clear my mind, too, settling into the present moment with him. We stay like that for a long while until I suddenly jump up, grabbing my notebook.

"What are you working on?" Jesse asks.

"Just thought of some lyrics for something." I think I figured out a hook for the song I've been writing about my relationship with my dad.

"Yeah?" Jesse says. "Let's hear it."

"Um . . . I don't think it's something I'm, like, ready to put on the album or anything."

Jesse nods. "I'd still love to hear. If that's okay."

I bite my lip. Keeping Victor's words in mind, I wrote these latest lyrics from a place that creates some distance between me and the issues I'm not comfortable sharing publicly. I don't think they're too transparently vulnerable for me to share.

I finally nod and sing out the words that just popped into my head about trying to sever the root of the shame loop I've been trapped in.

Jesse listens attentively and is quiet for a bit when I finish. "You really pinpointed how hard it can be to escape generational cycles. How helpless it feels to fight it sometimes, like trying to reverse the tide."

We look at each other for a long minute and I try to choke down the knot forming in my throat. I'm taken aback at just how much he understands the core of my lyrics and how clear it is he can relate to them. It almost makes me want to share more with him, but I stop short—my throat tightening like a physical warning that I'm not quite ready, that this is enough for now. I should probably keep pacing myself since this is so new to me.

"Reverse the tide," I repeat before focusing on my notebook again. "I think that's perfect for the hook, actually."

We work on it together for another hour until Jesse falls asleep around midnight. I'm just about to pass out, too, when my phone rings.

"Hello?" I whisper, trying not to wake Jesse.

"Happy birthday!" Aisha whispers back excitedly. She's a few hours ahead in Toronto so it's three in the morning for her. "Oh, and happy anniversary, too."

"Aw. Thanks, Aisha." I break into a goofy smile as I start to sit up.

I've been so busy I hadn't thought much about my birthday coming up. "Uh, my birthday isn't our anniversary, though."

"We first kissed at your party, remember?"

"Yeah, of course I remember. But that doesn't count because . . ." I trail off, hating that I'm reminding her what an idiot I was for bailing on her that night. "I mean, I thought our anniversary was in a few days. You know, when I first played 'On Repeat' for you?"

"Hmm. Okay, that can be our anniversary then. I like that better actually." I can hear the smile in her voice, and I imagine it lighting up her whole face, her beautiful eyes bright and shining. Suddenly, it feels like she's right here with me, erasing all the distance I've been feeling between us.

"I wish I could see you," I murmur as I get out of the van, sliding the door shut as quietly as I can.

"Me too. Ugh, I miss you so much," she groans.

I laugh quietly as I sit down, huddling on a bench near the van. "I miss you, too. Do you want to turn on your camera?"

"Why?"

"I don't know. I just wanna see you. Please?"

"Oh, fine. Just a sec, let me turn the light on." She flips on her camera and then buries her face in her pillow. "God, I look like crap. I'm so tired."

I shake my head and she finally lifts her face from her pillow to roll her eyes at me. "Hey, you look great. Thanks for calling so late, I know you've been busy."

"I guess, but it's not like I'm touring around the country or anything," she teases. "Where are you right now? It looks like you're outside—isn't it cold?"

"We're a few hours from Calgary. We're camping in the van tonight. It's really nice out there."

"Oh yeah? Calgary's pretty close to my old dance academy. I bet it's gorgeous out," she says.

I look back at the screen and grin at her. "Well. You're pretty gorgeous, too."

She pretends to gag then bursts into giggles. "Uh, no. *You* are. I like your hair that long."

Even before I left, I had been overdue for a haircut. I think it's the longest it's ever been, an inch or two below my ears. If I was at home, I know I'd probably be worried about my dad commenting on it looking too feminine. But I'm trying to focus on what I want to do. "Thanks. Anyway, how was your showcase? You didn't say much when you texted."

She tells me how it went and I'm relieved to hear she felt okay about it. "I've decided I'm going to audition for some contemporary ballet companies instead of classical. Which is so weird because I always imagined myself at a classical company. But I think I'm finally letting go of, like, all my mom's brainwashing," she says quietly.

"I'm so glad you're doing what you feel most passionate about. That's awesome, Aisha."

"Ditto," she says. "It's been so unbelievable seeing you out there in front of so many people every night. Oh, and how did your interview go? I didn't have time to watch it."

"Well . . ." I take a deep breath, reminding myself that this is safe to talk to her about. That I've been wanting to be more open with her and this is my chance to finally be real about what happened. "I got asked if I had personal experience with assault and I kind of froze. I said that I . . . that I didn't. I just wasn't ready to, like, tell the world. I know that's okay, but I still feel weird about it. And then at the meet and greet tonight, this kid shared his assault experience with me. I'm glad he shared, but it was just kind of heavy after the interview and everything."

"Ollie . . ." Aisha's giving me a solemn look, but it's not pitying. If anything, she seems moved that I opened up to her about it. "That all sounds like a lot. That's good that you felt okay setting that boundary in the interview. I'm glad a fan felt comfortable enough to share that with you. But yeah, I'm sure it was hard to hear. Do you want to talk about it more?"

I give her a small, grateful smile. "Thanks, Aisha. I . . . I actually do want to, um, talk more with you about what happened when I get back. Does that sound okay?"

"Of course," she says gently. "You know how much I love you, right?"

My smile gets bigger. "I love you too. I should let you get to sleep now, though."

"Yeah, you're probably right," she says regretfully.

After a drawn-out goodbye, we finally hang up. I let out a long sigh as I look up at the stars again. It's almost worse when we talk because then the sinking weight of how much I hate being away from her gets even heavier. I try to remind myself it's only a couple more months, but that doesn't help.

I am glad that I was able to start being more open with her about what I've been dealing with lately. She was just as great about it as I knew she'd be.

The cold starts to get to me after a few minutes, and I head back inside the van and try to get some sleep.

＊

Sophie calls me while we're driving to Calgary the next morning and starts singing "Happy Birthday" to me at top volume.

Jesse looks over from his spot beside me. "It's your birthday?"

I shrug distractedly as Sophie continues.

"So how does it feel to be eighteen?"

"Can't say I feel any different yet, but I'll let you know when I do."

"You sound a little grumpy. Are you okay?"

"Yeah, I'm doing good. Just tired of all the driving. How about you, how's school?"

"Just busy with midterms, nothing exciting. Are you sure you're okay, though? I saw that Anthony Rodgers interview."

I take in a steadying breath. "I'm doing all right." I'm glad I talked to Aisha last night, but I'm not ready to rehash it with Soph right now. "Thanks for checking in, I appreciate it." The phone beeps, and I check the screen. "Oh, that's Mom calling, gotta go."

"Okay, hope you have a great birthday, Ollie!"

"Thanks, Soph." I end the call and pick up the other line. "Hey Mom."

"Happy birthday, sweet boy!" she practically screams.

"Thanks." I wince at her volume and glance over at Jesse. I'm sure he heard, but he keeps his eyes on his own phone.

"Your father says happy birthday, too," she continues. "We miss you so much! How are you, have you been eating enough?"

I contain a sigh. "Yes."

"What have you been eating, though? I hope you're not only eating fast food—"

"Thanks for calling, but I can't really talk right now," I say quickly.

"Can I call you back later?"

"Okay, have a good day, wlidi!"

Jesse lets out a chuckle as soon as I hang up and my face burns. My mother never fails to embarrass me. We haven't talked on the phone in a couple weeks though, so it was nice to hear her voice.

"That was cute," he says. "Happy birthday. Why didn't you say anything earlier?"

"Thanks. I don't know, it's not a big deal."

"Your eighteenth birthday isn't a big deal?"

"I mean, I guess I can buy lottery tickets now. So that's exciting."

He lets out a big laugh. "Well, we definitely have to do something to celebrate after the show tonight."

His laughter is so infectious, I can't help but grin.

*
*

We arrive at the small club in Calgary a few hours later. Jesse's performed here before and knows some of the crew. Usually, the crew keeps their distance from the talent, but everyone is really friendly and they even let us help set everything up for the show.

"You seem to know what you're doing," one of the stage managers, Darren, says as I connect the looping equipment.

"I work at a small venue in Toronto. I help with lighting and sound sometimes."

"Nice," Darren says. "Let me know if you have any ideas for your lighting setup tonight."

"Really?" I've never been asked for input on stuff like this before. Back at work, I would sometimes imagine what it would be like to help build the atmosphere of a show. I never thought I'd get to do it for my own performance. "Awesome, I'd love to share some ideas."

We finish setting up the equipment then play around with the lights during sound check. As I rehearse my set with the lights changing at just the right time, I start to get chills. I have a feeling this is going to be a stellar show.

I live stream some of Jesse's rehearsal and then we head back to our greenroom before the show starts.

"Did you want to meditate for a bit?" Jesse asks.

I'm not feeling that nervous for once, but it couldn't hurt.

We sit on the couch in silence and I remain calm, the anticipation in my stomach slowly building. I visualize myself onstage, feeling completely at ease.

I open my eyes and see Jesse's already looking at me. Without any words passing between us, I know he can tell I'm ready to go. We both break into big smiles, and I feel breathless but in a good, excited way.

I head out onstage and the crowd gets as loud as it can possibly get. My heart's beating super fast, but I don't feel shaky as I take my place at the mic. I feel like I'm in the right place, like I'm supposed to be here. As I launch into my first song, the energy in the audience steadily rises, the crowd getting more and more into it. I fully relax into the moment, feeding off all the energy in the room and using it to fuel my performance.

The entire audience sings along as I finish "Until the Stars Burn." It's been turning into a fan favorite. I scan the faces in the crowd, and my eyes land on a pretty girl near the back. Her dark brown skin is radiant, bathed in the indigo lights swirling around the room. She has her long braids pulled back in a messy bun, the way Aisha wears her hair. My eyes connect with hers and my heart slows to a complete stop.

It's Aisha. She's here.

26

I stop singing for a moment and just stare at her. Her eyes are glistening, but she breaks into a huge smile.

"*Keep going,*" she mouths at me.

I finally snap out of it and continue the song, unable to look away from her. She's still smiling, even as she wipes at her eyes. I know we're thinking the same thing, that it feels like an entire lifetime since I first sang this song for her. I blink hard, getting choked up as I finish my last note.

The audience cheers, and I head offstage.

"My girlfriend just showed up! I'm gonna go talk to her, okay?" I say to Jesse in a rush.

"Aw, that's so sweet! I was wondering what happened when you stopped singing. You saw her out there?"

"Yeah, I'll introduce you after your set. Good luck!"

I pull my phone out of my pocket and text Aisha to meet me near the backstage entrance, then head there myself, letting the security guards know to let her in.

As soon as I spot her, I rush over and wrap my arms around her, picking her up off her feet.

"I can't believe you're here! Why didn't you say anything this morning?"

She laughs as she hugs me back. "To surprise you, dummy!"

We're interrupted by Greg herding us further inside so security can close the door again. I take her hand as I lead the way to the greenroom.

"How did you even get here so fast?" I ask, shaking my head in disbelief.

She avoids my gaze. "Um, my dad had some extra flyer miles on the card he lets me use. It's the same flight I used to take over to my old ballet school."

I look at her sideways. "How'd you convince him to let you come out here?"

Aisha pauses. "He's on a business trip this weekend. But I'll be back home before he knows I left," she says as we reach the greenroom door.

My eyes widen. "What if he sees online that you showed up?"

"Don't worry. He's not on social media and doesn't look at stupid gossip sites or anything like that. We're good."

"You're sure? But what if he checks the card history?"

"I don't care." She leans in and crushes her lips to mine, pushing me up against the door as soon as it shuts behind us.

When she pulls back, I lean into her again, kissing her more intently.

"I missed you so much," I murmur against her mouth. I wrap my arms around her even tighter.

"Okay, we should probably relax now," she says with a breathless laugh when she eventually pulls away again. She takes a seat on the small couch by the door.

I sit next to her, pulling her into my lap and resting my forehead against hers. "I'm so glad you're here."

"Me too," she says and then we're kissing again and neither of us is stopping. She grips my shoulders, then her fingers start to slide across my back, making me shiver.

"Oh, sorry!"

At the sound of Jesse's voice, Aisha and I fly apart.

Aisha covers her face with her hands. "Oh God."

"It's cool, I'll get out of your way," Jesse says quickly as he turns to exit again.

I shake my head, even as blood rushes to my face. "That's okay. Jesse, this is Aisha. Aisha, Jesse."

She jumps up to shake Jesse's hand. "Hi, it's great to finally meet you. Thanks so much for everything you've done for Ollie."

Jesse smiles, but it looks strained. I think I catch something a little sad in his eyes, but it's gone in an instant. "Don't mention it. It's great to meet you, too."

I'm still frozen on the couch. I can't exactly get up right now, so I just squirm in the awkward silence, unable to think of anything else to say. Being in the same space with both of them is breaking down the careful compartmentalization I've set up in my brain.

"I can meet you back at the van and then we can all grab some dinner?" Jesse suggests after another painfully long second.

"Sounds good," I say. "We'll meet you there in a few."

Once Jesse leaves, Aisha spins back toward me and squeezes the bridge of her nose. "That was *awful*."

I pull her back down next to me on the couch. "It's no big deal. Jesse's chill, it's fine." I do my best not to think about what I thought I just saw in Jesse's eyes and why it might be there.

She groans, leaning her head against my shoulder. "Dinner sounds like a good idea."

I wrap my arms around her again, just breathing her in for a long minute. Finally, I get up, pulling her with me. "Okay, come on."

*

"That was so beyond unbelievable, seeing you out there," Aisha says as she unwraps her shawarma. Security said it wasn't safe to eat at the Lebanese place Jesse suggested because there were too many fans there, so we got takeout. We're on the road to the campground we'll be staying at just outside the city. "I've never seen you perform like that—you looked so confident!"

"Gee, thanks," I blurt out darkly.

She winces. "Oll, I didn't mean it like that . . ."

"I'm just kidding, you're okay," I assure her quickly. I kiss her temple then glance at Jesse in the seats in front of us. "Jesse's been a big help."

He smiles, shaking his head. "It's all you, man. You killed out there tonight."

I shrug, uncomfortable with all the attention. I change the subject, letting Aisha tell Jesse about some of the dance programs she's hoping to get into next year. All of them are in New York, which I'm trying not to think about too much. Once I'm back home, we'll only have a few more months until she graduates and leaves. The thought makes me sick to my stomach and I put my shawarma down.

"That sounds fun, dancing in New York," Jesse says. "Do you model too? You'll probably find lots of work there."

Aisha squeaks out a high-pitched laugh. "That's nice of you to say, but I don't think I could ever model."

"Why not? You're super beautiful," he says.

Aisha's eyes widen and I spot a faint bit of color rising in her cheeks. "Oh. Uh . . ."

My stomach churns even more as I study Jesse. That moment when he caught Aisha and me in the greenroom had me worried that the three of us hanging out might be strange. And honestly, it is a bit strange . . . but they seem to be getting along just fine. Maybe more than I'm comfortable with.

I push the thought away. He was just stating the obvious. It's hard to ignore how stunning she is. Jesse notices me staring at him and he reddens, looking down. "Sorry, I, uh—"

"That's okay," Aisha cuts in. "I mean, thanks. It's just that modeling is a pretty toxic industry, and I've already dealt with a lot of that in ballet."

I rub her shoulder. She smiles a little before leaning into me and squeezing my hand.

"That sounds rough," Jesse says.

"Yeah, it's been kind of difficult, but things have been better lately. I'm enjoying dancing a lot more again."

"That's great," Jesse says as the van turns onto a small trail. "I think we're almost here."

*
*

Security stays near the entrance of the park, letting us camp on our own again. We pick a site with a great view near a tranquil little pond that reflects the dazzling night sky.

"This place is fantastic!" Aisha says.

I nod, slowly breathing in the night air. It's still unusually warm for so late in October.

"It's one of my favorite spots," Jesse says. "I usually pass through here and the park we stayed at last night when I'm traveling across the country by myself. A bit of a different experience in my own van without the pigs lurking around the bend."

Aisha nods sympathetically. "It must be weird having them around everywhere you go."

"I kind of hate it," Jesse mutters. "This is still a nice break, though."

"Definitely." Even though it's annoying to have security around all the time, I do appreciate them being there when fans get overexcited. I open the back of the van and grab my guitar and a couple of blankets. "Are you up to jam tonight?" I ask Jesse.

"I'm up for it," Jesse says, grabbing his own guitar.

We sit on the dock at the edge of the pond and dive into some of the new stuff we've been working on.

"I love this!" Aisha nods her head to the quickening rhythm then jumps up and starts dancing. "This is so good, you guys!"

I grin stupidly, unable to take my eyes off her as she spins and twirls to the beat.

She stares right back at me then leans down and takes my guitar from my lap. "Come here." Grabbing my hands, she pulls me to my feet.

Clumsy as always, I somehow stumble right into her. We both laugh. She wraps her arms around my neck, and my arms circle her waist as we steady each other.

"Careful!" she scolds me, still laughing. "We almost went right into the water."

"Speaking of which," Jesse says, "growing up, me and my friends back home had a little birthday tradition . . ."

"Uh, hell no." I know where this is headed. "This water has to be ice cold."

"It'll be refreshing!" Jesse takes off his jacket and then his shirt as he gets up. I quickly move my gaze from his exposed skin, pushing the dream I had about him away.

"Are you out of your mind?" I barely get the words out before he's cannonballing into the pond.

"*What the hell?!*" Aisha shrieks. She tries to jump back from Jesse's splash zone, but it's too late. Icy droplets spray both of us from head to toe.

I wipe water out of my eyes. "Dude. I can't believe you just did that!"

Thankfully, our instruments just barely survived unscathed. I shake my head as I set the guitars farther from the edge of the dock, where I stashed the blankets.

"Come on in!" Jesse waves at us.

Aisha shakes her head, shrugging off her wet coat. "No thanks. Not a fan of hypothermia."

"The shock only lasts for a minute," Jesse says. "It's the most invigorating feeling ever, you have to try it!"

I start to take off my wet jacket, too. "Well, we're already soaked, I guess."

"That's the spirit!" Jesse says. "Aisha, are you down?"

She lets out a defeated sigh. "Okay. Just for a minute though."

Jesse cheers as we take off the rest of our wet clothes and I try to ignore how deeply awkward I feel.

People go skinny-dipping. This is what fun people do. Just don't be weird and stare or anything.

Not staring proves to be difficult when Aisha steps right in front of me, beaming as she takes my hand. "You ready?"

Fuck no. I force myself to nod and then we hop off the dock together.

The water feels like a million needles piercing my skin. I can't think about anything besides the cold.

Aisha screams bloody murder, immediately scrambling back onto the dock and wrapping herself in a blanket.

"Why did I do that!" she barely gets out, her teeth chattering. "That was so stupid!"

I'm too frozen to even move a muscle, my internal systems panicking.

"You're good, just breathe through it." Jesse's treading water next to me now. "Think of it like meditating. If you focus on your inner body, the shock starts to wear off."

I nod, then close my eyes and concentrate on drawing air into my lungs. I slowly become aware of the warmth still inside them. I keep inhaling as deeply as I can, visualizing the heat in my chest spreading out to thaw my frozen limbs. After a minute, the needles are gone and this pumped-up high shoots through me. It's just like how I felt when I was onstage earlier. I finally pull myself up onto the dock.

Aisha sits next to me, sharing her blanket and then locking her arms around me.

"Are you okay?" she asks, still shivering violently. "How are you not shaking?"

"Yeah, I'm okay now." I rub her arms to warm her up. "Try doing what Jesse said. It honestly helped."

Aisha looks up and shoots Jesse a glare. "Do you not have nerve endings?" she grumbles.

He laughs as he climbs out of the water. I avert my eyes again as all the warmth inside me migrates to my face. "I told you, I used to do this all the time with my friends. Sometimes in the middle of winter."

"And you never got sick?" she asks.

He shakes his head. "Try the breathing thing, I promise it'll warm you up."

"Okay," Aisha says with a sigh, closing her eyes.

I close mine too, focusing on my own breathing again as I wrap my arms around her.

"It's like there's a heat source in your core, warming you from the inside out," I say, pressing my palms flat to her stomach.

She takes hold of my wrists with her icy fingers, keeping my hands pressed to her skin. "Well, you're helping, at least. How are you *always* warm? Even after that?"

After a few minutes she stops shivering, her breath slowing.

"Feeling better?" I ask, opening my eyes.

"A little." She smiles at me and then glances at Jesse, who's leaning back on his elbows with his eyes closed. "That wasn't exactly as 'invigorating' as you claimed."

He grins, not opening his eyes. "First time's always the toughest."

"More like the last time," Aisha mutters, punching him lightly on the shoulder.

Jesse just laughs, and after a second Aisha joins in.

I hear my phone ring in the pile of clothes behind us.

I pull on my jeans and retrieve my phone from the back pocket. "Hello?"

"Happy birthday, buddy!" Neil yells into my ear. There's loud music playing in the background.

"Who's that?" Aisha asks. She holds an arm out, gesturing for me to pass over her clothes.

"It's Neil," I say as I hand her stuff over. "Hey, thanks, man!"

"Tell him I say hi!" Aisha says.

"Happy birthday, Ollie!" a chorus of voices calls out.

"That was Ebi, Khadija, and everyone," Neil says, still shouting over the noise. "You having a good night with Aisha? She get over there okay?"

"Yeah, she's okay. Everything's good," I assure him. "Are you good? Ebi's having a theater party?"

"Yeah, just doing a trivia night at his place," he says. "Don't worry, everything's on the up and up."

I can't hear him that well, but he sounds completely sober. I need to stop worrying about him so much. He's been working his ass off to stay clean for a while now.

"That's cool. So, um . . ." I bite my lip. It feels kind of awkward since we never talk about stuff like this and have been talking even less since I've been gone, but I think I should tell him how much I appreciate what a good friend he's been . . . and about the song, since I've been meaning to for a while. "There's something I wanted to talk to you about," I finish, lowering my voice.

I pace in a slow circle a few feet back from Aisha and Jesse.

"Is it about the blog thing you're working on?" he asks.

"No, not that." I haven't gotten any feedback from Kamran yet, but he said he'd take a look soon. Things have been too hectic for me to obsess over it . . . so far, at least.

"Oh. Is . . . this about Sophie? I'm really sorry, dude. She asked me not to say anything after the festival. I didn't want to, like, lie to you."

I rub at my forehead, containing a sigh. "It's not about Soph."

"Oh. Shit." He laughs awkwardly. "God, she's gonna kill me. I'm sorry—"

"Neil, it's fine, she already told me," I say under my breath. I walk a few more feet away from Aisha and Jesse, who are chatting quietly. "I'm not mad."

"You're not?" he asks skeptically. "What's up then?"

"I just wanted to tell you I'm proud of you for how well you've been doing lately. I know it must be tough, but I really appreciate that you've kept at it."

"Thanks, Ollie," he says seriously, somehow refraining from making a joke to lighten the moment. "That means a lot, man. I'm proud of you, too. I know you said you're handling everything okay, but I get it must be a lot for you to deal with since you get stage fright sometimes. Playing all these shows and doing interviews. Plus, you know, people constantly prying and making assumptions about personal stuff that isn't their business."

"Yeah. It's a lot, but I'm still talking to my therapist and stuff so I'm good," I assure him. It's been tough to deal with, but I think I've been managing okay recently.

"Okay, cool. I get that you want to keep your private stuff private, but . . . if there's anything you want to tell me about, I wouldn't ever, like, judge you or anything. No matter what. You know that, right?"

I nod as my throat starts to clog with emotion. I know he partly means if I want to talk about what happened with Thomas, but I think he's also talking about me being bi. I appreciate him reaffirming that I can talk to him whenever I'm ready.

"I know. Thanks, man." I clear my throat. "What I wanted to ask you about is if it's okay if I mention you in a song for my album? Not by name or anything, it's just about, you know, us being friends and your recovery and stuff."

"Oh, okay. Yeah, that's totally fine by me. And that's really cool, I'm excited to hear the song." Even with the bad connection I can hear the sincerity in his voice.

We talk for a few more minutes before hanging up, then I let out a relieved sigh. That went better than I thought it would. I'm so lucky to have him. As stressful as the tour's been, I feel like I was able to be more open with Neil because of some of the experiences I've had on the road. Part of me still wishes things could be like they were before I left, even just for a little bit. But I know that's impossible.

27

When I get back to the dock, Jesse and Aisha are huddled close, sharing a blanket now.

Aisha scoots away from Jesse as I approach. "It's still really cold," she says in a rush. I swear her face starts to flush again, like when he said she was beautiful. "Everything okay with Neil? You were talking for a while."

I glance over at Jesse as he leans back on his elbows again, looking totally relaxed.

"Are you good?" he asks me when I don't respond to Aisha.

I nod slowly as a sour twinge of annoyance bubbles up inside me. I can't exactly tell if I'm jealous that Aisha seems to like being so close to him or if I'm annoyed that Jesse is paying so much attention to her and not me. Maybe it's a little of both. I push the feeling down and just try to be relieved they're getting along.

"I'm fine. I was just talking to Neil about a song I wrote." I sit next to Aisha and pull her into my lap, gathering her tightly in my arms. "It's about his recovery stuff so I wanted to make sure it's cool with him if I release it. He said it's okay."

"That's sweet," Aisha says, kissing me on the cheek. "Do you feel like playing the song right now?"

"I'd love to hear it too," Jesse says.

"Sure." I give Aisha's hands a firm squeeze then get up again to grab my guitar.

Aisha and Jesse listen quietly, my voice and the chords the only sound besides the gentle motion of the pond at our feet. The unease I felt earlier completely slips away.

Aisha wipes her eyes when I finish.

"That was perfect." She leans in and kisses me. "I'm glad you were there for him when I couldn't be. I'm so happy he's doing better now."

I just nod, feeling choked up as I put my guitar down and cuddle up to her again.

"That's really powerful," Jesse says softly, looking away. "I, um, have some friends who've struggled with addiction, too."

"Sorry to hear that," I tell him when he looks up again. "I know how difficult that can be, watching a friend go through that."

Jesse nods, his eyes far away. "Thanks. I had to distance myself from them just to keep my own sanity. I do miss them, though. Our show tomorrow night is near the area where I grew up."

"Are you thinking about maybe visiting while we're in Vancouver?" I ask carefully. "I mean, if you have time and if you feel up for it."

Jesse sighs. "I'm not sure yet. I guess I'll see how I feel when I get there."

I debate saying more but decide to let it drop for now. I want to be there for him the way he has been for me recently. But I know better than anyone that even the small bit he just shared probably took a lot out of him.

When it gets late, we head back to the van. Thankfully there's a small generator so we have a bit of heat, but from how Aisha's shivering in my arms I can feel that she's still not used to the cooler temperature.

"Are you gonna be okay?" I ask. We're cuddled up in the backseat while Jesse snores up front. "Do you want another sweater?"

"I'll be fine." She turns away so I'm spooning her.

When she snuggles even closer, my body starts to react.

I pull back a little. "Sorry."

"It's okay," she whispers, pressing herself into me again.

"Aisha . . ." I can't think straight. She's moving her hips against me now and I clamp down on a groan. "Aisha, I really wish we were alone right now."

"Why? What would you do if we were alone?" she breathes.

"You know."

"Say it, though. Tell me."

So I do. I whisper into her ear, and she keeps moving against me until I almost can't take it.

"You have to stop. You're making me crazy," I barely get out.

She turns and starts kissing my neck. I bite my tongue, doing my best not to make any noise.

Suddenly there's a flash of light right outside the window.

We both freeze.

"What was that?" Aisha whispers.

"I don't know." I sit up, my heart racing.

There's a bang on the door and Aisha yelps. "Oh my God, who is that?"

"What's going on?" Jesse asks, jolting upright.

"There's someone outside," I hiss. There's another bang on the door. I squint through the windows, but it's too dark to tell who's out there.

Jesse curses. "I'll go check it out."

"Wait!" I leap up, catching his arm. "We should call security instead."

Jesse frowns at me for a long moment but then sits back down, sighing. "Okay, you're probably right."

I call Tim and tell him what's going on. The light flashes again and there's more banging. Aisha holds on tight to my shoulder, shooting me a terrified look.

"Don't worry, it's gonna be fine," I assure her, even though I'm scared myself.

Blinding headlights appear a few minutes later. We hear car doors opening and what sounds like Greg and Tim talking to someone.

"Okay!" An unfamiliar male voice says right outside the van. "I'm going. You'll burn for this. You'll see."

There's another louder bang at the van door and we all jump.

"It's me," Tim calls out.

Jesse slides the door open. "What the hell happened? Who was that?"

Tim sighs, his face grim as he gets into the driver's seat and starts the car. "Some deranged fan. He tailed us from the show earlier. Said it was his 'mission to save you from sin' or something."

What does that mean? My stomach turns as my mind goes to the rumors about Jesse and me, wondering if whoever was out there was some kind of homophobic zealot.

"He might have tipped other people off about our location," Tim continues. "We should get out of here."

We're all silent on the drive out of the park. I squeeze Aisha's hand and she shoots me a weak smile, but she still looks freaked out. I am too—that could have gone a lot worse. Helen said people might try to follow us, but it didn't seem like a real possibility.

I'm one hundred percent sure Helen isn't going to be thrilled about this when we talk to her tomorrow. She's probably going to increase our security even more, which I know Jesse will hate. I don't love it either, but I'm willing to deal with it as long as we're safe.

*
*

Right before dawn, Tim finds us a cozy log cabin bed-and-breakfast with a few rooms available. Aisha and I are still pretty wired when we say good night to Jesse and head to our room.

We cuddle together in a big bed that's about a thousand times warmer and more comfortable than the backseat of the van.

"You okay?" I ask her after a few minutes of silence. Aisha's far-off gaze finally focuses on me, her face lit by the small fireplace by the window.

"Sorry, what?"

I tuck some stray braids behind her ear and study her. "I just wanted to check how you're feeling now. That was really scary."

"Yeah. It was." She sighs and presses her forehead to mine. "I guess I never really considered that stuff like that would happen now that you're famous."

I wince internally at her calling me famous. "I never thought much about it either."

Aisha leans back to look at me again. "How are you feeling though?"

"I'm a little freaked too. But mainly I'm just glad we're okay." I kiss her gently and she kisses me back, softly at first and then more urgently. Soon my brain is turning to mush and I pull away from her before I lose myself completely. "Aisha, wait. I . . ."

The way she's looking at me makes whatever I was about to say vanish from my mind.

"Remember what you said earlier?" she murmurs in my ear. "About what you wanted to do when we're alone?"

I just nod. I'm having trouble breathing, much less speaking.

"Oh. You mean, like, now." I finally get out. "Didn't you say before I left that you wanted to wait until I got back home?"

Aisha looks away, biting her lip. "Yeah, I was worried it was going to make it more difficult to be apart . . . But it's already been so much harder than I thought it would be." Her voice breaks. "How much worse can it get? And we're here now, so . . ."

I shake my head, taking her chin in my hand. "I get that it's been way harder than we thought. But just because we're here doesn't mean we have to. Are you sure this is what you want?"

She takes my hand, squeezing it gently. "I'm sure," she says, and a nuclear jolt goes through me. I can feel how much she means it. "Oll, you know I love you. And I completely understand if you don't want to right now."

"I love you, too. And—" My own voice breaks now, and I clear my throat. "I want to. It's just . . . remember on the phone last night when I said I wanted to talk to you about . . ." I close my eyes, mustering all my courage. I can do this. I want to share this with her and I know that even if it makes her sad, she'll be okay. We both will. "About what happened with my assault?"

She nods and keeps squeezing my hand while I tell her, holding space for me to voice the things that I used to think would destroy me if they were uttered aloud. But once the words are out, it's like all the power, all the shame Thomas held over me isn't as crushing anymore.

And afterward, when we stop speaking with words, we find ourselves communing in a space of our own creation where nothing goes untouched by the warm, safe glow of the firelight.

✳

"Morning," Aisha says, slowly sitting up in bed as I hand her a mug of coffee. "Thanks. Did you sleep at all?"

I shake my head. It's probably the lack of sleep, but last night doesn't feel like it actually happened. It's like we've been here for an eternity and a split second all at once. I'm doing my best to block out the thought of having to leave soon, allowing myself to stay as deeply rooted in the present as I can. "Just enjoyed the view."

I grin dopily as I sit next to her and she breaks into a big smile too, her face flushing even as she rolls her eyes at me.

"What a line."

"I meant the actual view," I say, pointing out the window at the majestic mountain range rising behind the B and B. We're right across from a steaming, natural hot spring too.

She turns to look and gasps. "Oh! It's like a postcard out there."

"But you're still a great view too," I add, breaking into another big smile.

She laughs, resting her head on my shoulder with a sigh. "I can't believe I have to go home today."

My heart drops painfully. I wrap an arm around her shoulders. "I know."

We stay like that for a while before she speaks again, pulling away from me to study my eyes. "How are you feeling about . . ." She trails off, looking worried. "I mean, are you feeling okay about last night?"

I nod, smiling gently, and her face relaxes. "I feel great. How about you?"

She fits her fingers through mine and looks at me in a way that she's never looked at me before. It's like all the distance between us—that we'd been feeling even before I left—has disappeared now that I've truly let her in. "I feel great, too."

We stare at each other for a moment, and it's hard to describe how grateful I am for her. But I know I have to try. "Aisha . . . thanks for never making me feel like there was something wrong with me for needing to take my time with stuff. For a while, I thought . . . I thought I would never feel okay enough to be with anyone like this. I love you so much."

She tears up and then whispers it back before capturing my mouth with hers.

28

"Ollie? Are you listening?"

I snap back to the present to see Helen frowning at me on Jesse's phone screen. We're sitting in the back of a new rental van, on our way to Vancouver. Tonight will be our biggest show yet, a three-thousand-seat stadium. My heart thuds painfully at the thought of being in front of that many people.

"Yeah, I'm listening." I was actually thinking about how hard it was to leave Aisha at the B and B an hour ago. When we came downstairs for breakfast, she said she was fine, but I could tell she was starting to dissociate. Saying goodbye was awful. We both cried in the parking lot before we had to get back on the road. We were supposed to drop her off at the airport in Calgary today but after what happened with the fan, we don't have time to backtrack. The B and B has a shuttle that will take her there later.

"Well? What do you have to say?" Helen asks.

"Oh . . ." Am I supposed to be apologizing for something? "Uh . . ."

"I'm sorry, but I don't see how this is either of our faults," Jesse says darkly. "How could we have known someone would end up spying on us swimming last night?"

I turn to him in confusion. I must have missed something. "Spying on us?"

"Yes, the pictures that fan who followed you posted online," Helen says exasperatedly.

Panic floods my senses, my breath growing shallow. Helen says more, but I'm not looking at Jesse's phone anymore—I'm scrambling to pull out my own. When I open my feed, I see them, the photos of Aisha, Jesse, and me on the dock last night.

They're taken from so far away that it's impossible to make out explicit details of our bodies, but it's still obvious that it's us and that we aren't wearing clothing.

This isn't happening. I can't breathe. I blink at the pictures like that will somehow make them disappear, but it doesn't. They're still there.

My eyes skim the comments and my face blazes. So many people are making graphic assumptions about what the three of us were doing. Some of the comments about Aisha are so mean and disgusting that my hands start shaking. I grip my phone so hard it feels like it might break.

"Look, I understand this doesn't seem like a big deal since normal kids do this kind of thing all the time," Helen says, her tone softening. "But you're not normal kids. You have to assume you're being watched. I know that's not an easy thing to deal with, but you're going to have to be a lot more careful if you don't want stuff like this getting out. We'll touch base again after your show."

She hangs up and Jesse lets out a frustrated groan. "This freaking sucks. Are you okay?"

"I guess." I'm still not processing. I wonder if Jesse's looked at any of the comments yet. Dealing with the rumors about the two of us was already awkward, but this is about a million times worse.

It suddenly hits me that people I know are going to see this. Oh God, I wonder if Aisha has already.

"You sure? I get that this is—"

"I gotta call Aisha," I cut Jesse off.

She doesn't pick up. I guess she's already on the plane. I try to spend the rest of the ride editing a video, but I can't concentrate. Sophie calls me, but I don't answer. My mom texts me shortly after that, but I'm too scared to even read it. I can't deal with talking about this with them and I don't even want to imagine talking to my dad.

We arrive at the hotel and have a bit of time to relax in our rooms before we have to head to our show. Not that I can relax. My phone starts ringing almost as soon as I set my bag down. I pray it's not Sophie or my mom again, then let out a relieved breath when I see that it's Aisha.

"Hey . . . Are you okay?" I ask cautiously.

"Not great." There's some traffic noise in the background.

"Where are you? I guess you saw what happened? I'm really sorry."

"I'm on my way home. And yeah, I saw when I got off the plane. I can't believe this is happening." Her voice gets shaky. "Oh my God. My dad is definitely going to see this. It's freaking everywhere, not just on gossip sites. It's on the regular news. He's going to kill me."

"It's gonna be okay," I try to assure her, even though I have no idea if it will be. I'm worried my own dad will hear about it, too. "I'm so sorry this is happening. Promise me you won't read anything else, okay?"

"It's fine. People have been saying a bunch of fucked-up stuff about me for a while because they ship you and Jesse and want me out of the picture." She forces out a thin laugh. "So I'm used to it."

"Aisha . . ." I squeeze my eyes shut for a second and sit up in bed, my stomach writhing with guilt. "I hate this so much."

"It's not your fault," she says with a sigh. "How're you doing? Are you ready for your big show tonight? I know you said you were nervous."

I sigh. "Yeah, it's gonna be so many people. I'll have to pretend you're in the crowd again and maybe that'll get me through it."

"Aw. You're gonna do great. Try not to think about all this crap— I'm sure it'll blow over." She's trying to put on a brave face, but I know she's still upset.

After she hangs up, I swear and throw my phone on my bed before rushing into the bathroom to get ready. I wish I could shield her from all this, but there's nothing I can do. I feel beyond useless. Shit like this feels like it could cancel out everything good about being on tour, about getting to live out this dream. But Jesse, Victor, and Serafina have all been able to get through it, so I'm praying I'll eventually figure it out too.

When I come out of the bathroom, I see that Kamran has sent me a message.

KamranTheSufi: Do you understand how jealous I am that you got to interview Victor from Midnight??? Your write-up was super relatable, too. It was cool to hear about how Victor inspired you with how open he is about his sexuality. I think you should go ahead and submit it to Dev. It looks great!

I'm still not feeling super confident about sending it in, but his message lifts my mood.

> **Cavalcader24:** Thanks so much, Kam! I've never really talked about my sexuality like this before. Even with a pen name it still feels like a lot.

> **KamranTheSufi:** I've been there. I appreciate you sharing it with me even if you don't feel ready to submit it for this issue. Take your time.

> **Cavalcader24:** I'll keep thinking on it. Thanks again ☺

I'm thankful he gets that this is still stressful, even though it's an anonymous thing. I don't know if I can put any more of myself out there in public right now, whether people know I wrote the piece or not.

*

During sound check, I stare out at the thousands of empty seats. The rows loom imposingly in front of the giant stage I'm standing in the middle of with Jesse and a sound tech. I nod along to everything the tech is saying, but I'm half-checked out, my nerves in shambles.

I don't get asked for my input on lighting and sound. The crew is distant and professional with Jesse and me; we're just expected to hit our marks and cues and generally try not to get in the way.

Then it's time for me to rehearse my set. The confidence I felt last night has disappeared entirely. I'm a shaky, sweaty mess the entire time. When it's Jesse's turn to take the mic, I notice he doesn't look that great either. He usually sings full volume for his rehearsals, but he's quieter than normal, to the point that the sound tech asks him to raise his voice.

"Hey, you okay?" I ask as he walks offstage.

He lets out a long sigh. "Freaking out a little. This will be the biggest show I've played, plus it's my hometown . . . It's a lot of pressure."

"I can imagine," I say as we get to the dressing room. "I know I'm probably going to be in my head for our final show in Toronto with all my work and school friends watching. I'm getting kinda anxious now, too." Not to mention how anxiety-provoking the last twenty-four hours have been, between the stalker-fan and the photo situation. "You down to meditate?"

"That sounds good," he says, collapsing into a chair in front of the lit-up dresser mirror.

I take the chair next to him, pulling up a meditation on my phone and turning up the volume so we can both hear. I close my eyes and focus on my inner body, trying to find that same awareness from last night in the freezing pond. Becoming conscious of the warm air in my lungs, I slowly exhale as much as I can. I pause for a beat then take in cool air through my nose, relaxing my shoulders. I broaden my awareness beyond my body, but I can't sense Jesse's calming presence beside me like usual. Bringing my awareness inward again, I refocus on my breath.

I'm feeling more at ease until the meditation is interrupted by a message coming through.

My eyes snap open. "Sorry," I say, grabbing my phone to silence it.

"No worries. I was having a lot of trouble getting in the flow anyway," Jesse says. "Do you want to start over?"

I'm about to restart the meditation when I see the text is from my dad. My heartbeat picks up its pace. It's rare for my dad to text me—something must be wrong.

He's linked a gossip article that has one of the photos from last night front and center.

The headline reads: "*Ménage à trois? Singer Jesse Jacobs gets NAKED with rumored flame Ollie Cheriet AND his GF!*"

My blood runs cold as I start to read the message beneath the article.

Dad: *Olia, what is this?! Your uncle sent me this article, how am I supposed to explain your disgusting behavior?*

No. No no no . . .

My hands start shaking so much I have to put my phone down.

This is so, *so* bad. It would be bad enough if my dad found out on his own, but it's a million times worse that my uncle told him. I've basically shamed him and embarrassed our whole family.

"What is it?" Jesse asks as I leap up from the chair and start pacing the room.

His words echo in my head and I feel like my whole body is on fire. I know my dad's suspected over the years, but it's completely unbearable having him actually say it. It feels like confirmation of all the worst things I've thought about myself.

I become aware of Jesse's hand on my shoulder and I still for a second.

"Are you okay? Tell me what happened," he says.

I shake my head, pulling away from him. I grip the edges of the dresser with both hands, trying in vain to slow my rapid breathing.

"Ollie, you're scaring me." Jesse's voice is distant now, my ears ringing as my throat starts to constrict.

I need my meds. I lurch from the dresser over to my bag in the corner. I open the pocket I usually keep them in, but the bottle isn't there.

Shit. I forgot them in the hotel room. I slide down the wall behind me, putting my face in my hands. I'm getting lightheaded now, my lungs seizing.

Jesse's crouched in front of me, his hand on my shoulder again. "Ollie, come on. What should I do? Should I call someone?"

I break away from him, using the wall the help me get upright. "Just . . . need to get some air," I wheeze out. "Gonna go outside for a sec."

I stumble out of the dressing room.

"Just stop, okay?" Jesse's right behind me, his voice frantic. "I'll go get security." He says more but I'm having trouble hearing him because I'm fully panicking now, unable to get enough air into my lungs. The edges of my vision start to blur, a sharp pain building in my chest. I can't walk anymore and then my legs give out completely. My body crashes to the floor.

29

"Ollie? Ollie?!" Jesse's voice echoes from somewhere above me, but my eyes are squeezed shut so tightly all I can see are stars. I'm hyperventilating, and I have no idea how I haven't passed out yet. I wish I would, so this would stop happening. I feel like I'm dying.

"What's wrong with him? Is he having a seizure?" Someone is talking to Jesse now, but I don't recognize the voice. "He's supposed to be onstage in two!"

"He can't go on—he's having an anxiety attack," Jesse says. "Ollie, can you say something?"

"An anxiety attack? Are you sure?" the other voice asks. "He looks really bad. Should I call 911?"

"Yes, call 911 and get security."

"No," I choke out. "Don't call 911." I don't want to cause a bigger scene. I know physically I'm okay, but my brain is trying to convince me that I'm not. I have to get it together and go out to perform.

Come on, breathe. You're not dying. You know you're not dying, just calm down. My body refuses to obey. I curl up into a ball, trying in vain to stop shaking. Frantic sobs bubble their way up my throat, but I keep my mouth clamped shut. *Don't cry.*

"Call 911," Jesse insists firmly. "Get help."

I hear a pair of footsteps running off, and then it's just Jesse's voice again. I feel his hands on either side of my face, turning me toward him.

"Hey, look at me."

I'm so embarrassed that I don't even want to open my eyes, but after a second, I force myself to meet his gaze. I don't want to scare him more by making him think I've become unresponsive.

Fear clouds his eyes. "You're gonna be fine, okay? I promise, just hold on."

I nod slightly and try to sit up. Jesse takes my arm, helping me lean back against the wall. I try to take in a full breath, but my breathing remains quick and shallow. *When the hell will this end?* This is one of the longest attacks I've ever had. My panicked thoughts start to ramp up again and I fold in on myself, pulling my knees up and wrapping my arms around them. I hyperventilate even harder and bury my face against my arms when I can't hold my tears in any longer.

I wish I would just black out, but instead I keep sobbing. This is beyond humiliating. I'm so fucking pathetic.

I can't concentrate on what Jesse's saying anymore. My brain is stuck in a hellish loop, telling me I'm about to die over and over again.

"Jesse, you have to go on." The sound tech's voice breaks through my daze. I'm suddenly aware that Jesse has his arms tightly wrapped around me. "It's too late notice to cancel the entire show."

"The ambulance is arriving." I hear Tim's voice now. "I'll take him."

Jesse detangles himself from me and then I'm being pulled to my feet.

"You're gonna be okay," Jesse says a final time, squeezing my hand as the sound tech herds him away.

"Can you walk?" Tim asks, his arm across my shoulders to keep me upright.

"I don't . . . need an ambulance," I pant, swaying on my feet. Tim's grip on me tightens.

"Looks like you do. Come on."

I sit out back in the ambulance with an oxygen mask on for a few minutes, which helps me finally regulate my breathing. Eventually, I take it off and head back inside. It was so stupid of me to forget my meds, even if I hadn't planned on using them. I thought I'd be able to get by on meditating with Jesse before shows, but I had been wildly unprepared for how horrible today would be. I don't want to start using them again, but I can't risk something like this happening at any more shows.

When I enter the dressing room, my phone is ringing on the dresser. I approach it slowly, letting out a breath when I see it's Helen, not my dad calling.

"I'm sorry I couldn't go on," I say as soon as I pick up the phone. "It won't happen ag—"

"Hey. Relax. Things happen," Helen says gently. "The security team explained. We're just glad you're all right."

I nod, thankful she doesn't seem mad. "Thanks, Helen."

"Do you feel up for doing the meet and greet tonight? Just to say hi to the fans that missed out on seeing you perform."

"Of course," I tell her. I hope I am. "Again, I'm so sorry. It's just been a stressful day. I didn't get much sleep and—"

"It's fine. Just try and get some rest, okay? I'll check in later."

Tim takes me to the meet and greet room and I wait in there for a few minutes before Jesse shows up.

He smiles at me but still looks worried. "Are you sure you're good not going to the hospital or anything?"

I nod as he takes a seat at the signing table next to me. "The paramedics said I'm fine."

"Ollie . . . I'm really glad you're okay." From the way his voice hitches, I can hear how much he means it. I freeze, unable to tear my eyes away from his.

"Can you tell me what happened?" he asks gently. "I know you saw something that upset you on your phone."

I finally break his gaze, my throat starting to tighten again as I shake my head. I can't think about this right now, much less talk about it.

"Ollie, come on . . ." he trails off as the doors open, the familiar sound of squealing fans erupting into the room.

Jesse sighs and then stands, immediately putting on a smile. I stand too, even though practically no one comes up to talk to me. Why would they? I didn't even perform. And since this is Jesse's hometown show, everyone's more interested in him. Watching him talk to the kids from the Indigenous youth organization he works with is a nice distraction from thinking about earlier. They're all so excited to meet him; it's really cute.

Everything's going well, until an older kid goes up to Jesse and starts talking to him quietly. I can't hear what he says, but Jesse's smile dissolves, and he shakes his head in disbelief. The kid moves on and Jesse just stands there.

"Hey. What was that?" I whisper beside him, and he snaps back into himself.

"Nothing." He smiles thinly at me before turning to the next group of fans.

*

Jesse's silent on the ride back to our hotel, staring out the window at the rainy sky. When we get out, I rack my brain for something to say after everything that happened earlier. I don't want to pry about what that kid said to him, but I wish I could do something to help. I don't know what to say about my attack either. I don't really want to talk about it, so I stay silent as we head back to our rooms.

"See you in the morning," he says softly once we're on our floor.

He heads into his room without another word.

I collapse on my bed and find myself thinking about how tightly Jesse held me when I was freaking out. How he squeezed my hand. And then that moment at the meet and greet, the tone in his voice when he said he was glad I was okay.

How am I supposed to explain your disgusting behavior? My dad's message repeats in my mind again and again. I squeeze my eyes shut so hard it hurts. I still haven't responded to him. I haven't gotten back to my mom or Sophie either. Aisha called me a couple of times too, but I don't even feel up to talking to her.

God, I wish most of today never happened. I dig my fingers into my eyelids, but that doesn't do anything to stop the tears.

*
*

I stumble out of my room early the next morning to pick up some much-needed coffee. I slept badly, unable to stop replaying yesterday's shit show. Just as I open my door, I see Jesse headed into his room across the hall.

"What are you doing up so early?" I ask.

He freezes, his shoulders tensing.

"Nothing," he says, avoiding my eyes. He's wearing a light army jacket that's completely drenched, like he's been out in the rain for hours.

Did he sneak out without security? Maybe he wanted to go visit his friends and family while he's in town and didn't want them tagging along. Or me tagging along, I guess.

His phone rings and he groans. "It's Helen. Come on," he says opening the door to his room and inviting me in.

"Hey guys, thanks for rallying last night," she says when Jesse picks up. "I know it was a tough one."

"I'm sorry again for—"

"You don't have to apologize for getting sick," she says. "Pierre did want me to check in with you, though. Is there anything we as a team can do to help out? We want to make sure you're healthy enough to continue the tour."

My heart pounds. *Shit.* I feel weird admitting I'm taking medication, but I need to get over it. I need to make sure the label knows I can do this.

I shake my head. "No, it won't happen again. I just, um, forgot my anxiety meds at the hotel. I'll make sure I have them on me from now on."

Jesse shoots me a reassuring nod while Helen jots down a quick note.

"That's good to hear you'll be more mindful," she continues. "So, I'm not sure if you two have seen the news this morning, but something else has started making the rounds."

My stomach drops. *What could it be now?*

"It seems someone on the venue crew leaked some pictures of you together when Ollie was having his attack."

What the fuck is wrong with people? I feel so violated that someone decided to get a photo op of one of the worst moments of my life.

"I know this isn't the first time you two have dealt with this," Helen continues. "But these photos are going particularly viral. Just so we can get ahead of this, are you two romantically involved?"

I shake my head, glancing at Jesse, who's gone beet red. *Wait, why is he blushing so hard?* The only other time I've seen him blush was when he brought up the online gossip when we were at Wanuskewin. I'd wondered then too what the source of his embarrassment was. If it was the awkwardness of the rumors themselves or the possibility of any truth that could lie behind them.

I don't feel any closer to figuring it out—but it doesn't matter either way. I don't have the right to care.

Jesse doesn't say anything, so I jump in. "No. All of this is just stupid fan rumors."

Helen nods. "Just to be clear, the team wouldn't have any problem with it if you were. RMA and Middle Path are welcoming and inclusive of all identities. We just want to make sure nothing like that affects your working relationship."

Jesse and I just nod silently.

"I understand all this press has been personally difficult," she continues. "But on the upside, the tour has been getting way more media coverage than we ever anticipated. That combined with how well you've been doing with your social posts has made us reevaluate the scope of the tour."

Wait, does that mean . . . "You want to extend the tour?" I blurt out.

Helen nods. "Yes, Pierre wanted me to tell you that we'd like to add fifteen American stops after the Canadian leg ends in December."

"Fifteen more stops?" Jesse glances at me excitedly. "That's incredible!"

I smile, but my mind races as I try to figure out the logistics. "I'd have to miss more school. When would the new end date be?"

"Late April."

"I'll have to talk to my parents again," I tell Helen.

"You're eighteen now, right?" she asks. "So legally you don't need them to sign anything."

"Right, but I still have to check in with them. How long do we have to get back to you?"

"We're moving fast with planning, so next week would be ideal. We'll have to adjust your contract to add the extra earnings as well."

I nod, my brain going a mile a minute. This is great. I'll be making even more income to help out my family and then hopefully support myself in continuing to pursue music. But I'm not sure how my parents will react. Especially my dad, who is so set on me going to college. But I'm not interested in that anymore. Or in doing what he expects of me.

My throat constricts when I remember my dad's last message. Damn it, I have no clue how I'm going to face him about that either.

"And how's everything with the album coming along?" Helen asks.

I come back to the present. "It's going okay. Still figuring out the last half." Since our weekend at Victor's, I haven't had a lot of time to work on it. The stuff I've been scribbling in my notebook lately—besides the song about my relationship with my dad—has been more removed from my personal experience than my other songs. I've been playing around with fictional narratives like the ones Victor told me he was working on.

Helen nods. "Let us know when you're getting closer to finishing up and then we'll talk about music videos for the singles. All right, so today is a no-show day. But your schedule is still packed with interviews. Tons of outlets are hoping to talk to Jesse since he's local to the area. Remember, do your best to steer the conversation away if they get into anything too personal. Call me if you need anything."

Great. Another day of dealing with weird, invasive questions. The thought alone makes me short of breath. I'm definitely going to need my meds today, and I'm going to try not to feel bad about it. I have to find a good balance of taking them when I need them without becoming too reliant on them. Especially with this unbelievable opportunity. I need to figure this out. I have to.

30

Before Jesse and I head out for interviews, I can't help but look at the pictures of us from last night. It makes my skin crawl that someone on the crew was snapping pictures of me in the middle of my attack.

In the photos, I'm curled up on the ground and Jesse's holding me, our faces inches apart. He looks terrified, but that doesn't mean he has feelings for me. Except . . . I'm not quite convinced that's true. I'm thinking about him blushing and going quiet when Helen asked if we're involved—and that moment at Wanuskewin. All of the times I could sense something palpable in the air between us even though nothing has actually happened. And can never happen.

Because of Aisha? Or because you're scared of being with a guy? The thought pops up like a fly that refuses to be swatted. Taking a calming breath, I let myself sit in the discomfort for a moment, falling back into my plan of trying to accept my crush. If I didn't know Aisha, or if we weren't together, how would I have reacted to my feelings for Jesse? Would my guilt be as intense?

My dad's message flashes before my eyes again, and shame hits me with a sickening thud, eclipsing all the support I've been getting from friends. I hate that his opinion still has so much power over me. His disapproval looms, impossibly large and threatening, and I'm not ready to face it.

I still haven't messaged him back.

The day is extremely long. We get the same questions over and over in each interview, and figuring out fresh ways to answer them is exhausting. Jesse's ever-professional, upbeat shield shows more and more cracks as the day drags on. I do my best to pick up the conversation whenever he gets weirdly quiet, especially when he's asked about how it feels to be back home.

At least the interviews are a distraction from my phone, all the endless gossip and my family's unanswered calls. The debilitating dread of having to talk to my dad still sits in the back of my mind. On top of that, I don't know how I'm going to get up the nerve to ask my parents about staying on tour longer. My dad might be so angry at me that he won't care what a blessing it would be. Not to mention telling Aisha about it. I hate the idea of being away from her even longer, that we'll have even less time together before she leaves for college. But there's still something deep down inside me that wants this. To do what I'm truly meant to do.

After the interviews are finally over, we get back in the van and then get on a ferry to our next stop in Victoria. Jesse sits a few feet away from me on the nearly empty top deck, staring at the freezing, blueish-black water of the Pacific, hunched over against the brutal wind.

He's barely looked at me since we boarded. I know he's got his own stuff going on, but I wonder if all the rumors about us are stressing him out, too. It's obvious he wants space, but I'm worried things will get even more strained between us by the time we get to the States if we can't figure out a way to stay on good terms now.

Before I can think better of it, I walk over to him. "Hey."

He starts a little at my voice, so caught up in his own head he didn't even see me approach. "What's up?"

"Mind if I sit?" I ask carefully.

"Of course," he says, and I take a seat next to him on the cold steel bench.

"Just wanted to check how you're feeling." I notice my breath, a ghostly cloud that passes over his face. "I get if you don't feel up for talking, though."

He stays hunched over but shifts a little in my direction, his knee brushing mine. "Feeling about what?"

"Uh ..." Everything I was planning to ask him about gets stuck in my throat. "I guess I just wanted to make sure we're okay."

He's been looking down, but now he focuses on me, his eyes questioning. "Why wouldn't we be?"

His knee is still against mine, his warmth seeping into me. I make myself ignore it, but then I'm focused on his face, his eyes just as inky dark as the waves beneath us.

Finally, his gaze softens. He knows I'm not buying his front that nothing's wrong.

"It's not you. Don't worry."

I nod, waiting for him to say more, but he looks down again. I let the sound of the ferry trudging through the water wash over us as we fall into a peaceful lull.

"Ollie?" he says eventually, and I turn toward him again. My movement brings us even closer, more of my leg pressed against his.

"Yeah?" I don't move back. It isn't a big deal. I'm not doing anything wrong, it's just really cold out here.

"If you don't want to tell me that's okay, but what happened before your panic attack at the show? I know you saw something on your phone that freaked you out."

I squeeze my eyes shut. My dad's message flashes in my mind like a neon sign. I inhale deeply and open my eyes again. I can't let my dad's opinion overshadow everything I've been working toward. The support I've been allowing myself to receive *does* matter. And I can see from the gentle curiosity in Jesse's eyes that all he wants is to be there for me too.

I clear my throat and try to be brave, meeting Jesse's eyes. "It was my dad. He saw the naked photos of us and got upset about it."

"I'm sorry, Ollie." Jesse's voice is almost carried away on the sharp wind, but I still make out his words. "What did he say?"

I can't make myself speak, but I know it's written all over my face. All the shame I wish I could tear out of myself.

He shoots me a look so full of compassion and understanding that there's no way to mistake it as simple pity. My shoulders relax, my nerves calming. He's not looking at me any differently now that I've silently revealed this part of me.

"You know," he continues, "I've been thinking a lot about that song that you shared when we were camping a few nights ago. The one about generational cycles. It really resonated with me. If you ever want to work on it some more together, just let me know."

I nod, my throat still too tight to speak, and then we're just look-ing at each other, our breath intermingling in front of our faces. It's happening again, whatever I've been feeling between us, and I can't talk myself out of believing it's real this time. Everything we're not saying rings in my ears so loudly I can hardly take it. His cheeks have grown rosy spots. I know it's not from the cold.

The boat horn sounds and I jump, finally moving my knee away and turning back toward the water. My mind races as I try and make sense of what just happened—the heady buzz of tension between us. I remind myself that what I'm feeling isn't wrong as long as I rein it in and my feelings pass. What's important is that we're talking, even if we're not up for hashing everything out tonight. That we both want each other to be okay.

*

At the hotel, I fall onto the bed as I finally give Aisha a call back. She left me a couple messages today.

"Hey." She sounds stuffed up. "I was worried about you. What happened at your show last night, are you okay?"

I hold in a sigh. "I'm okay." I should probably tell her about that horrible message from my dad, but I don't want to think about it anymore. "Just forgot to bring my anxiety meds to the show."

"You're taking meds again?" she asks, sounding surprised. "I thought you said you don't like how those make you feel."

"Yeah, but sometimes my breathing exercises and stuff don't cut it."

"When did you start taking them again?" she asks, her voice quiet.

I wince. "When the tour started. I'm sorry I didn't mention it earlier. I didn't want to worry you."

She sighs. "Oli, I thought we were past this. You don't have to keep things from me because you think it'll upset me."

"You're right. I just . . ." I don't know what to say. All my excuses sound so stupid in my head. The truth is that I felt scared and weak and I didn't want her to see me like that.

"What?" she asks when I don't finish.

"Nothing. I'm just sorry." I feel awful that I keep doing this, that I keep messing up and hurting her. "Anyway, how are you doing?"

"Okay." Her voice cracks a little.

"Are you sure? I know those photos of us are a lot."

"Uh-huh." She chokes back a sniffle.

"Hey, can you turn your camera on?" I ask gently.

"Not right now," she says, sniffing again.

"Come on. Please."

She turns it on, and I see her eyes are puffy and there are a few tissues on her pillow.

"What happened?"

She shrugs, wiping her nose. "It's just been a tough day. People at school were talking about the swimming photos. And . . . my dad found out that I came to see you. He's so upset about everything . . . God, it's so awful. He didn't even really yell at me. It's like he can't even *look* at me. And you know I haven't talked to my mom in a long time, but she sent me a message saying that I, like, ruined my reputation and that no good dance company would ever take me now."

I squeeze my eyes shut. "Aisha, that's not true. And I'm so sorry—"

"You don't know that. Maybe she's right."

I shake my head. "Don't let her get to you. I wish you would just block her number. And I'm sure your dad will get over it soon."

"Yeah, I guess," she says, her voice dull. "Anyway, tell me more about your day."

"Well . . ." This doesn't seem like the best time to tell her about the possibility of the tour being extended, but I want to stop keeping things from her. "The label wants to add some US stops to the tour."

"Wow, that's so great!" she says, but I can see the disappointment in her eyes. "I'm so happy for you."

"I haven't checked in with my parents about it yet," I admit. "I've been dodging them . . . you know, since the pictures got out." I push my dad's message out of my mind again.

"I get it. It's so fucking shitty that someone took photos of you when you were having an attack."

"It does feel really gross, yeah. And, um, you know that what people are saying is bullshit, right? Jesse was just trying to help me out while I was panicking."

She doesn't say anything for a second, her face grim.

"What is it?" I ask, my heart starting to pound.

"I'm glad Jesse was there to support you." There's the muffled sound of static as she blows out a hard breath, seeming to brace herself. "Ollie, I can't imagine how hard it is, having everyone online assuming how you feel. But I want you to be honest with me. *Do* you have feelings for him?"

"No," I say automatically, shaking my head.

Shit. All this time she's said she didn't believe the rumors. Why is she asking now?

All my rationalizations about whatever's been happening with Jesse are falling apart. I feel so gross for lying to her. God, I am truly an awful person. She deserves so much better than me.

She shoots me a sad look. "It's okay if you do. I get it."

I blink at her uncomprehendingly. "What do you mean you 'get it?'"

"I mean, I get if you find him attractive."

"Well, I know that *you* do," I say under my breath. I wince, immediately wishing I could swallow my words.

"That *I* do?"

"I caught the way you looked at him when you were here," I mutter. *Christ, why am I saying this?*

She shakes her head at me incredulously then lets out a defeated sigh. "Okay, fine, Ollie. I can admit it. I think he's attractive. You know what it's like being around him. It's impossible not to get drawn in. And you're with him *all the time*. For even longer now that your tour is getting extended. I could tell, when you were singing and when you were meditating together, that you guys have a different kind of connection. Like you just lit up in a way that I've never seen before."

I'm silent, hating every second of this conversation.

She shuts her eyes tight for a moment. "And I can't help wondering if you can't admit how you really feel about him because it's still hard for you to talk about liking guys?"

I stay quiet, blinking hard. Everything in me wants to deny it, but it's pointless trying to hide it from her anymore.

"It's just a stupid crush," I finally say, my voice trembling as I wipe at my eyes. "It doesn't mean anything. I love you and I would never do anything to hurt you."

"Ollie, I know that," she says, her own voice getting shaky now. "But I have to be honest, *everything* hurts right now. I feel like this is taking over my whole life. I can't think about anything besides what's been going on with you. I'm distracted in all my classes and rehearsals. I need to get it together and focus on my dancing right now. And . . . and it hurts that you still don't feel like you can trust me, even after—" She stops short, her voice breaking.

"Aisha . . ." I want to say something to fix this, to show her that I can do better, be better. But the words won't come.

"I think . . . I think maybe we should take a break so we can both figure some things out," she whispers.

"No." An intolerable pain stabs at my chest, so sharp that I can't breathe for a moment. "I get that you need space. But why can't we figure things out together?"

"I'm sorry," she chokes out. She's crying now too. "I just need some time to think, okay? I'll talk to you later."

She hangs up. I bury my face in my hands, letting out a muffled scream, my entire body shaking.

This can't be happening. God, I fucking hate myself. All of the horrible shit she's been dealing with is my fault. She's better off without me, but the thought of being without her makes me feel like my heart is being clawed out of my chest. I curl up into a ball and bite down on the sobs fighting to burst their way out of me.

✲

"Are you good?" Jesse asks during a break between interviews the next morning.

"Fantastic," I mutter, stuffing a big bite of donut into my mouth. I was too wired to eat breakfast at the hotel earlier, so I'm starved.

"You're acting kind of weird," he says.

I pause in the middle of chewing and slow down. I took a couple more pills this morning than I did yesterday. But with the US tour dates still not totally confirmed, I can't risk being a mess today.

After I cried myself to sleep, I could barely drag myself out of bed this morning. But since I took my meds, I feel practically nothing. Which is perfect. I've managed to get through our first couple of interviews without any issues. If anything, I was more talkative than normal.

"Well, you've been weird, too," I counter, my voice dull.

He's been down and distant since Vancouver, despite our moment of connection on the ferry. I've been patiently tiptoeing around his mood, but if he's going to call me out, I don't see why I have to keep acting like I don't notice.

Jesse just shoots me a dark look before the next interviewer takes a seat in front of us at the conference table.

We get through a few more interviews and then we have to head over to our next show. It's almost as big as the one in Vancouver, but I still feel pleasantly numb during sound check. I don't stick around to watch Jesse, going straight back to my dressing room.

I stand motionless in front of the mirror, my eyes drawn to the dark circles under my tired gaze. My face is placid, but beneath my medicated numbness I wish I could scream until my voice is gone. I don't move a muscle for a long time, zoning out.

My phone buzzes and I rush for it, hoping it's Aisha calling to say she's changed her mind. But it's just my mom again, so I silence it, collapsing into the chair in front of the mirror.

I do some deep breathing for a few minutes, but it doesn't help me get any more centered. I still feel disconnected from myself, like

I'm not quite in my body. When it's time to start my set, my feet feel clunky as I shuffle toward the stage.

I don't spot Jesse in the wings waiting to wish me luck like usual. I don't know what I expected since I didn't wait for him to finish rehearsing. He probably just went back to his own dressing room like I did. Hurt flares inside me. This is the first time he hasn't checked on me before a show.

A hand slaps me on the back and I jump.

"Relax." It's a stagehand, a sympathetic smile on his face as he holds a shot glass out to me. "Heard you got a bad case of stage fright at your last show. Here's a little liquid courage to get you started."

"What is it?" I ask. Not that it matters because I shouldn't be drinking.

"Just some vodka." He gives me a reassuring wink and places the shot in my hand. "Good luck! Cheers!"

"Introducing . . . Ollie Cheriet!" the announcer calls out to thundering screams.

My legs go weak and wobbly at the sound. The stagehand has disappeared. I'm on my own.

I heave out a sigh. *Fuck it.* I down the shot and head out onstage.

31

I don't remember all of my performance, but the thing that's most vivid is how unbearably hot it is, like the stage lights are about to melt my skin. Even as I blink in and out of awareness, my mouth moves on autopilot. My notes sound right, but the lyrics feel hollow and meaningless. Especially the ones about Aisha.

Sweat stings my eyes, and I walk out to the edge of the stage where the lights don't beat down on me as much. The audience kicks up a few notches as I get closer to them, everyone in the front row reaching out to me frantically. Nodding at their overjoyed faces, I keep my smile in place.

I feel like I'm floating away again but startle back into myself when a chorus of excited shrieking starts. My mouth is still moving, but now I'm seated at the edge of the stage. A chill passes over me and I'm suddenly aware that I'm not wearing my T-shirt anymore. It's balled up in my hand, but I don't remember taking it off.

I go to stand up, but lose my balance for a second, tipping forward. Suddenly there are dozens of hands on me, all over me. Some touching me in places I don't want to be touched. I'm frozen as strange fingers grab at me, trying to pull me into the crowd.

Security intervenes, untangling me from the audience. I straighten and back away from the edge. Thankfully, my final song is just ending so I sing my last notes and bolt into the wings.

Jesse catches my arm. "What happened out there?"

Avoiding his concerned gaze, I break away, moving toward my dressing room as quickly as possible.

✳

"Hey."

At the sound of Jesse's voice, I lift my head from the dressing room table. I've been hunched over, wanting to scream, wanting to cry, but still too numb to do anything.

"Security said we should head out soon. Are you ready to go?"

I slowly get up. "Yeah, I'm ready."

In the van, I rest my boiling forehead against the cool window, trying not to think about what just happened.

When we get to our hotel, Jesse finally speaks again. "Can we talk for a few minutes?" he asks.

I want to go hide under my covers so badly. But when I see how worried Jesse looks, I make myself nod. "Okay, sure."

Once we're in his room, he sits down at the edge of his bed and puts his face in his hands. I sit on the other bed, right across from him. The only sound is the rain outside, rhythmically tapping at the window.

When he finally lifts his head, his eyes are watery and red. "I told you that I've had a hard time dealing with friends with addiction issues. And I know you can relate because of that song you shared."

I nod, waiting for him to continue.

"Ollie, I really care about you. That's why I need to check in. Have you been on something today?"

"My anxiety meds, yeah. I may have taken a few too many because I was really stressed." I hang my head, staring at the carpet between us. "And then I was so nervous before I went onstage, I took a shot from this guy on the crew. It was stupid, I'm sorry."

Like he said, I know exactly how hard it is to have a friend dealing with substance issues. Even though I don't think I'm at the point of addiction, I still put Jesse in an awful position. And I'm lucky I didn't hurt myself.

Jesse nods. "It's okay. But if we're going to keep touring together, you can't do that again."

"I won't," I say, finally looking up and meeting his eyes. "I just haven't been coping well with some stuff that's been happening. I promise I'll get my shit together. I'll see if I can get my next therapy session moved up."

I know the way I acted was unacceptable. I have to start actually dealing with things. I'm going to have to come clean to Nadine about how much I've been relying on my meds, and about drinking tonight. Plus, I need her help figuring out how to handle everything else going on—and I won't get that unless I'm honest.

"I'm glad to hear that," he says quietly, not breaking my gaze. "And if you want to talk to me, I'm here. Sorry I've been so distant these last couple of days . . . I haven't been coping well with some stuff that happened either."

For a moment I wonder if it has to do with the two of us, but I get the sense it's related to whatever he's been stewing about since the Vancouver meet and greet. "That's okay. I'm here if you wanna talk, too," I tell him. "I mean, whenever you're ready."

"Thanks, Ollie. So, do you want to tell me what's been going on?"

I nod, thinking about that moment on the ferry again. How with so few words, he made me feel so seen and supported, opening the door for me to walk through whenever I needed to. Taking in a deep breath, I squeeze my eyes shut. "Last night, um . . . Aisha and I kind of broke up."

"Really?" he sounds surprised. "But you two are so good together! Like, I can't imagine putting myself out there and letting myself love someone as much as you guys love each other. It was pretty beautiful to see. What happened?"

I swallow down the lump forming in my throat. "It was a lot of things," I say, looking away. I'm trying not to think about what Aisha said she sensed between Jesse and me, but I can't think of anything else.

"Did it have to do with all the dumb stuff going around online?" He looks away as he says it, his face starting to flush. We both know it's not just gossip.

I say nothing, but I know he can tell that's part of it.

"I'm sorry," he murmurs. "Aisha's an awesome girl and it's really fucked-up she's getting all this hate. I . . . I shouldn't have suggested we go swimming that night."

"You couldn't have known. Don't put this on yourself."

After a silent minute, I speak again.

"Did you want to talk about what's been going on with you?"

He closes his eyes for a moment and then nods. "Okay. At the meet and greet in Vancouver, there was a kid who knew one of my childhood friends. And he told me . . . he told me that my friend passed away a year ago. I hadn't been in contact with anyone from home for so long that no one even bothered to reach out and tell me."

"I'm so sorry," I respond softly, not knowing what else to say. I've never lost anyone that close to me.

"That night, I went over to the rez to see some of my old friends who knew him. They basically said they thought I wouldn't care. Because I abandoned them. Because I'm too big-time now," he says bitterly. "Which is bullshit. They have no clue why it's been so hard for me to go back there."

"You said dealing with your friend's addiction stuff made it difficult to visit?" I ask cautiously.

"Yeah, that. And my family." He looks down, shaking his head. "If you can even call them that. We haven't spoken at all since I left when I was fifteen."

"That sounds awful, having to leave home that young."

"Being on my own was a million times better than staying with people who were supposed to protect me but never did," he says.

My heart drops as he finally looks up at me again.

"Ollie . . . when I first found your song, I connected with it because I know how it feels to be scared people won't accept you because of something that's happened to you."

My throat is too tight to speak, so I just nod, my eyes stinging.

"Thanks for sharing that with me," I say when I'm finally able to talk again. "Even though I wasn't ready to talk about it in the Anthony

Rodgers interview . . . I do know what it's like, going through something like that."

I close my eyes tight, suddenly flashing back to when I got pulled into the crowd at the show. At the time, I was too numb to process, but now it's hitting me how triggering it is and how awful and violated I feel—my skin crawls at the memory.

"Hey." Jesse gets up and sits beside me. "Sorry if it's too difficult to talk about. But I'm glad you felt okay to tell me."

I nod, realizing that he's holding my hand now. And then somehow, we're wrapping our arms around each other. I let myself stop worrying about all the unanswered questions between us and slowly start feeling grounded and steady again. We stay like that for a long time.

"We should probably get some sleep," he says finally.

"Yeah," I agree, getting up. "Let me know whenever you want to talk again. Or if you just need some more space. See you in the morning."

*
*

I book a last-minute session with Nadine the next morning. When I admit that I mixed my meds and alcohol she sounds disappointed, but ultimately she's understanding about it. She suggests replacing my current medication with a new one that's meant for daily use and isn't as potentially habit-forming. Even though I already tried a similar medication that made me exhausted all the time, I agree to try the new one. I'm hoping it doesn't have the same side effect, but we'll keep trying and hopefully figure out what works best for me.

I also tell her about the situation with my dad and what happened with Aisha. I'm glad I'm not in the office with her—I don't think I could hold it together if I had to talk about it face-to-face. It's hard enough over a video call. As I predicted, she advises me to call my family back and try not to catastrophize the fact that Aisha needs some time on her own.

After my session with Nadine, Jesse and I do a live stream and then head out to do a few interviews. In between, I finally risk a look at my messages, reading Sophie's first.

Apparently our parents want to have a "family meeting" when I have some time to video chat. We've literally never done that before, but I know it's basically just going to be me apologizing and trying to explain what happened with the naked photos.

I know I can't avoid talking to Sophie and my parents forever—I can't live in this constant state of anxiety about the inevitable. I'm feeling a bit more grounded after talking with Nadine, so I gather my courage and tell her I can chat that evening.

Even though confronting this is the healthy thing to do, when it's time for the call, I pace around my hotel room, trying not to throw up.

You can do this. Just tell them it's all made-up shit online. It is, for the most part.

I open my laptop and connect to the call to find my family already waiting for me. Sophie's in her dorm room and my mom and dad are sitting together in the living room.

"Sorry I'm late," I say weakly. Instead of waiting for my mom to start some awkward small talk, I decide to just launch into it, wanting to get this over with as quickly as possible. "I just wanted to let you know none of that article was true. It's just gossip. We were just swimming that night. So don't worry—"

"It's not just that one article," my dad cuts in. "People are talking about you and that boy you're on tour with all the time. Saying that you're involved with him."

"Isaac, he said it's just gossip." My mom shoots him an annoyed look. "Olia, we just wanted to make sure you're feeling all right."

"I don't believe it!" My dad erupts at my mom, then turns to glare at me. "I know something is going on and it needs to stop."

My mouth goes completely dry as I blink at him.

"Dad, you're being such an asshole!" Sophie shakes her head in disbelief. "What is wrong with you? Ollie's going through a lot right now. He doesn't need you accusing him—"

"Sophie, keep out of this," he yells at her before focusing on me again. "Are you acting like this because of what happened to you? Because of what they asked you about in that one interview?"

I stare at him uncomprehendingly. When it clicks, I gape at him in horror. I can't believe this is the way he decided to bring up my assault.

I eventually find my voice again. "That isn't how it works. Being assaulted isn't in any way related to who you're attracted to. That's such a messed-up thing to say."

"Screw you, Dad," Sophie chokes out.

Mom shakes her head, covering her face with her hands.

Dad lets out a frustrated sigh. "That's beside the point. You need to—"

"Just stop!" I explode at him. "Look, I'm not with him. But it's obvious you're not . . . you're not open to accepting me how I am."

Dad abruptly gets up and walks away.

Mom looks worriedly after him. "Isaac! What are you doing? Come back here!"

"Hey, Ollie," Sophie says as Mom keeps yelling after Dad. "I accept you. I love you and *nothing* could change that, okay?"

She's tearing up and so am I. "I know, Soph. Love you, too."

"Me too, Olia," Mom says, turning back to the camera. "I love you, sweet boy, no matter what. Don't listen to your father. What he said wasn't okay. I'm going to have a long talk with him, I promise."

I nod, forcing out a weak smile. "Okay, I gotta go."

I shut my laptop and put my head down on the table, my shoulders shaking with sobs.

I'm so grateful that Soph and Mom support me, but that was still really, really hard.

After a minute, I realize I didn't even tell my parents about the tour being extended. But now I don't feel like asking for my dad's permission. I don't even really care about helping him out with money anymore. Not that he acknowledged me helping in the first place. I'm going to continue with the tour and take care of the mortgage for my mom, but that's it.

After a while I stop crying and get up to go wash my face. I feel a little better afterward. As horrible as that was, part of me is relieved it's all out in the open. My dad's disapproval isn't hanging over my head anymore, casting a shadow over my ability to see the value in all the other support in my life. In everyone else who chose to accept me, including my mom and Soph. All the fear and shame that's been buried inside me is finally starting to shrink, freeing me up to start moving toward being my whole self.

32

I'm dozing off in the greenroom of a morning talk show when my phone jolts me fully awake. I check to see if it's my mom—when I told her the name of the show, she seemed really excited, so I invited her to come along. She said she'd try to make it if she could get someone to cover her shift, but she's not here yet.

The last month and a half has been a blur of eerily similar days in the van, random hotels, interviews, and concert venues. It's been tough to squeeze in enough rest when we're constantly on the road. So far, my new medication hasn't been as bad as the first one I tried, but it'll be a while before the effects fully kick in.

We were on tour for most of the holidays, so it was a relief to get back into town last night. Jesse and I crashed at my place. My mom was super excited to meet him. And to stuff us both full of as much food as she could manage. My dad is staying over at my uncle's—something he's been doing a lot lately, according to my mom. I'm trying not to feel responsible for the rift that's grown between them. Nadine suggested I invite them to family counseling. My mom agreed, but my dad refused. He still hasn't talked to me since that horrible video call.

My phone is still buzzing. When I check the caller ID, I see it's Neil.

"Hey, man!" I greet him brightly. "I don't think you've ever called me this early in the morning."

"I'm on my way to school," he says unhappily. "I'm choreographing a group performance and I asked everyone to come rehearse earlier than usual. We're not looking too hot and our next showcase is coming up fast."

"Good luck. Wish I could be there."

"Sophie could record it for you, if you're really that interested."

"Sophie's going?"

"Uh, yeah . . ." he says slower now, like he's not sure if he should have offered up that information.

"Okay," I say, taking a breath. "Soph told me it was a one-time thing with you at the festival, but are you guys a thing now? I don't mind, she just hasn't said anything to me."

"No, but are you sure you wouldn't mind if we were?" he asks, his voice quieter than normal. "I haven't asked her yet."

"Well . . ." Neil's my best friend and all, but he doesn't exactly have a great history with girls. "Do you, like, actually like her? Or do you like her like you liked Gwen?"

Gwen is this girl from school that Neil used to hook up with a lot in tenth grade but never officially dated. I wasn't a particularly big fan of hers since she would say some pretty ignorant things. Thankfully, Neil stopped hanging out with her last year.

"No, it's not like with Gwen," he says quickly. "God, this is so cringe . . . but I think she's incredible and I care about her a lot. I wouldn't risk acting like an idiot and screwing things up. Or hurting her."

I'm quiet for a second. I feel like he really means it. "That's cool, then."

"Not that I'm in a rush to tell her any of that," Neil says. "If you can keep that between us. I have no idea if it's even that deep for her. Or if it's just too weird for her since she's already in college. But I'm glad she wants to talk to me at all."

"That makes sense." I find myself thinking how I feel the same way about Aisha. She's only called me a handful of times since she asked to take a break. They were friendly but short talks, just catching up. I should be counting my blessings, but there's a part of me that still can't stand the fact that our relationship isn't what it used to be. "And don't worry, I won't say anything to Soph. She said she's coming to the show tonight, too."

"Thanks," Neil says, sounding relieved. "Sophie's coming tonight? Okay. Cool, cool. So Ebi, Khadija, and I should just say our names at the door and they'll let us come backstage?"

"Yep, you're on the list," I assure him.

"Beth begged me to ask you to add her, too. I understand if you don't want to, though. I feel like she'll literally faint when she meets Jesse."

I laugh. "Nah, it's fine, she can come along. And uh, is Aisha coming with you tonight?" I texted her that I'm in town and that I'm hoping she'll make it to the show, but I haven't heard back.

"She hasn't said anything to me about it. Sorry, man."

My heart drops, but I keep my voice upbeat. "No worries. I gotta get going—see you tonight."

I hang up and try to push down my disappointment. Last time we talked, she told me she's starting an apprenticeship at the Dance Theatre of Harlem in the fall. She said she wants to keep things between us casual for the time being. I'm not exactly sure what that's going to look like yet. She did say she still loves me but doesn't want to hold me back from having new experiences. And she wants to be open to meeting new people, too. That was kind of devastating, but it also alleviated some of my guilt about still having feelings for Jesse.

I glance over at him. He's on his own phone on the other side of the greenroom with his earbuds in. It turns out Aisha was right—my feelings for him have only grown in the last few months. But nothing has actually happened between us. We've begun to open up to each other more, getting into a rhythm of songwriting and meditating together between shows, which has only made it scarier to think about telling him how I feel. He's become such a vital support for me that I'm not willing to risk ruining what we already have. Plus, I'm prioritizing my commitment to this tour and finishing my album. I'm still finalizing the last few tracks. I want to keep making music for as long as I can and I don't want anything to mess that up.

Since that night on the ferry, we still haven't outright talked about how either of us identify. I did take Jesse up on his offer to work on my song about my relationship with my dad together, and his insights really helped some things click for me. There's this unspoken understanding between us that we know we're on similar journeys. Songwriting has kind of become our way of talking about things we aren't quite ready to confront. With Jesse's help—and Victor's idea about using elements of fiction to create some personal separation with my work—I've been able to put a lot of stuff I've been struggling with into the last half of my album in a way that feels safe.

But we have spoken about some pretty heavy stuff, too. Jesse's told me a little more about his family situation. And I felt okay talking to him a bit about what happened with Thomas. First opening up to Aisha about it and more fans trusting me with their stories has really helped me to get more comfortable speaking about it with Jesse and working through it more with Nadine.

Jesse beckons me over. He's on a call with Helen.

"There you are," she says. "Just checking in before you guys go on—no big news stories or anything this morning."

She's letting us know because Jesse and I haven't been using our social media unless we have to post about the tour. It's a struggle not to look whenever there's new gossip, but I've been doing well with avoiding it lately.

After she finishes going through the day's schedule, Jesse and I are retrieved from the greenroom. I check my phone one last time for messages from my mom, but I don't have any notifications.

"I guess my mom couldn't get work off after all," I tell Jesse. It was probably difficult trying to find someone last-minute during the holidays.

"Aw, that's too bad. She seemed really excited about it," he says as a crew member fits us with mics.

"Yeah. She can still watch it later, I guess."

Jesse nods and then smiles a little. "Hey, you're not sweating."

"Guess it's a holiday miracle," I say wryly.

After the host introduces us, she gets right into asking us about the tour.

"How are you feeling about starting the US leg next week?" she asks. "You must be thrilled that it's been extended."

"Yeah, I'm hyped," I tell her. "But I'm really thankful to finally be back home for a few days first."

"Are you pumped for your show at The Vinyl Underground? You used to work there, right?"

I guess she's done her research. "Yep, it's gonna be sort of bizarre performing there myself."

She nods, turning to Jesse. "And how are you feeling about the tour continuing?"

"Super psyched. I'm still in total shock at how much my fan base has grown in just a few months. Excited to meet even more of them. It was cool to be able to invite some youth organizations—"

"Speaking of your fan base," the host interrupts, "I did want to get your take on that article going around."

God, what now? I guess it's something Helen and the team missed.

When we look at her blankly, she continues, "The piece is about fan speculation that the two of you have been queerbaiting to garner more media attention for the tour. There're some theories going around that Ollie tripping and almost falling in Montreal was a set-up stunt orchestrated by your label. Same with the skinny-dipping incident and Ollie's panic attack before the Vancouver show."

Blood rushes to my face, and I shake my head in utter disbelief. It's bad enough people were making weird comments about all that, but now they have the gall to suggest it was all planned? I swear, some of these people need to go outside and get a hobby. This is truly unhinged.

"Would either of you like to comment on that?" the host asks, looking between us.

From how strained Jesse's smile is, I can see that he's at his wits' end.

"None of that is true," I jump in. "The truth is, the way those situations were talked about online was very hard to deal with and made us deeply uncomfortable."

The host nods. "I'm sure it must be hard to have people constantly speculating about your sexuality. Especially since you're both so young."

Jesse nods. "To be honest, we would love if our fans could focus on our music. All this other stuff really prevents us from being able to connect with our supporters."

"A lot of young people in the spotlight have been forced to come out of the closet when they weren't ready because of accusations like this," the host continues. "Is there anything else you want to say to fans about respecting your boundaries?"

My heart thuds at the mention of coming out. I don't think I'll be ready to talk publicly about my sexuality any time soon. Even though I've felt really supported by the people in my life I've opened up to, telling the whole world is still way too much for me right now.

"Just adding on to what you both said, stuff like this really creates distance between us and fans. It's awful. It feels very violating. It's not anyone's business," I say, keeping my voice firm. "Moving on though, let's go back to what Jesse was saying about the youth organizations. It's been great to see the work he's been doing. He's inspired me a lot. So, I talked to our label recently and we'll be giving some of the proceeds of my album to a few organizations that help survivors of sexual assault."

I'm starting to sweat now—bringing this up for the first time. I'm glad I have the opportunity to do this, but I'm still not ready to talk publicly about my own experience. Because my fans have been so brave sharing their stories with me, though, I think I could be ready to share my own someday soon.

After our segment finishes, we head offstage and I spot my mom waiting for me in the small hallway between the audience area and the greenrooms.

She's grinning ear-to-ear, her eyes damp as she traps me in a giant hug. "I'm so glad I was able to catch you out there! You did so well. I'm so, so proud of you!"

"Thanks, Mom," I say as I detach myself from her.

"And you." She reaches out to Jesse and pinches his cheek. "I'm proud of you, too. You were both wonderful."

"*Mom.*" I shoot her a mortified look.

Jesse laughs. "Thanks, Mrs. Cheriet. I really appreciate that."

She waves a hand and shushes him. "I already told you, call me Anissa."

I sigh. "Jesse and I have to grab our stuff and then we'll meet you back out here, okay?"

"Okay," she says before giving one of my ears a light tug and smiling brightly again. I almost forgot that I have the earrings I got from Wanuskewin on. I've gotten a lot more comfortable wearing them. "I'll be here!"

"Sorry about that," I groan as we step into the greenroom.

"It's totally fine," Jesse says, smiling. "It's really sweet how supportive she is."

His phone starts ringing and he picks up.

"Hey, Victor! Yeah, all good."

I grab my coat from where I left it as Jesse starts laughing at something Victor said. Even though I exchanged numbers with him and Serafina after our weekend at his place, I haven't had the nerve to reach out to either of them. But Victor and Jesse seem just as close as ever.

"Yeah, sure. Ollie's right here," Jesse says. He's looking at me from by the door. "Victor wants to say hey! I'll put you on speaker."

"Hey, Ollie!" Victor's voice rings out. "Just wanted to tell you I read your interview—it was a great piece. Thanks again for asking me to do it!"

I totally forgot Ebi and Dev said the issue would be coming out this week. After Kamran gave me that encouraging feedback on my piece, I finally submitted it. But things have been so hectic with the tour since then, it's barely been on my mind. I did share it with Neil and he was really cool about it. Dev and Ebi and the rest of the group were supportive too.

Jesse glances at me, his eyes going wide for a second, before his face quickly returns to a friendly neutral. From his reaction, I guess Victor told him all about it and he wasn't sure if I would be comfortable with him knowing since it got a little personal and it was supposed to be anonymous. Victor must have assumed I'd told Jesse about it first. I've thought about mentioning the piece to him a couple of times, but I hadn't said anything yet.

"Thanks so much, Victor," I finally say.

"I'm so pumped you guys are doing some US tour dates now. We definitely have to meet up in a few weeks for your New York show. Sera said she can make it too."

"That would be sick," I blurt, unable to contain my excitement.

"We'd love that," Jesse chimes in.

"Sweet! Catch you guys later," Victor says before hanging up.

Jesse puts his phone in his pocket and shoots me a cautious smile. "Do you mind if we talk for a sec before we go meet up with your mom?"

"Uh, sure," I say, biting my lip. "Look, I meant to mention the interview—"

"You didn't have to mention it," Jesse cuts in. "It's just . . . I wanted to come clean and tell you that I already read it."

"Oh." I scratch the back of my head. "Yeah, I figured Victor told you about it."

He shakes his head. "No, he didn't say anything about it before. I've just been following your friend Dev's blog since we visited their studio. And yeah . . . I came across the interview yesterday. Sorry, I know it was supposed to be anonymous. But I thought it was great. I really identified with what you said about trying to find healing and self-acceptance about . . . you know, your sexuality."

We've tiptoed around this for a while. Both of us always on edge, our guards up to face all the public scrutiny we just talked about on the show. But I'm glad he trusts me enough to finally be more open with each other about it outside of the context of songwriting. "Thanks, Jesse. I'm glad you liked it."

"Cool." He looks relieved. "Maybe . . . you could interview me?" I can't help the surprise that shows on my face. "I mean, not like right now or anything. But maybe sometime soon."

I smile a little. "Sure. That sounds great."

33

When we arrive at The Vinyl Underground, my old coworkers make a big fuss about me returning; they have a cake for me and everything. It's a lot of fun introducing them to Jesse and catching up. Since I know the sound and lighting setup so well, the stage manager lets me have free rein on that front. During my rehearsal, I start to get really pumped. I have a feeling this might be one of our best shows yet.

After I finish, I watch Jesse rehearse his set. He asks the crew to change the lineup so he can debut a new song. I'm wondering why he never mentioned he was working on something new since we've been writing together so much recently. The song is much more stripped down than most of his stuff, with just the acoustic guitar he's strumming as accompaniment.

I can't look away from him as he croons into the mic, lit by a single spotlight. He's so beautiful that for a second I'm not even registering the lyrics; I'm too busy staring at him. Finally, it clicks what he's saying. It's the first song of his that mentions someone in a romantic way. He doesn't say any names or pronouns, but something in me is completely sure he's talking about me.

When he finishes and heads back over to me, I don't know what to do with myself. My entire face flames as I focus on my feet.

"That was gorgeous," I murmur, still unable to look at him.

He reaches out, his fingertips brushing mine for the briefest second. My breath catches and I finally meet his eyes.

"Thanks." He breaks into an easy smile. I can feel that he doesn't expect a response from me right now. That he's okay with just letting things stay how they are between us, that he isn't trying to rush while we figure ourselves out—and what exactly we could mean to each other in the future. "Do you wanna meditate before your friends get here?"

I nod, holding his gaze. "That sounds perfect."

*
*

Ten minutes later, Neil and the rest of the theater gang burst into our dressing room in a flurry of singing and screaming and hugs.

While Ebi, Khadija, and Beth gush over Jesse while he signs their albums and poses for pictures, Neil comes over to me.

"Sorry, I didn't hear from Aisha," he says quietly.

I shrug, pushing away the sharp pinch of hurt. "It's cool. Soph should be here soon."

Just as the words leave my mouth, the greenroom door opens again.

"Ollie!" Sophie grins then wraps her arms way too tightly around me. "I missed you!"

"You too," I say, smiling even as I forcibly remove her from me. "It's great to see you."

"Hey," Neil says, waving awkwardly at Sophie, his face reddening. "What's up?"

I step away to let them talk, heading over to Jesse and the rest of the group again.

"You guys get enough pictures?" I ask, laughing.

"Almost," Khadija says as she and Beth squeeze in next to Jesse and snap another.

Ebi rolls his eyes then comes over to give me a hug. "It's great to see you, Ollie. I saw you on TV this morning. That initiative you're donating to sounds cool—congrats."

"Thanks, Ebi. That means a lot. And thanks again for all your support with my piece."

"No worries, it turned out great! I know you're busy, but feel free to pitch some more ideas whenever."

A stagehand pops her head into the room. "Hey Ollie, you're on soon, good luck!"

Everyone walks with me over to the backstage area, talking around me while I do a few breathing exercises.

"You nervous?" Neil asks.

I smile. "Actually feeling pretty excited."

"*Let's go!*" He high-fives me. "You're gonna absolutely smash it, dude!"

My friends wish me luck before I head out onstage, and I look out at the completely packed house. I've been on this stage a hundred times as crew. I still thought it would make my stomach drop, being under all the lights alone. But somehow, I'm perfectly okay. As the audience roars, I soak it in. All of their support lighting me up.

The start of my set goes off without a hitch. I'm hitting my notes and letting myself get fully caught up in the emotion of each song. I feel like I could stay here forever, like I never want this moment to end.

I scan the crowd, feeling overwhelming appreciation for each and every person in the room. My eyes lock with a girl making her way to the side of the stage and my smile grows into a surprised grin.

It's Aisha, grinning right back at me.

"*Sorry I'm late,*" she mouths. She says something to the security guard who nods and lets her through the barrier.

I keep singing. When I'm about to start my last song, "Only Now," I look over and see Aisha has joined Jesse, Neil, and the rest of our group in the wings. I give them all a grateful smile then turn back to the audience. I'm fully embodying the lyrics—unadulterated joy illuminating me from the inside out. I can feel it as it hits everyone in the room. I'm suddenly struck by the absolute surrealness of this moment. It's the complete opposite of my first shows, when I felt like I was outside myself, watching someone else live out my fantasy. It's not surreal, I realize—it's hyperreal. My reality has somehow merged with my wildest dreams. I'm fully here, completely present as I take total control of the stage.

Acknowledgements

Special thanks to:

AUTHOR SUPPORT
Mariko Turk
Aleema Omotoni
Daniel Aleman
Alechia Dow
Derrick Chow
Ryan Douglass
Alexandra Mae Jones
Trynne Delaney
Eliza Martin
Kayla Ancrum
Riss M. Neilson
Rod Pulido
Eric Smith
Jen St. Jude
Louisa Onomé
Liselle Sambury
Courtney Summers

BETA READERS
Loretta Fisher

Eli Matilda Ridley
Kristopher Mielke
Bella Galbraith ,

WRITING COMMUNITY
InkWell Workshops
Toronto Writers Crew

AGENTS
Lesley Sabga
Julie Gwinn

EDITOR
Claire Caldwell

ANNICK PRESS TEAM
Kaela Cadieux
Amanda Olson
Yousra Medhkour
Bailey Hoffman
Stephanie Myers

Sarah Dunn

Serah-Marie McMahon

Brendan Ouellette

Heather Davies

Gayna Theophilus

Rick Wilks

David Caron

Michela Prefontaine

Monica Charny

Diana Itseleva

And everyone else at
Annick Press

COVER ILLUSTRATION

Otesanya

COVER AND INTERIOR DESIGN

Sam Tse

SERIES DESIGN

Zainub's Echo

COPY EDITOR

Hope Masten

PROOFREADER

Dana Hopkins

EXPERT READERS

Myra Saada

Harry Weaver

CHARACTER ART ILLUSTRATORS

Marian Sloane

Reneé Simmone

About the Author

Maya Ameyaw is a Ghanaian Canadian author born and raised in Toronto. Her debut novel *When It All Syncs Up* received starred reviews from *Kirkus* and *School Library Journal*. She is a former bookseller and currently works as a writing group facilitator. Maya has edited several literary anthologies for a number of Toronto-based community arts programs including InkWell Workshops.